Cactus Heart

Books by Jon Talton

Concrete Desert
Camelback Falls
Dry Heat
Arizona Dreams
Cactus Heart

Cactus Heart

Jon Talton

Poisoned Pen Press

Copyright © 2007 by Jon Talton
First U.S. Edition 2007
Large Print Edition 2007

10 9 8 7 6 5 4 3 2

Library of Congress Catalog Card Number: 2006933929

ISBN: 978-1-59058-353-1 Large Print

Poisoned Pen Press
6962 E. First Ave. Ste. 103
Scottsdale, AZ 85251
www.poisonedpenpress.com
info@poisonedpenpress.com

For Susan

Acknowledgments

Paying my debts: The retired Phoenix Police officers of the Big Apple breakfast club, especially Glenn Martin, provided valuable insights into law enforcement in the 1940s. The Phoenix Police Museum helped me see and touch the era. Any errors or deliberate changes in descriptions or procedures are my responsibility.

Retired Phoenix officers Steve Fotinos and Cal Lash, along with retired Mesa detective Bill Richardson, have regaled me with stories of Arizona law enforcement history, which inform this and future Mapstone novels.

Also, I'm grateful to Jana Bommersbach for her path-breaking work on the Winnie Ruth Judd case, which provides a window into the often sleazy workings of old Phoenix. Bill Stephens, a legendary Arizona lawyer, was generous in his memories of the city. Dr. Jack August, Jr., the director of the Arizona Historical Foundation, continues to inspire me with what a real-life historian can accomplish.

Finally, I give special thanks to Barbara Peters, my editor, who in no small measure made *Cactus Heart* possible.

Chapter One

Throughout history, the desert has been a place of trial, penance, and hard-won revelation. God lives in the desert. But Satan does, too. In the American West, conquistadors and cowboys were tested, and often broken, by the desert. Its vastness hid no cities of gold. Its implacable heat and drought were hostile to the white man's crops and cattle. Even as the frontier disappeared, the Sonoran Desert remained a wild and unknown place, the home of strange gods, a waterless world of danger and mystery.

But now it is the turn of the third millennium, and the desert in this far corner of the Far West is air conditioned, irrigated, and comfortably crisscrossed by interstate highways and transcontinental air routes. It is the prosperous, high-tech engine of the New Economy. Even the Indians are in business. It is a playground for beautiful people: a tan, happy place of endless second chances and easy redemption. Sometimes, late at night after Lindsey has fallen asleep, I wonder if we can change the order of things so easily. But it's the kind of thought that's gone by morning.

It was the third week of November, the best time of year in Phoenix. The days were mild and sunny, the nights wrapped in the enchanted dry clarity that made the mountains stand out blacker than the dark sky. Although the tourists and snowbirds were arriving in force, traffic didn't seem too bad. Arizona State University had a good shot at the Rose Bowl. The newspaper even seemed to take a holiday from the day-after-day recounting of drive-by shootings and rapes and drug murders. It was the time of year when you could almost forget the noonday heat of July and say, yes, this is paradise.

I was in-between cases, having just uncovered new evidence in a thirty-year-old jewelry store robbery, which, for the moment, satisfied my boss, Maricopa County Chief Deputy Mike Peralta. That's what I did: researched unsolved crimes that had fallen into the memory hole of the law-enforcement bureaucracy. They called me a consultant, but I also carried a deputy sheriff's star.

A year ago, I had been teaching history at a

university in San Diego. But that was a year ago. Now I was back home in Phoenix, a place I never thought I would be again, living in the stucco house just north of downtown that had been built by my grandparents. Now it was just home to me and too many books and, sometimes, Lindsey Faith Adams.

On Monday night, the Peraltas took us out to a big Mexican dinner at the Tee Pee, and then downtown to America West Arena, the "Purple Palace" the locals called it, where we watched the Phoenix Coyotes squeak by Toronto, 3-2. Peralta had been trying hard to become a hockey fan since the NHL had come to town and the Suns had traded Barkley. And he had been looking longingly at the new ballpark next door for the Diamondbacks. But this night had also been business: Several times during the game, he had buttonholed a county commissioner or state legislator sitting nearby, or had been glad-handed by a moon-faced Republican fund-raiser. Peralta denied that he wanted to run for sheriff next year.

After the first period, Peralta and I made a food run—Sharon wanted a carrot-and-celery pack and Lindsey craved nachos. But on the way to the concession stands we nearly collided with Bobby Hamid coming out of the men's room. Bobby Hamid is one of the nastier scumbags in the entrepreneurial world of Phoenix organized crime, and when he barely avoided slamming into us, I caught something scary and primal in his eyes. Then he dropped back into character and smiled, as comfortable as the black Halston suit he was wearing.

"Chief Peralta," he said. "And the history professor, Dr. Mapstone."

Peralta put on his cop face, something that had its own frightening aspect, all beefy jowls and black eyes perched atop a two-hundred-fifty-pound frame. "Come to blow up the building, Bobby? Fight the jihad for your Arab brothers?"

Bobby Hamid chuckled. "Always the bigot, Chief Peralta." He seemed like a man chatting at a cocktail party as the spectators passed on either side of us, laden with food and Coyote memorabilia. He was moussed, manicured, and did not look like a hockey fan, even in Phoenix. "As you well know, I am a Persian who is now an American citizen, and as Dr. David Mapstone knows," he smiled mockingly at me, "Persians are the inheritors of a great and ancient civilization, and we have a very complicated history with the Arabs."

"Fuck," Peralta said under his breath and stalked away. I followed him.

Behind me I heard Bobby: "Call me sometime, Dr. Mapstone. We must discuss history."

The first time I had met Bobby had been in an interrogation room when we were trying to link him to a pair of murders, a kidnapping, and a million dollars in drug money. He and his lawyer had dismissed us like a bothersome business annoyance. Now the whole thing encouraged Peralta to buy himself an extra beer.

After the game, though, Peralta was almost celebratory as we spilled out onto the street and walked west on Washington Street toward the county government complex, where we could park for free. The night was as good as it gets in the desert: cool, dry, and magical. We spread out, me and Peralta up ahead smoking cigars and talking work—the Harquahala Strangler killings still went on and he said he felt further from an arrest than when they began three years before. Lindsey and Sharon Peralta walked a quarter of a block behind us.

I had known Mike and Sharon for twenty years, long before he was chief deputy in one of the nation's largest counties and she was the most popular radio psychologist on the West Coast. But it was harder for Lindsey. Peralta always seemed awkward around her, always the boss, uncomfortable that I was dating one of his deputies, even if she was the best computer braino in the department. And Sharon, with her nonjudgmental judgmentalism, disapproved that Lindsey was ten years younger than I.

At the corner of First Street and Washington, we waited at the light for Sharon and Lindsey to catch up. I looked back at Lindsey fondly. Walking long-legged and insolent with her black jeans, black, shoulder-length hair and tiny gold nose stud: my young-old soul, my dark star. Peralta looked back with me, and I could tell he was about to say something. Then I looked ahead again to see, over Peralta's shoulder, a man with a large brick in his hand. The man was walking nonchalantly out from an alley toward a black Mercedes idling in traffic at the light.

The man with the brick was an Anglo, maybe around twenty, with an odd-looking blond buzz cut and wearing heavy black boots and a ratty Suns T-shirt. He had that lean, hard-muscled look that is created in the weight rooms of state prisons. At first I didn't put it together, but Peralta's face tensed and he pushed past me. Just then the man heaved the brick into the passenger window of the Benz, and two more figures ran out from the alley.

A lot of things happened at once. The car

window shattered and a woman screamed with a surprised, high-pitched keening. I could see two young women in the car, which jerked forward maybe two feet and stopped again. The guy with the buzz cut reached in the passenger side and pulled a blond woman halfway out, hitting her several times in the head.

"Get out of the car, you bitches!" he shouted.

Another man, a Latino with extravagant tattoos on both arms, was on the other side of the car, yanking open the driver's side door, while a third man, his skin gleaming black against a white T-shirt, brandished an Uzi machine pistol. I think a car honked. The light changed and the rest of the traffic sped away. Peralta had his gun out.

Peralta walked deliberately to the Benz and cracked the Anglo in the back of the head, dropping him unconscious onto the pavement. He aimed the automatic at the two men on the other side of the car and said, in a conversational voice, "Die, assholes." It wasn't exactly the way they teach you at the academy to identify yourself as a peace officer, but what the hell. With his left hand, Peralta produced a pair of handcuffs that I applied to the guy on the ground. The other two men watched us with the eyes of animals caught in a trap. The guy with the Uzi squinted toward Peralta. Tattoo cursed in Spanish. My knees felt noodley.

"How progressive," Peralta said. "A multicultural gang."

"Sheriff's deputies! Lay down your weapon!" It was Lindsey, off to my right. She was in a combat crouch, gripping the baby Glock 9mm she always carried in her backpack. I had never seen Lindsey draw down on anyone before. This was the same woman who had spent yesterday morning lying next to me in bed, legs entangled in mine, quietly reading my dog-eared copy of Dante while I went through the Sunday *Times*. Now she chambered a round with a decisive snap of metal on metal. "Put down your weapon!" Her voice was a tense half-octave above normal.

"Shit," the black guy hissed, shook his head and slowly lowered the Uzi to the pavement. We all relaxed just a notch and instantly the two men bolted across the street, running south.

I ran after them, kicking in the adrenaline that had been gathering over this very long three minutes. I wished I hadn't eaten that second chili relleno. I wished I had a firearm. I could hear Peralta yell "get help" to Sharon and then his heavy tread catching up behind me. Lindsey quickly passed me, she was so agile, and about half a block down the street she caught one of the scumbags and leaped on his back. He growled and twisted, throwing her into a wall. I was just about there but he took off. I stopped to make sure she was all right, but she was already up and we were both running again. We quickly left behind the nice real estate around the arena. The streets became darker, the pavement broken, the buildings forlorn and abandoned.

They ran west on Jackson, then dashed across the railroad tracks and zigged to the north again, past the old warehouses around Union Station. The two suspects weren't very fast, otherwise I never could have kept up. I lost them past the cone of light of a streetlight half a block ahead. A heavy, metal door slammed. Lindsey grabbed my arm and we slowed to a walk. She nodded toward an old multistory brick building. I gave a little start as Peralta caught up and the three of us stood for a moment in silence under the streetlight. Lindsey silently mouthed "there" to Peralta and he nodded toward the building. "I wish we could still shoot fleeing suspects," he whispered in a wheeze.

Lindsey pulled a little flashlight out of her backpack. We walked cautiously into an entrance set back from the street. An ancient fire door gave against Peralta's grip and we stepped inside.

The air wasn't as stale and close as in an Egyptian tomb. The blackness wasn't as total as on the dark side of the moon. Peralta started to take the flashlight but was apparently satisfied that Lindsey was holding it correctly, away from her body so it wouldn't attract a bullet. We tracked carefully down a hall framed by crumbling plaster and bricks to another door, wood this time, half ajar. Out onto a wood floor in a larger room. The flashlight leaped out onto old cartons, broken loading pallets, a fair-sized rat ambled lazily away from us, we avoided a black widow web. We all stopped and listened. Somewhere water was dripping. I wondered why the hell we didn't wait for the city cops, but Peralta and Lindsey went ahead.

Just then something heavy fell on me and the momentum drove me toward what looked like a wooden fence, but then I realized it was a gate to an old freight elevator and I crashed through it painfully and there was no elevator. Behind me, I heard a gunshot, high-pitched, and then several more, deeper blasts. And I had a man on me and we were falling. I smelled his sweat and rancid breath. We dove into the empty darkness and the floor came up suddenly and hard.

Maybe he broke my fall, or maybe I broke his, but we both lay there for a moment, stunned and gasping for breath on what felt like damp concrete. My knee was throbbing and my ankle felt like it was sprained. I swear something slithered across my forearm. I fought panic. I couldn't see.

Suddenly I felt the air rush of his fist, searching for me. He swung again, so hard I could hear him grunt, and his fist glanced painfully off my shoulder. I jabbed in his direction and connected with cartilage. He cursed—*hijo de puta!*—and spat. With my other hand I followed my fist and grabbed onto some hair. He screamed and smashed me in the eye. Instantly, my face was a hot gob of pain. But I didn't let go. At six-foot-two and two hundred pounds, I was bigger than he was, but he was strong as hell and I was out of shape and scared. We wrestled around ineffectually, stirring up dust and cobwebs, bumping into a wooden barrier. Bumped it harder, harder again, and it collapsed into something beyond with a loud crash.

He broke away and I was alone in the blackest dark I could ever imagine. I was desperate to see him, hear him, even smell him. Nothing but darkness. I kicked behind me into the empty air. I knelt down—God, that knee hurt—and ran my hand in an imaginary circle around me. Stepped right. Stepped left.

Just then I touched his rough forearm and involuntarily drew back. He grunted angrily and I sensed his bulk coming toward me. Strong hands found my throat and pushed me back. I gagged and drove my fists upward, breaking his grip. Then I found his eye sockets and fought dirty. He screamed and shuddered. I drove the fleshy heel of my hand toward his head, did it again, and we lay still in the darkness.

Chapter Two

An hour later, we were outside on the street, scattered like debris that had been deposited by an explosion.

Peralta sat on the bumper of a Phoenix Police squad car, bent over and holding a bandage against his arm. His bulk strained at the fabric of his shirt. Six feet away, Lindsey sprawled out on concrete steps, staring up toward stars hidden by the city glow. I sat next to her, holding a cold-pack to my face and examining the damage in a compact mirror borrowed from Sharon. The skin around my left eye was beginning to show red and black swatches and that whole side of my face felt like it was inflated with air. I handed back the mirror. I never had rock-star looks. Old ladies said I was handsome—what did that tell you? Dark hair, regular features. Lindsey said I had great eyes.

Right at the moment, I looked like I'd been

dragged through a coal mine; a sixty-dollar pair of corduroy pants ruined and it wasn't as if I were still married to a millionaire's daughter. Only Sharon Peralta still looked reasonably put together, preppy and professional in chinos and white blouse, with her black hair pulled back and a flush of exasperation in her fine cheekbones. She regarded us as one would a curious and potentially dangerous tribe.

"I was thinking about hockey as a complex adaptive system for controlled violence, but then I stepped out on the street with the Mod Squad." She turned to Lindsey. "That's a baby boomer pop-culture reference." Lindsey ignored her.

"It's Mapstone," Peralta groaned, waving his hand at me. "He spent fifteen years teaching college and now he just can't get enough action."

"Stop," I said. It hurt to smile.

"He's right, Dave." Lindsey stroked my un-bruised hand. "You seem to be a magnet for this kind of thing."

"I've never seen you draw down before."

"I've never had to before," she said quietly.

We were right across from Union Station, a charming Spanish mission-style building from the 1920s that sat dark and closed. The last passenger train had been canceled a few years ago. The building's old stucco front glowed yellow-white in the reflected light of the street lamps. Off behind it, a freight train slowly trundled along, steel wheels clanking across steel rails. Several police cars and a fire truck were arrayed on the street in front of us. The cops were all in the building and the firemen, tall and bulked up, milled awkwardly around their truck, not sure whether to go or stay. A figure slumped in the back seat of one of the PPD cars, safely behind locked doors and Plexiglas prisoner screen: my antagonist from the elevator shaft.

Peralta and Lindsey filled me in on what had happened. They saw the bad guy too late, as he jumped out of the darkness and landed on me. It hurt all over again to hear them describe our roll into the wooden gate of the elevator shaft, and then through it. About that time, the guy's partner took a shot at Peralta and got the hell out of the building before Peralta canceled his ticket for good.

Somewhere in the melee Peralta tore a nasty gash in his arm. Then there was nothing to do but try to get me out of the elevator shaft, a task that had to wait for the fire department. It was a good fifteen feet down there. Somehow I got out with just a twisted ankle, some bruises, and a black eye.

"At least we got two of the dirtbags," Peralta said. "With any luck, PPD can find out who their friend is. They say there's been a smash-and-grab gang of carjackers working downtown for a month. This is probably them."

Peralta sniffed. "So much for their little bicycle patrols. You want a job done, call a deputy sheriff."

"What about the women in the Benz?" I asked.

"The one on the passenger side went to the hospital unconscious," Sharon said. "The only place you can beat somebody that badly and she ends up fine is in the cartoons."

"Two doctors' wives out on the town," Lindsey said. "Just stopped at a traffic light. Wrong place, wrong time, adios."

Mike and Sharon were bickering over whether he should get a tetanus shot when a young, crew-cut PPD sergeant stepped out.

"Chief." He approached Peralta tentatively. "Don't mean to bother you, but there's something in here you'd better take a look at."

If Lindsey and I had gotten into this mess alone, the city cops might have treated us with annoyance. Our escapade would have caused much report writing by our colleagues in blue and they wouldn't have appreciated the county mounties butting into their jurisdiction. But Peralta was chief deputy of Maricopa County and a presence that could impress, intimidate, and manipulate just by walking in a room. He looked at the sergeant, rose stiffly from the squad car bumper, and suddenly his stride was all business. I followed them back toward the building. Just standing up caused my face to start throbbing painfully.

"This building has been abandoned for years," the sergeant was telling Peralta. "Looks like the last use was as some kind of warehouse."

"It was once a hotel, back in the twenties, when the railroad station opened," I said.

Peralta flashed me a look of annoyance. "I hurt too much for history lessons, Mapstone."

We stepped around old packing cartons and rotting wooden pallets. The fire department had set up some emergency lighting; it cast a harsh halogen glare and stark shadows around the big room. At the mouth of the elevator shaft, a ladder provided easier access than I had found an hour before. The sergeant climbed down, followed by Peralta. I went next, then Lindsey. Sharon, I noticed, stayed outside.

It was still gloomy and close at the bottom. Cops' flashlights played off piles of trash and ancient, greasy cables and pulley wheels. It was maybe ten feet by ten feet. Big enough for two men to find each other in the dark. The sergeant led us through a wooden barrier on one of the shaft walls. We stepped through, crossed down maybe half a dozen small steps. That led into a narrow hallway of rough red brick and what looked like a dirt floor. I stooped to fit. Peralta filled the hallway, scraping the walls like an aircraft carrier transiting locks made for pleasure boats. Lindsey, at five-seven, could just stand up.

"We found this when we came down," the sergeant said. "There's several passages down here. Looks like they might have been sealed off from the rest of the warehouse. If there's another way up, we haven't found it. One of my guys leaned against part of the brick and it gave way. That's when we called the detectives."

We walked maybe twenty feet and made a sharp turn. Here the passage opened into a slightly larger room where four other Phoenix cops were clustered. Part of the wall had collapsed and I could see, in a flashlight beam, some debris beyond.

We approached silently. The opening in the wall was small, just big enough to hand through a nineteen-inch TV set. The bricks had fallen in, exposing a cavity inside the wall. On the other side were some wooden framing and more old brick. The cops shone their lights and we peered in. It was a small skull, human looking, along with more bones, all a yellowish color, collapsed into a heap. There was some unidentifiable fabric or maybe leather. Then I saw another small skull.

For a long time nobody said anything. We stooped in silence and stared through the hole in the wall, as if we expected the flashlight beams to re-animate the dead.

"Look at that, off to the side," Lindsey said.

"Don't touch anything!" It was a patrolman who looked like a young Jack Kerouac.

"Oh, okay," she said sweetly, her sarcasm lost on a roomful of cops. She plucked away Jack Kerouac's flashlight and focused it on an object that looked a little larger and thicker than a silver dollar. It was metal, tarnished and brass-colored under a coating of dust. My eyes were getting too bad to make out the design on its head.

"Pocket watch," Peralta said. "See, there's the watch chain off in the dust. Looks like some initials on the cover, but I can't make 'em out."

"It looks like a large Y and a small H," Lindsey said. I could hear the scratching of a cop's pen on a notepad and a memory compartment rattled open in my head.

"Y-H?"

"No," I said, absent-mindedly standing up straight, nearly cracking my head on the low ceiling. "It's H-Y. It was a cattle brand."

Everybody was looking at me now, the passage thick with cologne and dust.

"Hayden Yarnell," I said. "The cattle baron."

Cop faces stared at me impatiently.

I nodded toward the bones. "These must be the Yarnell twins. His grandsons. They were kidnapped back in the Depression and never found."

Lindsey whispered what we were all thinking: "Oh my God."

Chapter Three

Hayden Winthrop Yarnell burst into Arizona history on an April day in 1889, the year my grandmother was born. That day, at a desolate one-shack siding on the Southern Pacific Railroad grandly called Gila City, a gang of robbers attacked a train as it took on water. They wanted the express car, which they heard was carrying payroll strongboxes bound for the mines at Bisbee. The gold was there, all right, but so was Hayden Yarnell with two Colt Peacemaker revolvers.

A photo of him taken two months later shows a clean-shaven man with delicate lips and a long, strong nose, looking uncomfortable and stern in a high collar, string tie and suit coat. But something behind his eyes burned with the obstinate clarity of the pioneer—that's the way I've always pictured him at Gila City.

The leader of the outlaws, a murderer and

rustler named Three-Fingers McMackin, shot a
deputy in the face and strode to the door of the
express car. When Three-Fingers slid the door
open, Yarnell put a .45 caliber bullet between his
eyes. Another desperado nearly severed Yarnell's left
arm with a rifle shot, but the young guard managed to get back in the express car and close the
door. For the next half-hour, the outlaws emptied
their pistols and rifles into the car as Yarnell clung
to the floor by the payroll boxes. But they didn't
have the guts to try to open the door again, so they
rode away empty handed.

This wasn't the last Arizona would hear of
Hayden Yarnell. With reward money from the
train robbery, he talked his way into becoming a
partner in the Copper Queen mine, the legendary dig that for a time made Bisbee, Arizona, the
most important city between St. Louis and San
Francisco. Five years later, Yarnell cashed out a rich
man, not yet thirty years old. By that time he also
owned three saloons in Brewery Gulch, Bisbee's
notorious pleasure district, and was a director of
the town's biggest bank. Every history of Bisbee in
the 1890s had a Hayden Yarnell story or two: about
the day he faced down a gang of outlaws trying to
rob the Goldwater-Castenada Department Store,

his marathon poker games that would go for days, the orphanage he quietly bankrolled.

With the Apache subdued and the coming of the railroad, a young Anglo with vision and money could build many an empire. Yarnell chose cattle, one of the touchstones of the West. His first ranch, Rancho del Cielo, spread two thousand acres across the high southern Arizona grasslands around Tombstone. Eventually, he had more than a hundred thousand head of cattle scattered across ranches and pastureland from the Mexican border into the Arizona high country two hundred miles north. And every one of them bore the distinctive brand of his initials—the large Y, the small h—looking just as we found them engraved on the pocket watch beside two small skeletons.

I was telling this story over breakfast at one of my favorite morning spots, an unassuming little eatery on Glendale Avenue called Susan's. It had recently been called Linda's. Such are the comings and goings in the Valley of the Sun. Peralta sat across from me, occasionally nodding as he munched on a giant skillet breakfast, picked through that morning's *Arizona Republic* and made notes in a stack of manila files spread out among the salsa, ketchup, jam, and coffee. The television was tuned to CNBC. Susan came by to fuss over my black eye.

Peralta was decked out in Brooks Brothers and had the annoying energy of a morning person. I was in a suit, too, charcoal gray with a subdued navy tie that had been an early gift from my ex-wife, Patty. In my years away from Phoenix, I had come to love suits. Now it made me stand out as an oddball in a town of golf-course attire. I didn't mind.

"Mapstone, your mind is a wondrous thing." His tone was ambiguous. "How do you know these things?"

"I wrote a paper on Hayden Yarnell in college. Then my dissertation was on the Great Depression in the West, remember? Of course not. Anyway, he was one of the most important cattlemen in the state's history."

"This Hayden Yarnell is related to Max Yarnell, the businessman?"

"Where do you think Max got his money? Max Yarnell is a grandson. If I'm not mistaken, he's a brother of the twins who were kidnapped."

Peralta crooked his mouth down and squinted at me. "So why the hell haven't I ever heard of this Yarnell kidnapping case?"

I shrugged. "I only know about the kidnapping

because my grandparents used to talk about it. It happened in 1941, right on the eve of World War II. The cops caught the guy and he was executed, so there was no real mystery aside from where the bodies were buried. Then the war changed this town forever. You know ancient history in Phoenix is three years ago."

"I can't imagine not seeing Jamie and Jennifer grow up," he said, speaking of his grown daughters. It was a stunningly introspective remark for Peralta and I made no reply. He went on, "Don't you want to have kids, Mapstone?" He didn't even wait a beat. "You seem to know a lot about this case. So go down and help our friends at Phoenix PD. You can use the money."

It was my deal with the county: two thousand dollars if my research into an old case led to some substantial new information; five thousand if it closed the case. I did need the money. But I ate my omelet in silence, which would annoy him; he was a quick-answer man. Finally I said, "There's nothing to be done. We have the bones. Find a Yarnell relative and test the DNA. Looks pretty open-and-shut."

"That's even better," Peralta said.

I was losing my appetite. "This is a city case, and

the only thing they want less than a sheriff's deputy sticking his nose into it is a sheriff's consultant."

Peralta shook the ketchup bottle violently and doused his concoction of eggs, ham, peppers, and potatoes. "Let me see your wallet." I played along and handed it over. "I see a star—a good-looking badge, if I may say so—that says 'Maricopa County Deputy Sheriff.' I see a deputy sheriff's ID card with your name on it." He tossed it back at me. "As I recall, you graduated from the academy and worked on the streets for five years before thinking you wanted to go off and teach college."

"Four and a half years."

"Any teaching jobs out there you want?"

"I got a call from a Bible college in Houston," I said. He almost smiled.

"Anyway, your help on the case has been requested by Chief Wilson himself." The big enchilada of Phoenix PD. Peralta added, "After I volunteered you. He liked the work you did on the Phaedra Riding case."

Peralta was just being himself, but I couldn't hide my annoyance. "You are the master of the hidden agenda. I should have known we weren't just having breakfast to raise our cholesterol levels and gossip."

"We work for America's Toughest Sheriff, remember? So theater is important."

"I'm so glad I bring something useful to the department," I said sourly.

"You do!" he said, stuffing another forkful into his mouth. "We've got the chain gang, the tent jail, the women's chain gang. And we've got the nation's only cold-case expert who's a history professor and a sworn deputy—just to show we're gentle and intellectual, too."

"Oh, Christ!" I dreaded the hostility of the city cops to an outsider.

"Just do that history thing you do." He waved a meaty hand. "Write the local and national stuff going on at the time of the case, give a nice timeline, list of characters, new evidence, what it all probably meant, blah, blah, blah. The media eat that shit up. Your buddy Lindsey can make it a PowerPoint presentation and we can do color handouts."

"Blah, blah, blah," I mocked him.

"David." Peralta hardly ever called me by my first name. He sighed deep within himself and his broad, expressive face seemed instantly old. He rapped his knuckle on the newspaper. "We're taking serious heat on this serial killer. Harquahala Strangler. The media's even given the cocksucker a

name. It's a sheriff's investigation and we're suck-
ing wind."

"How many now?"

"Twenty-six women. All strangled, sexually
assaulted, and mutilated, dumped in the desert
west of the city. Last week he murdered a housewife
from Chandler."

"And you've got nothing?"

He glared at me. "We've got file boxes full of
reports. We've got computers full of reports. We ain't
got dick. We have an FBI serial-killer team living in
my shit, and they think we're morons." He made an
extravagant wipe with his napkin and slurped coffee.
"So we need some good press. This is a notorious
unsolved case, a rich family. If you help close an old
kidnapping—remember, you were front-page news
during the Riding case—maybe we can buy some time
before the politicians start calling for our hides."

"The trained egghead, to the rescue."

We settled up and walked to the parking lot
in silence, my ankle shooting pain bullets into my
brain with every step. Peralta's shiny black Ford sat
officiously next to my silver BMW convertible, the
flotsam of a failed marriage.

"This car, Mapstone."

"Don't start…"

"No deputy can drive a BMW. People will think you're dirty."

"Patty bought it for me. You know that."

"No way would I let a woman buy me a car!" Peralta snorted.

"Your wife makes ten times what you make, and she's bought you everything but your guns."

"That's different," he sniffed. "Anyway, Patty's your ex now. And it's…" He waved his hand at the car. "It's just not what we drive in this family."

"I need a good beat-up jeep, huh? With a gun rack and a 'Peace Through Superior Firepower' bumper sticker?"

"Exactly. You know, you could have gotten killed last night, being unarmed. It's department policy for deputies to carry a piece at all times."

"Even consultants?"

"Well, you're kind of in a gray area." He took off his suit coat, exposing the nine-millimeter Glock automatic in a shoulder holster. He tossed the coat into the Ford.

Finally, he said, "That woman died."

I looked at him blankly.

"The doctor's wife. She never came out of her coma. Died of massive head trauma. So now it's a murder rap."

"Oh, no."

Peralta said, "When you and I started out in this business, the world was still safe enough that there were some places where you had to carry heat and most places where you didn't. And you could tell the difference, know what I mean? Nowdays, hell, nobody knows when you'll meet some socio-path who doesn't even know enough to be afraid. Carry a gun, Mapstone. I don't want to have to save your ass over and over. It was hard enough when you were twenty-one."

Chapter Four

I climbed into the BMW, slid in Coltrane's *Blue Train* CD and took Seventh Avenue downtown. Dammit, I liked the car. Somewhere, the cold autumn wind was whipping leaves down streets scented with chimney smoke: the genuine fall of our movie-and-TV-seeded collective memory. But in Phoenix, it was seventy-five degrees and intensely sunny. The desert did change with the seasons, but the transformation was very gradual: autumn was a sweet mildness in the late afternoon, a change in the quality of light, a wistful abbreviation of the day. You had to pay attention.

When I hit Indian School, the cell phone rang.

"So, David," a woman's voice said, "I hear you got into some trouble last night."

"I didn't think Pulitzer Prize winners got up this early," I said to Lorie Pope of the *Arizona Republic*.

She laughed without humor. "Yeah, well, the

fad-du-jour over here is re-engineering the news-room into 'teams,' where we all get to rotate into the cops beat. It's supposed to make everyone feel equal. I feel like I'm twenty-one years old again."

"I remember when you were twenty-one."

"And I remember you, my love," she sighed in her husky alto. "But I digress. So what about it? A robbery downtown last night? The heroic Chief Peralta saving the distressed damsels in a dramatic showdown. Then something about a chase and a couple of skeletons being found? A certain history-professor-turned-deputy involved. Something tells me it isn't just another body drop here in sunny Phoenix. Tell me something I can put in the paper."

Idling at a red light, I flipped down the sun visor and used the mirror to check the damage to my face. Not too bad: a cut on my left cheek, ugly bruise under my left eye, a little swelling. Hurt like hell. The light changed and I said, "You know how Peralta is. Go through the public information officer."

"They'd just send me to that damned sheriff's Web site for a press release."

"Or buy me a drink off the record."

"That interesting, huh?" she said. "So how

about tonight? Or do you have plans with that X-er girlfriend, whatshername, Ashley?"

"Lindsey."

"Whatever."

"You ever hear about the Yarnell kidnapping?"

"Sure," she said.

"What do you know about it?"

"You're the historian, David. Weren't they grandsons of Hayden Yarnell? Twin brothers, right? I think a guy was finally caught."

"Jack Talbott," I said. "He was a handyman, who did work at the Yarnell place. He was arrested for some minor thing down on the border and they found some of the ransom money on him. But he never admitted to the kidnapping and they never found either the bulk of the ransom money or the twins."

"So, why are you telling me this?"

"I am preparing your mind," I said. "I'll call later."

Ten minutes later, I parked outside Phoenix Police Headquarters, a sterile monstrosity of the 1970s that uglies up the corner of Seventh Avenue and Washington Street. On the Washington side, about thirty protesters walked in a long circle, carrying signs: "Stop killing us!" and "NO Police War on Minorities." In a vacant lot off Van Buren Street last night a sixteen-year-old Hispanic kid decided to get in a gun battle with the cops. Nobody knew why. The newspaper said he was hit by sixteen bullets. Sixteen years and sixteen bullets. I limped around the corner, feeling the Advil I had taken for my ankle wear off, took the side entrance and checked in with the desk cop.

Half an hour passed before I was given a visitor's badge and sent up to the investigations division. It took up most of a floor, but with its cubicles, computers, and neutral-tone decor, it looked more like an insurance office than a police station. A receptionist sent me back to a glass office where a man sat staring at a messy desk. All I could see was the top of his head: dark, straight, dry hair, parted on one side. The name-card on the door said, LT. AUGUSTUS HAWKINS. He sure as hell didn't look like a Roman emperor.

I rapped on the doorjamb and stepped inside. "David Mapstone, MCSO."

"I know who you are," the lowered head spoke.

The bullshit cop hazing was well under way. The long wait downstairs. Now he would let me stand awkwardly while he balanced his checkbook or wrote to his girlfriend, or whatever. It was like dealing with a tenure committee and I was really bad at it.

I waited at least a minute before speaking. "Look, Hawkins, I don't want to be here any more than you want me to be. But I've got orders, same as you do."

The dry, dark hair went back and a face rose up. A most ordinary, suburban face with thin, pale lips, and blotchy, pale skin. A face that would always be just a few hours ahead of needing a shave. Below the face was a wrinkled gray dress shirt and a goldish pattern tie with an enormous knot. The face regarded me and nodded grimly.

"Yeah, well, right. Sit."

I did.

"This is a city case."

"No!"

"We have a cold-case squad."

"Seriously?"

"We don't need your help."

"I'm crushed."

"We don't want your help."

"So call Chief Wilson and tell him that."

He sighed heavily from somewhere south of his lungs and went back to staring at his papers. He didn't like eye contact. "My orders are to cooperate. I follow my orders. This is just a job. Not a crusade." He signed a document and looked at me again, briefly.

"And this is your lucky day," he went on, "because I have way more homicides than I have detectives. We have three thousand open-unsolved cases, and they're from five and ten years ago, with living loved ones who care about what happened. I sure as hell don't have time for my guys to be mucking around with some bones from sixty years ago. So if you stay out of the way and write your little report, we'll get along fine."

"Yessir," I said. "Out of the way, little report, get along fine."

He looked up and his eyes narrowed down to slits. A pillbox face ready to resist invaders.

"Look, what do you need to get this over with as fast as possible?"

I told him: access to records, somebody to push through the testing of the crime scene and the skeletons, and time to interview the Yarnell family.

He leaned back and expelled a breath. "You're talking about one of the most prominent families in the state. What do you need to talk to them about?"

"You know, we talk to family members in murder investigations. At least at the sheriff's office we do."

He shook his head and his voice became whiny.

"Jesus. It's virtually a closed case. We just need to tie up loose ends. There's no mystery here. We don't need to make waves or piss people off."

"I can be quite charming," I said. "Look how I'm winning you over."

He rubbed his neck. "You will wear your MCSO identification in the building at all times. There's no smoking in here. No using our office supplies. You will gather evidence and take no action—none—without informing me first."

He smoothed the papers before him. "No cowboy tactics, no Peralta shoot-em-ups. This is a nine-to-five job, a professional, civil service job. I'm taking my kid to soccer practice tonight, right on time. I expect that from everyone on this floor." He added: "We'll get the lab work moving ahead."

I rose and started to leave.

"You're an outsider times two, Mapstone," Hawkins said. "You're not a Phoenix officer. And you're not really even a deputy. You're some kind of professor. Outsiders don't do well in this department."

"There goes my self-esteem," I said, and left him staring at his desktop.

Chapter Five

The cases were so old the files were kept in the city records warehouse over on Jefferson Street. At least, that's what I hoped. I drove over, checked in with another civil servant at another desk, and, after some searching, went to work. I slipped the CD of Ellington's Carnegie Hall concert in my Walkman and spent the afternoon picking through records.

The physical memory of the case was located in dusty folders inside a single cardboard file box: papers that had once been the center of somebody's work, but now sat dusty and neglected. Lindsey was a master of search engines, databases, spreadsheets and the Internet. But most records older than ten years were still on paper, microfiche and microfilm, and research was done the way I had learned it in college. Suited me fine. There was something almost mystical about the tactile search through old records for historical truth—the idea of touching the same piece of paper that was touched by the man or woman who lived the event. But, as Peralta said, maybe I was just strange.

The files were a mess, out of chronological order or their proper folder. It looked as if they had been tossed haphazardly into the box years ago and forgotten. The dust attested to that. I was sneezing and wishing I had taken a Sudafed. So I spent more than an hour sniffling, sneezing, and sorting the files into some kind of order. I separated them into piles: handwritten call logs from uniforms, type-written accounts from the detectives, photostats of FBI forms, crumbling newspaper articles, frag-ments of court transcripts, a booking record with fading blue fingerprints, the judge's execution order and black-and-white photos. Then I organized the reports chronologically—those with dates, at least. Ellington's orchestra went smartly from "Take the A Train" through "Stardust" and "Ring Dem Bells." The concert had been recorded in 1943, two years after the Yarnell kidnapping.

This was not like the case files of a modern police agency. There were no pre-printed inci-dent reports for the beat cops to fill in, or any lab or forensics reports. Trace evidence beyond a detective's sense of smell would have been a science fiction dream. I looked in vain for a chronology of the victims before the kidnapping. Even for a crime from 1941, this one seemed to have generated little paperwork, much less the kind of files that would go with what one newspaper labeled it: "Arizona's Crime of the Century." But my brief time back at the sheriff's office had taught me how case files became misplaced, lost, and picked apart as time went on. The files were obviously incomplete. I made a note to check for files at the county courts and in historical archives. Then I got down to reading what I had.

On December 4, 1941, a radio car was called to the home of Hayden Yarnell. The officers were told that a kidnapping had occurred and they immediately summoned detectives. Yarnell's twin grandsons, Woodrow and Andrew, had gone missing the previous Thursday, Thanksgiving. They were four years old and wearing matching cowboy outfits, but there was no mention of a pocket watch.

I skimmed through a detective's report typed on a machine with a crooked r key, looking for a reason why it had taken the family so long to call police. The boys' father, Morgan Yarnell, said he had put the twins to bed Thanksgiving night around eight o'clock. When his wife checked on them after midnight, they were gone. The grounds of the Yarnell house were searched, as were the adjoining citrus groves. At seven the next morning, Friday, November 28, Morgan Yarnell received a phone call from a man who claimed he had taken the boys. He demanded a hundred thousand dollars, deposited in a locker in Union Station. Morgan Yarnell complied, but the boys were never returned.

The reports yielded no good answer for the week's delay. But several were signed by a detective named Joe Fisher. That was a name I had run across before. He was a legend in the Phoenix department, an investigator who had worked on all the big cases in the 1930s and 1940s. So it made sense he would pick up the Yarnell case. I unconsciously ran my fingers across the flimsy paper. Joe Fisher. This would require a trip to the Police Museum, to learn more about the man who came into the case with the impossible delay of a week.

At the bottom of one typewritten sheet, dated December 5, were the words "see officer's observations" but I couldn't find those pages. Damn.

Next I read the arrest report from the little border town of Douglas. It was dated December sixth. A Japanese fleet was taking its position to attack Pearl Harbor. Back in Arizona, a man named Jack Talbott was arrested for being drunk and disorderly in his Douglas hotel room. The cops found five hundred dollars on him in hundred-dollar bills, with serial numbers matching those in the bag that Morgan Yarnell had left at the train station. They also found what were described as "bloodstained children's clothes." A news clipping said the boys' father identified the clothes as belonging to Woodrow and Andrew.

Next I picked through the photos to find a mug shot from the corrections department. It showed a thin, sharp-featured young man with dark hair. He had mocking, merry eyes, not the look of zombie-like disorientation common to many who face the booking camera, whatever the era.

Talbott wasn't alone. A news story told of a young woman found with him, Frances Richie, age twenty-four. She was called his girlfriend, and charged as an accessory in the crime. She was pictured in a smart suit with a slouch fedora. Beneath the hat was a pretty face with delicate lips and large eyes. She didn't look like Talbott's type, but I had been wrong about that kind of thing before. After searching in vain for any police report on Richie, I set her photo next to his.

The trial transcripts and the newspaper accounts were unanimous in portraying Jack Talbott as everything that would horrify stolid Depression-era America: young, male, rootless, with a penchant for liquor, gambling, loose women, and the company of petty Phoenix hoodlums. Nowadays, he'd just be living an alternative lifestyle. He grew up in an orphanage back East and did time as a teenager for burglary. Then he hopped a freight train for the desert.

Talbott ended up doing odd jobs around the Yarnell house, sometimes filling in as chauffeur for the family. Meanwhile, he had gotten in over his head with gambling debts. To the county attorney, those things spelled opportunity and motive. In 1943, Talbott was executed at the state penitentiary in Florence. Richie received life in prison. Talbott's last meal was a steak, which the authorities apparently fulfilled despite wartime rationing. He never confessed to the crime. He never told where the boys were buried.

The files contained no mention of the old building where we found the skeletons. Nor was there a report of a missing pocket watch. Most of all, I wondered: Why had this powerful family waited a week to call the cops?

I rubbed my eyes, nursed a paper cut, stood up and stretched, then sat back down to go through it all over again, this time making notes. By the time the clerk came by to tell me the warehouse was closing, I had several pages written and I was ready for a break. As Hawkins said, just a nine-to-five job.

Chapter Six

There weren't many old buildings left in Phoenix, but I worked in one: the old city-county building at Washington and First Avenue. Finished in 1929 just before the stock market crashed, the five-story courthouse was a mélange of Jazz Age ambition and Hoover utility under a vast red-tile roof. On the city hall side, art deco Phoenix birds rose up grandly to bolster the brown sandstone. It must have been the most imposing building in Phoenix when this was a farm town with a population of 48,000. Later, it served as Phoenix police headquarters into the 1970s. Now, with nearly three million people spread across the Salt River Valley, the building sat like a museum piece surrounded by the monotonous glass and concrete boxes of downtown.

It was Wednesday and my ankle hurt worse. The elevator was still out; with the building nearly empty except for the marriage license bureau in the basement, the county wasn't in a hurry to fix it. I limped up the winding staircase, leaning on the wrought-iron railing as I climbed past the empty hallways of dark wooden doorframes, 1930s light fixtures and Spanish tile floors. I was on the fourth floor, which was mostly used as storage for who-knew-what old city and county records. Outside my office at the end of the hallway, a county maintenance crew had attached a new sign that said, DEPUTY DAVID MAPSTONE, SHERIFF'S OFFICE HISTORIAN. It still looked strange to me.

The office was big and airy, with large windows looking out on the arid Patriots Square across the street, and the massive new ballpark several blocks east. Other walls were lined with law books and old records, long forgotten by the county. The furnishings were strictly courthouse castoffs: large desk, a couple of tables and straight-back chairs, all of dark, heavy wood. I had brought in a watercolor print by a Santa Fe artist. It reminded me of a trip to New Mexico a few years before, but it bugged Peralta, who had no taste for even the slightly abstract.

I certainly didn't need the office—I could work at home on the laptop or find a cubicle at the sheriff's headquarters a block south—but I liked it. It had a wonderful dingy, 1940s quality.

Years before it had been the sheriff's private office before it was relegated to storage and then forgotten, until Peralta commandeered it for me. "It will give you structure," he had said. But I also knew it would allow him to keep an eye on me but not have me close enough to make the regular deputies at Madison Street uncomfortable.

I cleared off a scuffed wooden courtroom table as my Yarnell workspace. Lindsey was trying to teach me to use computerized spreadsheets and expert programs to organize my information. But I still found comfort in index cards, sheets of paper, a white board, and a cork bulletin board. If the stories about computers melting down on New Year's Day 2000 were true, my old-fashioned tools might be best. Still, I used my Mac PowerBook for writing, e-mail, and surfing the Net, using about ten percent of its capabilities, Lindsey chided me. Whatever worked. I wanted to deliver a report to Hawkins and Peralta in two weeks at the most.

"Hey-yo, Mapstone."

Carl, the building security guard, was standing at the door. Flush-faced and white-haired, with a thin British army officer mustache, Carl was retired from the Arizona Highway Patrol. He still carried himself with the bearing of a member of an elite law enforcement agency, but he was also very lonely and could talk the entire morning away.

"Another beautiful day in Phoenix," Carl said, examining the doorjamb for who-knows-what. "God, I hate days like this. It'll only make those damned people from the Midwest want to move out here for good. Then they'll bring all their problems. Then they'll enact a slew of new laws and make things just like what they wanted to get away from in Minnesota or Illinois."

"I know." It was an old discussion, among Arizonans and between Carl and me.

He moved into the office and leaned against the edge of the desk.

"I see you found the Yarnell twins Monday night."

He pointed to the copy of the *Republic* sitting on my desk. Lorie Pope had a Page One story on the discovery of the skeletons. It included photos of Peralta and me, as well as historic shots of young Andrew and Woodrow Yarnell, looking premonitorily unhappily at the camera. I didn't feel guilty about giving the story to her—we had been helping each other for twenty years, since she was a cub reporter and I was a rookie deputy thrown together on a long-ago crime scene.

"It was a hell of a case," Carl said. "I was here when it happened."

"You would have been…?"

"I was born the same year they finished this building," he said firmly. "That was 1929. I was 11 years old when the kidnapping happened. Nothing like that had ever happened in Phoenix. Those two poor little boys…"

I politely motioned for him to sit down, but he ignored me and kept standing. "It was all my parents talked about at the time," he said. "The Lindbergh kidnapping was still fresh in people's minds, you know. And everybody also felt so sorry for the kids' grandfather, Old Man Yarnell. The kidnapping just killed him. Died of a broken heart, they said."

"I know he died in 1942," I said. "Did you ever run across him?"

"Oh, my goodness yes," Carl said. "A living legend, that's what he was. Phoenix was a nice little city, but we still had some cowboys and Indians. Real ones. The West wasn't completely gone." The words sent a little stab of melancholy through me.

"And Hayden Yarnell…" Carl went on to recount the gunfight at Gila City. Then he told of a scary confrontation that he, Carl, had near there as a young highway patrolman in Eloy back in the 1950s. I tried to steer him back to Hayden Yarnell.

"I knew the man!" Carl said. I sat up a little. "Not personally, I mean, but I worked a summer as a bellhop at the Westward Ho, and Mr. Yarnell kept a room there and would give me dollar tips—a lot of money in the Depression."

"Wait, Carl. I thought Yarnell had a mansion of some kind. He was living in a hotel?"

"He did have a grand house. Sat on a bluff down by South Mountain. Burned in the early forties, as I recall. But he kept a suite at the Ho. Most of the big shots in Phoenix did."

Carl went off on a story about young Barry Goldwater. I let him talk himself out, and after a while he went away. The tragedy of lonely retired cops. I told myself again I wouldn't end up that way.

◇◇◇

I wrote a list of people to interview, made a couple of calls, and had started a timeline on the kidnapping when I heard footsteps coming back down the hall. Some days the only way to disengage from Carl was to feign a meeting over at Madison Street.

But it wasn't Carl. It was a cowgirl.

She looked to be in her early thirties, with reddish-brown hair flowing out from the brim of her hat. Large, brown eyes were set nicely atop high cheekbones in a Midwestern pretty face. Her mouth was wide and dug dimples as she smiled. Her light-blue denim shirt and jeans fit her well enough for me to indulge in several introspective lustful moments. She leaned against the door like we were old friends. Then she crossed the room with a confident stride and shook my hand, a firm shake. I was standing now, and noticed she was tall, maybe five-ten, maybe more.

"I'm Gretchen," she said, her voice holding the unaccented tones of the West Coast. "Gretchen Goodheart. I'm with the city archaeologist's office. I'm fresh out of business cards."

I invited her to sit. "There is such a thing as a city archaeologist's office?"

"Yes there is," she said, running a hand across the stack of history books on my desk. "You read books."

"And I'm housebroken."

She sat in one of the straight-back chairs, instantly making it a more interesting piece of furniture. She took off her cowboy hat and let her hair fall freely. Not a trace of hat hair. "This city is built on top of its history, as you well know," she said. "Rose from its ashes. We work with the

Indian sites, the ruins and the canals. But we're also interested in the city's early years after modern settlement. We've found lots of artifacts during the building of the ballpark." She gestured toward the window. "It's being built where the city's old Chinatown stood."

"So how can I help Gretchen Goodheart of the city's archaeologist's office?"

"It's how can we help you," she said. "Sounds like you had quite an adventure the other night. That must really hurt." She indicated my black eye, touching her cheek with an elegant finger. Then she frowned for a moment and the dimples went away; her face was wonderfully expressive. "Didn't Lieutenant Hawkins call you?"

"Nope," I said. "But sometimes it takes a while for word to get from the PD to the sheriff's office."

"I'm sorry," she said. "He said it would be all right if I offered our help."

"We're pretty lonely up here on the fourth floor, ma'am," I said. "And happy for help from an archaeologist."

"Actually," she crossed a long, denim-encased leg, "my undergraduate minor was in history. I was a junkie about the Old West. I've got every book on the subject I can find. I even read your book,

Rock Hard Times: The Great Depression in the Rocky Mountain West."

"Good God, who made you do that?"

"It was a good book."

"Sold in the dozens. I have a garage full if you want a few more copies."

I was way too pleased. I hoped it didn't show.

Chapter Seven

I fetched a flashlight out of the desk, and let Gretchen drive me down to the warehouse where the skeletons had been discovered. It was only a few blocks away, but my ankle was feeling all fifteen feet of that drop into the elevator shaft. She drove a white Ford Explorer that dwarfed the police evidence technician's van sitting outside the old building.

It was anything but forbidding in daylight. It was four stories tall, with a blond brick shell and aging wooden doors and windows painted dark green. The wall at the roofline had an ornamental curve, attempting to mimic the arches of Union Station across the street, I supposed. On one wall, fading white paint announced "AAA Storage" and a phone number with the old "ALpine" exchange for the first two numbers, two-five. A relic from the time when men wore hats and rode trains. It was surrounded by lots of nothing, something downtown Phoenix had in abundance.

Downtown's decline began in the late fifties, when Park Central mall opened a couple of miles north and the Rosenzweig brothers got the city's permission to develop skyscrapers on nearby land they owned, the first of the "uptown" towers that march north on Central Avenue for five miles from the old city center. But in the years I was gone, the eighties and most of the nineties, the decline had turned worse as the city and landowners had cleared block after block of old buildings, including some lovely territorial-era apartments near the Capitol, hundreds of historic bungalows just south of my neighborhood, and much of the old warehouse district around the train station. Now downtown Phoenix was an odd assortment of new buildings—each year's fresh attempt at revival—sitting alone amid emptiness. It made me ache for all that was lost.

Gretchen seemed to read my thoughts. "Not much here," she said.

"Not now. Want to go in?"

"Is that all right for a civilian?" An officious sign proclaimed the building a crime scene and offered various punishments for trespassing.

"If the techs are about done, it should be fine. I would leave your hat. Clearance is pretty low in there."

I pushed open a door and flashed my star at an evidence technician, a platinum-haired butterball in a dark blue jumpsuit who called me "honey" three times in three sentences. Her partner was a large black woman. I don't know how the two got into the smallest of those passages. They were clearing out. I could lock up. I signed a form with name and badge number.

"I'll tell you this, honey," she said. "You got enough bones for two skeletons. I have been doing this for twenty-five years and I know it before the medical examiner even gets into it. And they looked like children's bones."

I asked her for copies of the crime-scene photos, including a snap of the pocket watch with the Yarnell brand. She promised to send them over in the morning.

Gretchen and I stepped into the big room as I narrated the events of Monday night. A couple of bare bulbs in the ceiling gave a murky view of the cartons, pallets, and nameless junk that lay scattered around. Crime-scene tape was draped across the opening to the freight elevator shaft, and two feet of a ladder extended above the floor.

"No way would I have come in here," Gretchen said.

"I have aggressive friends."

We started down the ladder. "And they are? Your friends."

"Mike Peralta, he's chief deputy now but once upon a time we were partners. It's a long story. And Lindsey Adams. She's a deputy, really a computer specialist. We met a few months ago on another case."

"You like her."

I was at the bottom and helped Gretchen step off onto the broken concrete. The dusty smell of the first floor changed to something more moist and earthy. "How can you tell that?"

"The way you say her name." She smiled and the dimples came back.

"Watch your head." We went down the narrow steps into the passage. My cop's black, three-cell flashlight provided the only illumination, and the corridor felt even more claustrophobic than Monday night.

"Look at this." I ran my hand against the rough wall. "How old the brickwork seems. Doesn't even seem part of the warehouse building."

"It's probably not," Gretchen said. The dark corridor didn't echo. It swallowed up sound, making words stand out starkly for a moment before they disappeared.

She went on, "When they cleared the buildings for Patriots Square back in the 1970s, they found this little underground city of tunnels and chambers."

"I remember," I said. "There were old saloons and brothels and opium dens."

"They dated from the 1880s, when there was no air conditioning and it was cooler underground. And as the town grew, the new buildings were just built on top of the old basements, then they were gradually sealed off and forgotten."

I let out a breath, just to remind myself I could. The passage was amazingly close. People were smaller a hundred years ago.

We followed it down one direction, maybe fifteen feet, where it made a hard turn into a larger room, another step down. Here, the brick was mingled with what looked like adobe and the floor was dirt. Ancient wooden citrus crates were stacked precariously in one corner; I could make out the words "Arizona Pride" on one label and an illustration of a Gibson Girl-like redhead holding out a bounteous tray of oranges and grapefruits. Spider webs were everywhere, so we didn't venture far. There didn't appear to be any other way out.

Gretchen followed me as we tracked back the way we came, then turned again and followed the passage to where the skeletons were found. Now it was just a hole in the wall: bones, fabric, bricks, dirt—everything had been photographed, diagrammed and hauled away for more tests. The crime lab could do things today we didn't even dream of when I went through the academy in the mid-1970s.

"This is where they were found?" Gretchen asked.

It jarred me a little, this reminder that those bones were a "they." They once had eyes that saw and cried. They had parents, and a grandfather, who grieved for them. I nodded and played the flashlight around in the little compartment inside the wall. The space inside was maybe a foot deep and three feet wide and high, no larger. It really looked like a careless bit of workmanship: the far wall inside appeared to be dirt. Whoever built the basement didn't extend the brick all the way into the hard soil.

"Andrew and Woodrow Yarnell," Gretchen said softly. "They were four years old when they were kidnapped. Taken from their grandfather's house. Never found alive again. And all this time, they were right here."

The light bounced heavily off the brick. Winston Churchill did brick masonry to relax, but I didn't know beans about it. The bricks in this wall looked a little newer than the ones down the passage. Maybe. The mortar was crumbling. It would make sense: Jack Talbott walled them in and re-laid the bricks hastily.

"Do you think they were alive when he put them in there?" Gretchen asked.

"It's hard to know." I hesitated telling more to a civilian. Talbott had been found with the twins' pajamas. So maybe they were murdered immediately and the ransom demand was a ploy. That was almost a comforting scenario, considering the scraps of rope and leather that had been found. Those might mean the little boys had been tied up and walled in while still alive, without even a blanket against the cold desert night underground. I kept it to myself.

I tried to stand upright and almost knocked myself in the head. "The other thing I can't get out of my head is this pocket watch we found. Why would it be there?"

"Well, wristwatches didn't come into widespread use until after World War I," Gretchen said. "So there were probably lots of pocket watches still in use in 1941."

"Right, my grandfather loved his. His father gave it to him. And railroad men used them, too. But…" I stared out at the blackness of the passage. You would never find your way out without a flashlight. "But why would two four-year-olds have a pocket watch? Could they even tell time?"

"I see what you mean."

"And if this Jack Talbott, the kidnapper, was after a hundred grand of Yarnell money, why wouldn't he have taken the watch, too? It looked gold."

She moved toward me and took my hand. "David, I need to get out of here. It's creeping me out."

We went back out the way we came, Gretchen holding my hand tightly. I helped her back up the ladder and then started up myself. The rungs were slippery and cold. I felt an involuntary chill wrapping around my back, a sense of climbing out of a black place where murder had lived undisturbed for nearly sixty years, a sense of not wanting to look back down the ladder behind me. I stepped onto the hard concrete of the main room and had forgotten about the shooting pain in my ankle.

"Sorry," she said when we were out on the street again. She wiped each cheek. Her eyes were red. "Sorry."

"Don't worry." I patted her shoulder. "It's pretty intense. I shouldn't have taken a civilian down there."

No," she said, a marked steeliness in her pleasant voice. "I wanted to see."

Chapter Eight

I got back home late, feeling a little guilty about my appreciation of the way Gretchen Goodheart filled out her blue jeans, and a little edgy for reasons I couldn't exactly define. I was working on a dull headache that I ascribed to too many hours spent reading old records about an open-and-shut case that was actually growing more complex with every scrap of paper that I accumulated.

Central Avenue was a river of impatient lights headed out of downtown, but Cypress, my street, was dead. I crept along past the neat, darkened houses, the palm trees tall and soldierly in the narrow parking lawns between the sidewalks and the street. This was my old neighborhood. When I was a kid, I knew everybody on the block. There were the eccentric heirs to the railroad fortune on the corner; they moved away to the fancier Palmcroft district when I was ten. There was the old hound-dog in the backyard two houses down who barked if anything was wrong in the night. I knew a story for every house, and every notch in a hedge or passage between fences held a memory. The city was smaller then.

Now there were new neighbors to know. Most of the old owners had left or died in the years I had been away from Phoenix. Many of the houses had been restored beyond any former splendor, pools added, and all in all Willo was much more affluent than it had been. Yet the neighborhood had gained a self-conscious quality, too: It was a historic district, an urban homesteading success story. I wasn't sure if that was good or bad. I felt a constant sense of familiarity and strangeness, and tonight the block just felt empty and sad.

Lindsey's old white Honda Prelude was parked in front of my house and Lindsey was sitting inside. She had a key to the house but didn't use it. I parked and met her on the sidewalk, where she held her hand gently against my chest as if she were taking some internal reading, then she ran an index finger down my nose, across my lips, into my mouth. She wore baggy jeans and a gray sweater, and her pale skin glowed from the street light. Without a word she led me up the walk and we went inside.

Later, we sat on opposite ends of the sofa, our bare feet resting on each other's laps, easily naked together, sipping the Macallan from shot glasses. We were in the living room, the grandest room in an otherwise small house, with a twelve-foot ceiling and bookcases rising behind a wrought-iron staircase. Sometimes I could feel Grandfather and Grandmother in the room, not as ghosts but as missed beloveds. It was a room that put me in a mind to realize the fleeting preciousness of our connections.

"How was your day, honey?" She arched an eyebrow in parody.

"Oh, the usual, dear. Returning to the scene of the crime. Picking through old bones, serving the public trust. The Phoenix cops don't like me, but they also don't have much interest in old bones."

"I read today that in ancient China the historian held an honored place in the emperor's court," she said.

I smiled. "Born in the wrong time and place, I guess."

"History Shamus." She stroked my leg. "What time and place would you be born in?"

"Oh, I'm greedy. I'd want to see everything:

Rome, the time of Christ and Mohammad, ancient China. I'd want to swap stories with Dr. Johnson and serve with George Washington. Live in the thirties and forties, ride the great old trains, see Arizona before we spoiled it."

"You could stop by and prevent the Yarnell kidnapping," she said.

"But I wouldn't want to live in another time because I couldn't be with you."

She smiled and looked away. "You're a romantic, Dave. I like that."

"And I wouldn't want to live in the past because I'd give up the benefit of modern dentistry."

She laughed out loud, a wonderful sound. "Spoken like the grandson of a dentist."

I told her what I had learned today about the kidnapping. Then we sat in silence, listening to the house breathe and, outside, sirens run down Seventh Avenue. I studied her face, a face so different from the battalions of fresh-eyed, tanned sun-bunnies that Phoenix seemed to produce like General Motors produced Chevys. Hers was a face of contrasts: dark lipsticked lips, full but set in an economical mouth; creamy skin and precise dark brows; cheek-bones appealingly wide; a classical tapering toward the chin; her dusk blue eyes too far apart to be considered conventionally beautiful. All this was framed by the stunning black hair parted in the middle and falling with the barest hint of a curl down to where her neck met her shoulders. And that gold stud in the left nostril—someday I would ask about that, if we had enough time together. The first time we met, I was a year out of my divorce. I watched that face as she did her computer magic for me. And then one day I found her watching me.

"What are you thinking about?"

"Important things," I said. "How was your day?"

"A new assignment, actually," she said. "And I am so glad to get away from Y2K."

"If I had your skills, I'd be rich."

"You're good looking." She smiled. "You're great in bed, on the floor, whatever."

God, she made me feel lucky. "All because of you," I said.

"It's the Harquahala Strangler case," she said, her voice half an octave lower. *"El Jefe"*—her secret nickname for Peralta—"has assigned me to help. I've been teamed up with Patrick Blair."

"Whoa, the alpha hunk detective of the sheriff's office?"

Lindsey smiled a passable Mona Lisa impersonation. "Are you jealous, Dave?"

"No," I lied. "Hell, I thought he and that partner of his—what's his name? Tony Snyder—were gay. They both look like they stepped out of *GQ*. Remember they're in that calendar the sheriff is selling? *Beefcakes with Badges*, or something like that."

"I thought it was cute," Lindsey said. "Anyway, Tony has a nice wife and two babies in Peoria. He's on leave to finish his master's thesis. I think you're jealous, Dave."

I felt a hotness moving across my face and knew I was busted. She gave a delighted giggle.

"So why are they teaming you with Patrick Blair? He seems about as interested in database research as he'd be in studying history."

"They think this dirtbag gets his victims over the Internet."

"Serial killers keeping up with the times."

"If you tell Peralta I told you that, he'll murder me. It's the biggest clue we've held back from the media." She gave me a mischievous smile. "And no leaking it to that old girlfriend of yours, Lauren."

"Lorie."

"Whatever."

"I think you're jealous, Lindsey."

We made love again, a slow, wordless, carnal thing that was the basis of us, as much as the books and the dry humor and the cynicism that hid some shocking hopefulness. Like home: that's how it felt.

Then she was up and sliding back into her clothes, slinging her backpack over her shoulder. I was half asleep and reached out a hand.

"Stay with me, Lindsey."

"I can't, Dave," she said. "I've got to go to work."

"You always worked bankers' hours."

"New job, new hours."

I stood and cinched up the robe. "Peralta's degrading my quality of life. I can't believe he's making you do this."

"I volunteered, Dave." She pulled me toward her for a kiss. "No lectures, History Shamus. I don't want to just be seen as some propellerhead nerd girl doing computer systems."

"I think you proved that Monday night."

"Dave, don't worry. I'm a deputy sheriff, too. And this murderer is out there, right now."

And then she was gone, the front door echoing hard after her.

I wanted to say, "Please be careful."

◇◇◇

I fell into a deep sleep, and I was hiking across huge grassy hills strewn here and there with piñon and scrub oak. A California landscape, not like Arizona. I was acutely aware of the carpet of rough grass beneath my feet and the nervous sense of height, the world falling off in every direction down hillside and arroyo. It was getting dark and a few lights were visible far down the valley, but I felt compelled to walk. I fell, grabbed a scrubby branch, pulled myself back up, set out again. I wasn't afraid. Then there was a banging and jangling that didn't go with the dream, and finally I realized it was the doorbell. I swung off the sofa, slipped on my old, dark-blue Nordstrom robe and walked unsteadily toward the door. I noticed it was two in the morning, and something made me go to the bedroom and get the Colt Python .357 magnum.

I opened the little wrought-iron peephole in the door, saw Peralta, and wondered if I was still dreaming.

"Mike?"

"It's not the fucking Girl Scouts."

I opened the heavy door and he walked in. He was wearing a rumpled suit and carrying a gym bag.

I had seen Peralta in meetings and interrogations and even gun fights. But I had never seen him with the bare hint of vulnerability that surrounded him this moment. He seemed to read me and merely held out a finger, commanding silence, as he moved into the living room and sat heavily in Grandfather's old green leather chair.

"I need a place to stay," he said. "I don't want to talk."

"Are you okay? Is Sharon okay?"

He looked at me like I was an idiot. I held up my hands in surrender and we sat in silence. Finally, I went into the kitchen and came back with two beers. He took one in his massive hand, studied the label with disgust—it was a Sam Adams—but he drank.

I was suddenly aware that I was naked under the robe and my crotch was still delightfully wet from Lindsey, and all in the presence of the chief deputy. He didn't seem to notice. I had never been good at guy talk, where everything real was submerged subtly beneath words of sports and work and women. And I was particularly at a loss in Peralta's company, where his sheer presence overwhelmed everything like a mountain dropped into flatlands. So we sat. I thought of Lindsey, of her body and expression as she pleased herself atop me.

The twelve-foot-tall bookshelves that Grandfather had built kept watch over us.

"Tell me you own a television, Mapstone," he said at last. "Even you'd want to watch the History Channel."

So I took him into the little study and he took over Grandfather's desk chair. With the tube on ESPN, he became a contented self-contained unit. I went back into the living room and read for a while, James Morris' *Pax Britannica*, immersing myself in the adventures, characters and follies of the British Empire. It was the kind of book I wish I could write, but now, at forty, I knew I might never have the time or the talent. Still, Lindsey gave me a bookmark with George Eliot's quote: "It is never too late to be what you might have been."

Later, when I could hear Peralta snoring, I went to the linen closet, pulled out a comforter, carefully spread it over him and shut down the house for the night.

Chapter Nine

The trill of the phone pulled me out of a hard, dreamless sleep into a sun-filled room. I was just in my bedroom, seven forty-six on the digital clock next to the photo of Lindsey from the San Diego trip.

Lorie Pope's voice jumped at me. "David, did I wake you?"

"No," I groaned and swung out of bed onto unsteady feet.

"You always needed at least seven hours of sleep, as I recall," she said. "So last night must have been interesting."

"Not the way you think."

"Really?" she said. "Isn't that a wonderful word? *Interesting.* May you live in interesting times." She laughed her fine, crystal laugh.

I pulled on some shorts and walked to the kitchen, where I poured orange juice and drank it in one long swallow.

"I don't have anything new to leak, my dear."
I pulled aside the blinds and looked into the yard.
The oleanders and bougainvillea needed trimming,
the joys of a nine-month growing season.

"I'm calling to make a deposit, my love," Lorie
said. "It's only fair."

I could hear computer keys clattering in the
background of her voice.

"Remember your skeletons in the wall? And
the man who was executed in the kidnapping? Jack
Talbott? Remember he had a girl with him?"

"Right. Frances Richie."

"She's still alive," Lorie said.

I sat at the wicker kitchen table, my heart pounding a little harder. "Really?"

"I shit you not," she said. "She is still at the women's
unit at Florence, where she has been since 1942."

"How did you find this out?"

"I'd like to say it was terrific shoe-leather reporting, but actually, somebody called and left the tip this
morning. One of the clerks passed it along to me."

I thanked her and hung up. Frances Richie had
been twenty-four when she was arrested with Jack
Talbott in Nogales. That would make her about
eighty-two now. A true life sentence.

My head a little clearer, I went to see if everything

of the night before had merely been a strange dream. The living room was sunny and serene behind the picture window, the ceiling-high bookshelves familiarly pleasing. I walked into the study and there was no Peralta. But the comforter was left folded on the chair with military precision and the newspaper was set precisely in the middle of the desk.

May you live in interesting times.

◇◇◇

Over at the Starbucks at Seventh Street and McDowell, I stopped to buy my usual vente, non-fat, no-whip mocha. I sat outside at a round table surrounded by trim, young white professionals, all attractive, all well off, all unsure whether they really want to live in this wonderful little historic district of stucco homes surrounded by the inner city. They clutched their lattes and the alarm buttons to their Range Rovers and hurried in and out.

And why not be afraid? Look at this morning's *Republic*. In addition to another story about the discovery of the skeletons, it was chock-a-block full of post-modern mayhem right here in paradise. The centerpiece was about the pressure to catch the Harquahala Strangler. There was more in the B-section: some teenagers in Gilbert thought they were vampires and murdered a twelve-year-old girl to prove it;

a visiting nurse was raped and killed in Mesa; some gangbangers tried to ambush two Phoenix cops out in Maryvale. And a string of shootings on the west side had been tied together and now police were seeking one suspect. He now had a name, too: the Grand Avenue Sniper. Otherwise, the Cardinals were losing, the big Indian casino south of town was booming, everything with a "dot-com" attached to the name was making millions and the desert was disappearing into the city at the rate of an acre an hour.

I finished the sports section when the cellular phone rang. I hoped it would be Lindsey. It was Peralta.

"Progress," he demanded.

"What? It's not even nine in the morning." I was cranky. "I could have briefed you at the house last night. Or this morning, I mean, at two o'clock."

"You're a tragic fucking figure," he said.

"Fuck you. I'm sure we've found Andrew and Woodrow Yarnell, but PPD is going by the book. DNA tests and all."

Peralta grunted through the cellular system.

"The case was initially investigated by Joe Fisher. He was a legendary detective on the Phoenix force. That's cool."

"If you say so, Mapstone."

"Why do you care?" I asked.

"Because you're my project."

Before I could respond, he said, "I see your old girlfriend had a big story about the Yarnell case. Funny how that happens."

"Well, Mike, we work for America's Toughest Sheriff. Theater and all that."

"Why do they keep using that bad photo of me?"

"I want to go out to Arizona State Prison," I said. "Can you grease the skids?"

"What? You teaching history to the cons?"

"I'll laugh when I wake up. Frances Richie is still alive out there. She was the woman arrested with Jack Talbott in the Yarnell case."

"Jesus. We have judges letting murderers out in seven years. What the hell is she still doing in prison?"

"One of many questions I want to ask."

"What questions?" I could see him sitting back at his big desk, shaking his head. "We know who did it. What else is there to know?"

"Hey, you want me to work the case. Let me work the case. I want to know how the bodies got into that old warehouse. I want to know where that pocket watch came from. I want to know why the chief deputy doesn't seem to have enough to do so he has to micromanage me."

"All right, let me call the warden," he said. Then, "I put your Lindsey on the Harquahala case."

"So I heard," I said. "I don't know if she's 'my' Lindsey, though."

"Really?" His voice changed. "Why is that?"

"Because these are the nineties. At least for a little while longer."

Now it was his turn to search for a comeback. I said, "Three years is a long time to come up dry on a case like the Harquahala Strangler."

"Yeah," he said, "and you haven't had every law enforcement agency and media outlet in the West second-guessing you, either."

"You're a tragic fucking figure, Chief Peralta."

He ignored me. "It's a serial killer: some nerdy, unemployed, impotent white guy with a rage, like Kirk Douglas in that movie they show on cable."

My mind went blank for a moment. "I think you mean Michael Douglas."

"Whatever. We'll catch him."

"So let me drink my mocha."

There was a long pause. "Mocha?" Then the line went dead.

Chapter Ten

The highway from Phoenix to Florence once traveled for miles through citrus groves until it hit Apache Junction, then turned south into the desert. Nothing but two lanes through the cactus and hard cracked earth for another hour or more. Now the highway was a freeway. The citrus groves were gone, replaced by closely spaced subdivisions and trailer courts, shopping centers and fast-food restaurants. The only familiar sights came from Superstition Mountain looming in the east and the desert at the end of the urban pipeline, and these seemed at risk. I'd always been an Arizona libertarian, reared on Barry Goldwater values of individual freedom and cussed independence. But every day that Phoenix ate another twenty-four acres of desert I was turning into an environmental extremist.

In another hour, I rolled out of the desert into Florence. It's a typical one-industry town, but instead of coal or textiles, it depends on the forcible detention of human beings. Some of them are bad-break losers who never connected with the Franklin Planner map of life, others are as feral as the guys we met on the street Monday night, who'd literally just as soon kill you as look at you. Either way, they were the commodity that allowed these desert Florentines to scratch out a living.

Not too many years ago, the Arizona State Prison was a tough joint cut off by bleached walls and miles of arid wasteland from the fine people of the Grand Canyon State. Now it was one of many facilities run in the area by the corrections department. But if humanity regained its virtue tomorrow, the entire non-convict population of Florence would be out of work.

Frances Richie was neither in the big central prison nor in the women's unit. A guard directed me past a half dozen one-story modern buildings— they were right out of the Cold War missile silo school of architecture—until I came to one with a sign that said: UNIT 13. An appropriate sign of bad luck for what had been a twenty-four-year-old woman who fell in with the wrong kind of man. I checked in, showed credentials, signed papers, and was shown into a large, sunny room stocked with institutional tables and chairs. In a moment, a door buzzed and a woman in a loose denim jumper and clogs came in and shook my hand.

"I'm Heather Amis," she said. "I'm a social worker here." She was in her thirties and so tan that her skin, lips, hair, and eyebrows were varying shades of brown. Only her eyes stood out a bit, two green orbs amid the brown. She had a learned calm, but her words weren't: "I have to tell you, I was hoping you wouldn't come."

"It's always good to be wanted," I said.

"You were very insistent on the phone that you come today," she said. "I read the *Republic*. Finding the bodies of the Yarnell twins."

She motioned me to sit and I folded into a hard plastic chair made for a midget with a strong back.

"Miss Richie is in her eighties. She has diabetes and a heart condition. She can't be in the general population at the women's units. She's senile. So she's here."

"What is here?" I asked. "It's not exactly prison-like."

"We're kind of a nursing home," Heather Amis said.

"Why not just release her?"

"She was an accessory to a capital crime and for

years the Yarnell family opposed it. Yarnell money has elected a lot of governors and legislatures. Parole boards pay attention."

"Do they still oppose it?"

"I don't know, Deputy." A flush of anger crept into her tan cheeks. "She's been left to rot in the system for decades. I may be the first person who ever took an interest in her."

Then she kind of deflated. "Anyway, Miss Richie has nowhere to go. She was an orphan. No family. No friends outside the walls. What would she be released to?"

She shook her head and ran slender brown hands through curling brown hair. "You're a cop, so you have no reason to cut anybody a break. And most of the people I see in here, I can understand that. But, Jesus, the state of Arizona has taken this woman's entire life. Can't you just let her die in peace?"

We sat in silence for a moment. There was nothing to debate. The truth is, cops routinely deal with the marginal, the ignored, the alone, the people who fall through the cracks, as Lindsey says. But Frances Richie was all that in the extreme. Finally, I said as gently as I could, "May I see her?"

"She's not really responsive," Heather said. "I've been working in the unit for six months, and she's never said more than five words to me. But, whatever."

She walked out in a whirl of loose denim and clopping clogs and came back in about ten minutes, backing in the door, pulling a wheelchair.

Somebody said a great novelist could see the beautiful young girl inside the old woman. It would have been difficult with Frances Richie, even though the old news photos showed a young woman who was somewhere between cute and beautiful. Now her face was dominated by an enormous double chin, bulbous nose and battleship gray eyes poking from bony temples—the skull starting to come out at last—all mounted on a body long since overtaken by starchy food, inactivity, and disease. Heather Amis turned her toward me, knelt down and told her who I was.

She just stared and nobody said anything for a long time. In the silence, the room's smell of Lysol covering urine became apparent. Somewhere in the background, an electric something-or-other hummed.

Finally, I said the only thing that seemed to matter. "We found the bodies of Andrew and Woodrow Yarnell."

Frances Richie just stared that watery, unfocused stare, her eyes fixed on a place we couldn't see.

I went on: "We found them bricked up in a wall, down in a tunnel in a building near Union Station in downtown Phoenix."

Heather shot me a nasty look. I could see Frances Richie breathing harder, her bulky chest laboring to fill her lungs.

"Miss Richie," I said, "tell us how those boys got in that building."

"Is this really necessary?" Heather whispered, looking at me like I was the vilest man alive. "I'm going to get some coffee. I can't listen to this." She clopped off down a hallway, and I was alone with Frances Richie. But the old woman looked out into the sunlight, her face an unreadable ruin of wrinkles and fat. I stood and walked maybe ten feet, to a grimy window.

Outside, brand-new sidewalks cut across the flat brown earth of the desert, heading to other buildings past barbed wire, elaborate gates and security cameras perched like electronic vultures. On the other side of the parking lot, a group of male convicts wearing orange jumpsuits were doing something in a cotton field. What was the tunnel into Frances Richie?

I said, "I saw the photo of you in the dark dress the day you were brought back to Phoenix. Seemed like a very pretty dress."

I continued to look outside, just like she was doing.

I heard a word that sounded like "blue." Then she said, very clearly and not in an old-lady voice, "It was navy blue. It was the first store-bought dress I ever had in my life."

I didn't turn around. I didn't want to break the spell.

"You bought it in Phoenix?"

"It was a present. From someone very dear to me."

I spoke carefully. "From Jack? Jack Talbott?"

I turned to face her and she merely shook her head. Then her voice seemed to gather strength and timbre from being used again. "Jack Talbott. I haven't thought of him in years."

Now it was my turn to be silent.

"He was just a boy, really. We were so young then. He had a hard life and didn't know any other way of getting by in the world, so he drank, he ran with women, he fought, he had a very quick temper." She paused.

"He was your lover?"

She strained to hear. "Lover?" she asked loudly. "They told me never to talk about that, never."

"It's okay."

She inhaled loudly. "He always treated me like a lady, like a queen."

"How did you meet him?" I leaned against the wall. Maybe the distance between us made her feel safe.

"I worked at the Owl Pharmacy on Adams Street," she said. Her sentences had a very even cadence until the last two words, when they felt an emphasis whether they needed it there or not. "Is it still there?"

I shook my head.

"We'd come from Oklahoma in 1936 and papa worked off and on in the produce sheds down by the railroad tracks. But a truck backed over him one day and he died." She paused and breathed heavily. "So mother worked as a maid, but she died of TB, and I got a job at the drug store. I could eat lunch for free at the soda fountain."

She reared her head up a little and took another deep breath. "He was walking by one day on the sidewalk, and I was inside by the pharmacy counter, and we saw each other through the window. And he turned back and came inside. I didn't want to seem easy, but I couldn't stop looking at him, couldn't stop smiling. And he couldn't either. What is your name?"

"David Mapstone." I could see Heather starting back in the room, but she picked up on my eyes and came in slowly, quietly, behind us.

"Jack Talbott worked for Mr. Yarnell. Jack wanted to open his own garage someday." She raised her head again, as if inhaling the memories. She paused. "Mr. Yarnell took kindly to him. Mr. Yarnell was a kind man."

She licked her mouth with a huge gray tongue. "Do you believe in love at first sight, David Mapstone, sheriff's deputy? Do young people still believe in that?"

I shrugged not-so-wisely. "I've seen it happen."

"Never met a girl in stir who didn't believe," Frances Richie said. It was strange to hear a woman who looked like a grandmother use a word like *stir* so casually. But she was nobody's grandmother.

"Why did Jack take the twins?" I was so damned clever. Just toss in the hard question after the softballs.

"Jack." It was the only thing she said. She rubbed her eyes.

I repeated the question and she stared at the wall.

"Did you know he was kidnapping Andrew and Woodrow Yarnell?"

Her heavy head seemed to slip down a bit. Then she started to snore and for a long moment I thought she was gone. Then she raised her head and met my eyes, and her gaze was suddenly intense.

"I had a hat with that dress, David Mapstone," she said, sounding the syllables of my name like they were a strange, lost language. Her eyes were bright with tears. "It was the prettiest thing I ever owned. A little, blue felt slouch fedora, but for a girl. Like in the movies. I felt like a movie star. The jail matron in Phoenix took it."

Chapter Eleven

As I flew back at eighty miles-per-hour across the waterless expanse, it sank in how little Frances Richie had really told me. I had conversed with living history. But I had learned about a twenty-four-year-old's beloved hat, not about the most notorious kidnapping in Arizona. Then the old woman was asleep again. I gave a list of questions to Heather Amis, and she grudgingly agreed to ask them.

It didn't feel as if a millennium was coming to an end, but the year 2000 was only six weeks away. I didn't have much to show for it. It was an arbitrary piece of calendar, to be sure: the year 2000, A.D., Anno Domini, the Year of the Lord. Or, for historians, the more inclusive C.E., for "common era." Still, it felt amazing and strange to be alive to see this arbitrary turning of the calendar. As the homely sprawl of Mesa flew by the car windows, I thought about what was happening in the world at 1000

C.E.: the Middle Ages in Europe, and widespread fear of the end of the world. Leif Erickson supposedly discovered America. *Beowulf* was written. In what would become Phoenix, the Hohokam civilization was thriving. I was deadly in any trivia match.

Back in the city, I spent what was left of the afternoon showing photos of the pocket watch to jewelers. One shot showed the watch open: the hands were frozen at eleven-fifty. The owner of an antique jewelry shop in downtown Scottsdale identified it as a Waltham, Model Ninety-Two, eighteen size with twenty-one jewels.

"It's a beauty." He looked at the photos with a magnifying glass. "Railroad quality. Solid gold hunting case, and I would assume that's fourteen-karat gold. Double-sling porcelain dial. Very nice."

"Is it rare?"

"Waltham made a lot of watches. In fact, they were the first company to mass produce watches in America, did you know that? But they also made some exquisite watches, too. The Ninety-Two, it's not a terribly rare watch, but it's not that common, either, especially with the gold case. I'd bet fewer than a thousand of that model were made. Looks like yours is in very fine condition."

"When was it made?"

"Around 1892. Model Ninety-Two, get it?"

I asked him if the serial number could be traced. He wasn't optimistic. "The company went out of business in the fifties," he said. "I could tell you more if you brought it in."

Sure, I thought, I'd be happy to bring in, when Lt. Hawkins lets me check it out from the evidence room. When hell froze over. But I knew this much: The watch found with the twins' bodies was not just a workingman's brass watch, not something likely left behind by Jack Talbott. Yet there was nothing in the reports about a missing watch from the Yarnell house. The watch was never mentioned at all.

I drove downtown with the top down on the BMW. The day had turned cooler with a line of high clouds from the west, and it was hard to imagine that one hundred ten degrees or the raw sun of July were even possible. By the time I reached the courthouse, the streets were jammed with office workers heading out to the suburbs, out to one of those new cul-de-sac developments carved out of saguaro cactus forests. The days were definitely getting shorter, even in the Valley of the Sun. I could tell it by the dusky texture of the light in my office, which just a month before had been filled with sun at this time of day. Now, not yet five-thirty, the room felt faded and tired. Or maybe it was just me. I walked to the substantial old desk, set my notes down and sat myself, feeling the weight of all the violence and loss. I wished Lindsey didn't have to work tonight.

The old jail had been located on the floor above me, the jail where Jack Talbott would have stayed during his trial. Ugly legends surrounded the place, and one day I had toured the cells with Carl. They still possessed a shadowy smell of captivity. For a minute, I just listened to the old-building sounds, waiting for a ghost to appear and explain everything. And that's when I realized I wasn't alone in the room. Sitting elegantly in a straight back chair ten feet away from me, staring out the window and picking a piece of lint off his cuffed pants leg, was Bobby Hamid.

"I hope I didn't startle you, Dr. Mapstone."

"What the hell are you doing here?" I said, too damned obviously startled. I wished I hadn't left my Colt Python at home.

"Forgive me," he said. His accent was vaguely of the British public schools. "I came here looking for you, and the security guard, a very nice fellow named Carl, let me in to wait." It was just screwy enough to be true. "I made the assumption that you would not walk in the door and start shooting, like our friend, Chief Peralta."

I looked around the room, as if anything there could be of interest to Bobby Hamid. Sixty-year-old murder cases, books on Arizona history, aging police logs and reports, empty Starbucks cups. My laptop was where I had left it this morning.

"You have balls the size of Tucson," I said.

"Very good," he said. "The Arizona allusion."

"What do you want?"

He stood and walked over to the desk, then chose another chair and sat, posture perfect, dark suit set off with a conservative, polka-dot navy tie, any sense of menace only to be imagined by me.

"The sunsets this time of year remind me of Iran when I was a boy," he said, looking out the window. "Before the revolution there. But we live in revolutionary times, do we not, Professor Mapstone? Can you think of a time with more upheaval than our own? Even Europe in 1848? 'Things are in the saddle and ride mankind.' Do you recall who said that?"

"Emerson," I said. "I'm not going to have a graduate seminar with a drug dealer. For all I know, you broke into a county office. I'm sure the Crips and Bloods down in the holding cells would love to help you off with that five-thousand-dollar suit."

He laughed softly. "Ah, David, you do not wear the tough-cop mask with the ease Chief Peralta does." He crossed his legs and folded manicured fingers atop one knee. "Why would I need to be a drug dealer when I can get rich legitimately in the nation's sixth largest city? And for my pleasures, I have Indian art, beautiful women, the knowledge of good acts done for the community." In the dimness of the room, he looked like a young Omar Sharif.

He raised an arm expansively, indicating the view out the windows. "Look at downtown coming back. A new baseball stadium, science center, nightlife. And that doesn't even take account of my portfolio of tech stocks. My goodness, the return I get from investing here is far superior to what I hear one might receive from, say, smuggling heroin. Once you factor in the true business costs and risks, of course." A narrow smile played across his handsome features.

I reached for the phone on my desk. He said, "It was you who found those skeletons in the old building down by the Union Station, no?"

I eased the phone back into its cradle.

"I imagine it is true what the newspaper says, that they are the famous Yarnell twins that were kidnapped in 1941. A man was caught with some of the ransom money, and with a woman, if I recall what I read. He was executed. Yet the bodies were never found."

I reached for the phone again.

"My problem is strictly business, Dr. Mapstone. That building, the Triple A Storage warehouse. I want to buy it. I want to develop that entire area. And I nearly had a deal with the owners, then this. Now the city has the building sealed. I cannot move ahead. I am losing money every day I cannot act. Do you realize how fast downtown real estate prices are rising because of the baseball stadium?"

"I don't care, Bobby." I let the phone be. "And even if I did, how could I do anything?"

"You have influence with Chief Peralta, and he has influence everywhere. Do you think it is easy for me to come asking a favor from the Maricopa County Sheriff's Office?"

"Well, I'll be happy to mention it to Peralta. Now, I really need to get some work done."

He raised a hand deferentially. "I do not wish to waste your time. I know Chief Peralta has a lot on his mind, what with his marital troubles and all."

He studied my face. "Oh, yes, I keep track of the people who, uh, do not wish me well in achieving my American dream. Frankly, I find his wife shrill and pedantic, at least on her radio show.

Perhaps she is different in real life." He shook his head slowly. A philosopher. "Ah, Americans and marriage, so much difficulty. American men confuse the things a wife can do with the things one needs from a mistress. And then those murders he can't seem to solve. He has seen his reputation take a bit of a beating in the press because of that. I feel badly for our friend right now. I really do."

"I bet."

"Maybe your pretty, young friend—Lindsey, is it? —can help him trap this madman. She certainly made the difference on the Phaedra Riding case, did she not?"

"You claim to know a hell of a lot about sheriff's office business," I said, feeling a deep tension conquering my neck and shoulders.

"The Harquahala Strangler is a dangerous case, Dr. Mapstone. If I could help Chief Peralta stop these killings I surely would."

I should have thrown him out of my office. Instead, I sat there like an idiot and let him talk. He had more than balls—there was a reckless intelligence and charisma to him that was both compelling and disarming.

"You have heard from him every bad thing about me, whether true or imagined," Bobby Hamid went on. "But like me, Dr. Mapstone, you are an educated man, a man of the world. You know the purely evil man, like the purely good one, doesn't exist."

He sat back a bit in the chair and the wood creaked loudly. Then for a long time we just regarded each other across the desk, his eyes in shadows, me feeling my heart pound. Yes, Peralta had told me much of the bad about Bobby Hamid: a college student at Arizona State in the late 1970s, he stayed in this country after the fall of the Shah. He was reputed to have come from an upper-class Iranian family, but nobody knew for sure.

At first he ran a doughnut shop, but his immigrant's success story quickly verged into owning topless bars that were notorious for prostitution and drugs. Around the mid-nineteen-eighties, he was reputed to have had a lock on the cocaine trade for half the city. Along the way, there was a trail of cruel murders of assorted informants, rivals, and narco-groupies. Yet he could never be tied to any of it—never did a day in jail, as Peralta put it. And he slowly bought himself into respectable business and civic life. He was Peralta's obsession. I could understand why.

Finally, he said, "Tell me what you thought of the Yarnell heirs you met."

"You know I can't discuss a case." The truth

was, I still couldn't get an appointment to meet Max Yarnell.

"You do know that Yarneco, the family development company, owns that warehouse."

Well, no, I didn't. Against the coolness of the room, I could feel sweat forming against my chest.

I said, "The records say a real estate investment trust in Baltimore owns it."

"And Yarneco is majority owner of the REIT," Bobby said. "Just thought you'd want to know. They own a lot of the property down there. Once they were produce warehouses. Now everybody wants the land. Even the county, to expand Chief Peralta's jail."

I felt a flush spreading into my cheeks, hoped the dark of the office concealed it.

Bobby said, "You are an intelligent man, David, not merely a prisoner of books and ideas like most intellectuals. Sometimes things are not as they seem. It would be worth your time to reconsider your assumptions about me, about many things."

He stood up and bowed slightly. "Dr. Mapstone, it is always a pleasure. Do have a happy Thanksgiving."

I wanted to have a smart-ass comeback but all I could think of was getting him out of the office.

"By the way, someone left you a present."

"What are you talking about?"

I followed his gaze over to the court table I had set up for the Yarnell case.

"What the…"

It was a doll. An ordinary baby doll, maybe a foot tall, with a big head and a silly smile. It had a little blue bow tie and blue overalls. And a little sheriff's star. It made my skin crawl.

"Are you mind-fucking me, Bobby?"

"Oh, the English language is wonderful, isn't it?" he smiled, perfect teeth looking predatory in the half light. "Farsi has many wonderful words and sayings, but not like this. 'Mind fuck.' No, Dr. Mapstone, I am not mind-fucking you. This doll was sitting on your doorstep when I came in. No card attached. I merely brought it inside. It is from a friend with a peculiar sense of humor, perhaps?"

"Perhaps."

"I have never liked dolls," Bobby said. "Those dead eyes."

Then he was gone, his footsteps echoing like gunshots down the hall.

Chapter Twelve

The worst sound in the world is a ringing telephone after midnight.

"Dave."

Lindsey. "Are you all right?"

"Did you read the fourteenth Canto without me?" she asked. We'd been reading Dante to each other, a little bit at a time in bed. I said, "I'd rather wait for you."

"That's why you're my History Shamus."

A minute passed by with nothing but the electronic buzz of the phone line.

"Are you okay, Lindsey?"

"I guess I'm not."

I sat up in bed, awake with worry, the house silent and dark around me.

I waited for her. She said, "So how was your day?"

Something bad. Lindsey is the most direct

person I've ever known. When her conversation turns elliptical, it is a bad sign.

"I tried to call you," I said. "I figured you were tied up."

"Tell me about your day, Dave."

I imagined the bit of frost that came into her dark blue eyes when there was only one path she was prepared to take.

"I found Frances Richie, the woman arrested with Jack Talbott in the kidnapping? She's still alive. Still in prison."

I could hear her faintly breathing. Steady, shallow.

"She didn't have much to say. She remembered a slouch fedora that was taken from her by a jail matron after the arrest. I want to know how the bodies got in that wall, and she remembers the hat."

"Do you remember what you wore the first time we ever made love?"

"I remember more what you were wearing," I said. "And then not wearing."

"You wore chinos and a light blue shirt," she said softly, "and you looked impossibly preppy. But I knew inside you were a bad boy."

I felt myself smile against the cool plastic of the phone.

I waited a moment, hearing the line buzz emptily, and went on. "I learned that the building where the skeletons were found is owned by the Yarnell family." Thanks, Bobby. "I also tried to find out something about the pocket watch you noticed." I paused. "I guess it's all a fool's errand. When the DNA profile comes back, we'll know for sure. PPD is testing the DNA found on the skeletons against a sample from the surviving brothers. Then the case can be closed. I'm just trying to keep Peralta off my back."

"Why is *El Jefe* so freaked out by me?"

"Oh, he's that way with everybody. Even his wife."

"Well, she doesn't like me, either," Lindsey said. "But that I can understand. It's that thing with older women who are insecure about their husbands."

"Dr. Sharon? The highest functioning woman in Phoenix?"

"Trust me," Lindsey said. "I know."

She had distracted me just enough that I launched into a story about Mike and Sharon from years ago, when he was just a deputy and she was a mousy housewife. It was a funny story. An illuminating one.

"Dave."

I stopped talking.

"Linda died today."

Her mother.

It took about fifteen minutes to drive through the deserted streets to Lindsey's apartment in Sunnyslope, an eclectic neighborhood strewn across the high ground rising up to North Mountain. I had a leather jacket over a sweatshirt and jeans: It was colder outside, a definite chill from the High Country. I was wide awake.

She had about a dozen candles burning in the book-filled apartment and music on the CD player from a band that I had learned from her was called Pavement. I've lost enough people in my life, hell, I started with losses even before I was out of diapers. So it's second nature to know there are no words that really give comfort and many that can make things worse. I'd be worthless as a writer of sympathy cards. So I just made her a martini, dry with Bombay Sapphire, and held her, slowly stroking her soft, straight hair. She didn't cry.

Then we ended up making love on the hardwood floor in front of her sofa. Clothes halfway off, her miniskirt bunched up around her waist, her heavy black shoes still on and cutting into my back. It didn't seem right, appropriate, whatever. But I lost myself in it. She came with an angry, anguished screaming, clinging so tightly to me I thought my neck would snap. But I let her hang on, and she did for a long, long time. She says I am a "dark, sensual creature." But that's really a description of her.

We'd been together for only five months. She was my ally on that first case last summer, when I was newly back in Phoenix, a year out of the divorce with Patty and still feeling my way back into the cop world. Lindsey was the one holding my hand when I woke up in a hospital with a bullet hole in my shoulder. We read books to each other, made love with an athletic joy, and shared a rebellious sensibility that verged on the misanthropic. But she was also an unfolding mystery and I liked that.

She wanted me to teach her history and we shared a love of literature. But she drew the line at jazz. Her musical tastes tended toward indy rock, a campy love of 1970s disco and even some rap. So we carried on an uneasy truce across a green line of music and love. Neither of us had spoken that word yet, "love." We hadn't had the conversations that once were a given at certain points in what our age calls "relationships": the "where are we going?" talk, the "what do you mean to me?" talk, the "forever" talk.

That was fine with me. Maybe it was a naive hope that if we didn't abandon the mystery of early courtship we wouldn't lose its passion. Maybe some of it was our age difference, but not the way people would think. Most of it was the knowledge that comes after you realize that love doesn't last forever, that lovers move on, parents grow old, children die. That we live in a time of disconnection and abandonment. Maybe people in her generation seemed to come to that knowledge sooner. I didn't know.

"She killed herself."

I stroked her hair and said quietly, "Oh, baby."

"She used a gun."

I had never met her mother. Another of the rituals of courtship we never consummated. I knew her parents were divorced. Her father had been killed in Vietnam when she was a baby and her mother became a hippy—she was a true child of recent history. Lindsey and her mother weren't close. I could remember no visits or phone calls, just a passing reference to her mother living somewhere in the suburbs, Chandler, I think.

I felt her swallow hard. "Women usually use pills," Lindsey said.

Then, in a different voice, "Tell me about your case, History Shamus. What did we find down there under that warehouse?"

"Lindsey, tell me about your mother."

I could feel her tense a little, then let it go.

"Oh, Dave." She sighed. "God, I wish I hadn't given up smoking." She drummed her fingers on my calf. "I hardly knew her."

She flashed the blue eyes at me. "She heard voices. It scared me when I was little. I didn't know what it was all about. She took us from place to place. I used to see the different men she'd bring home, and she'd moan and screech behind the bedroom door. I thought they were hurting her. And she'd go into rages. She'd just walk away for days at a time. It was years before she got help, and she didn't always take her drugs. The legal ones, I mean. She did really well with the illegal kind. My upbringing wasn't *Leave It to Beaver*."

I just listened. She stroked my leg with a light, detached touch, making my leg hair stand up straight.

"It was all properly seventies and absurd," she laughed low and humorless. Then, in another voice, "I don't hate her. She was younger than I am now and she had a thing for drugs and booze and bad men. She sure didn't want to be a mother. It's just that I couldn't bring myself to love her, and if that makes me a monster, fuck everybody. Fuck everybody."

The room was as fragile as old crystal. I looked

around for some reassuring signs of Lindsey as I had known her, realizing that everything had changed somehow. Shelves and shelves of books: fiction, poetry, philosophy, a little history. Photos of Mayan ruins from a trip she made three years ago. Photos of us on the beach in San Diego from earlier this year. Mexican Day of the Dead art, one of her many eccentric enthusiasms. Two personal computers, CD-ROM, printer, scanner and modems on a butcher block suspended on a pair of old filing cabinets. X-Files calendar. A large print of Emily Dickinson. A barrel cactus with a blue ribbon around it. Her big tomcat Pasternak fell against me and purred loudly.

"The more you know about me, the less you're going to want to be with me." She leaned in against me.

"That's not true," I said. "And you're not a monster, Lindsey."

"You wouldn't know, Dave. You love my legs." I needed to laugh and we both did. There was a fundamental kindness in Lindsey and she would always let me off the hook.

"Just hold me," she said softly. "Don't try to make any sense of things. Just hold me all night."

Chapter Thirteen

She was gone by the time the alarm went off next morning. For a long minute, I luxuriated in her scent, our scent, embedded in the sheets. Then the memory of last night's bad news came back and I sat up quickly. There was a Post-It note on the pillow: just the imprint of her lips in dark lipstick. I tucked it fondly in my pocket. Then I showered, fed the cat, locked up and drove downtown.

If weather really matched our moods, it would have been cold and gray outside. Instead, it was just another beautiful Phoenix day: seventy degrees, fourteen percent humidity, not a cloud in sight. The radio was playing the pop love song of the season—hard to believe I once measured my romances by such things. All the way down Central, I was stuck behind a car with Quebec tags, my first snowbird sighting of the season. The tag was imprinted with *Je me souviens*—"I remember"—a reference to the French defeat on the Plains of Abraham in 1759 that ensured British domination of North America. Somebody appreciated history. I remembered Lindsey's kisses, the softness of her black hair, the sensation of my fingers lightly stroking the downy skin on the small of her back, the sound of her love moans and gasps. I remembered too damned many good-byes in my life.

Over on the AM, Dr. Sharon was lecturing a caller about people needing to act like adults and take responsibility for their actions. I agreed with her, but I also knew human beings are remembering animals. With memory comes baggage and fear. I didn't know if any two people could make it for long nowadays, but if they did, somehow they had to find a way to make peace with their individual histories and make a new one together. Then they only needed all the luck available in the world. The romantic philosophy of Deputy David Mapstone—fat lot of good it's done me. Dr. Sharon signed off with her trademark: "You can do it!"

I could do it. I had stopped by home for a change of clothes when the phone rang. It was the sheriff's communications center and a message had been left for me: Mr. Max Yarnell, chairman of Yarneco and brother of the kidnapped twins, would see me at eleven o'clock. I changed clothes again, this time into a suit.

Yarneco took up the entire 20th floor of the Yarneco Tower on North Central, only a few blocks from my house. The skyscraper had been built for Dial Corp. in the early 1990s, and it resembled a copper-colored deodorant stick, or a vehicle for deep-space travel, or maybe a marital aid—anyway, it was the most dramatic building on the Central Corridor. I liked it.

When the elevator opened, Hayden Yarnell was waiting for me. He was entombed in an oil painting that took up the better part of a darkly paneled wall in the reception area. Snowy-haired and dressed in a dark suit and stiff Herbert Hoover collar, he gazed out at a future that had seen the Yarnell Land & Cattle Co. evolve into an international concern. His eyes looked black. A gold watch chain dangled tantalizingly from his vest.

Next to the patriarch was a museum-quality display of the company's history and present-day structure. This was the age of the dot-com, but somehow Yarneco made piles of money the old-fashioned way. Yarneco owned mines in Arizona and Chile, defense contractors in California and Ohio, and a land development division responsible for huge projects around the Southwest. It was, a panel said, the largest privately held company in the state.

Before I could read further, I was met by a pleasant-looking young blonde in a very pleasant-looking powder-blue suit with a short skirt. She introduced herself as Megan, Mr. Yarnell's assistant. He was running late, but I could wait in his private conference room. She led me through another dark-paneled room, where I couldn't help noticing behind a counter two muscular, short-haired young men in suits with roomy jackets—roomy like Peralta's, designed to conceal substantial firearms. They looked me over carefully as I followed Megan up a spiral staircase and through two heavy wood doors into the Yarneco inner sanctum.

The room was dominated by a sleek boardroom table big enough to accommodate a minor-league hockey game. Then there was the Indian art, large, intricately carved kachinas. Luminous Acoma pottery on dark pedestals. Basketwork that looked old enough to be very pricey. And two walls of glass.

From up here, Phoenix looked like the exotic capital of an imagined land of sun and prosperity. Glittery towers, a sea of green treetops, the mountains bare and rough and purple-black, witnesses to their volcanic heritage. Maybe this was what Coronado was after when he roamed the Southwest in search of the Seven Cities of Cibola. Only he was four hundred years too early. I could easily see my house three blocks away on Cypress.

I broke out of my reverie when a tall man strode into the room and gave my hand a peremptory but solid handshake. He had his grandfather's long nose and full head of hair, but his hair was the color of lead and his face was tan and handsomely lined more from sailing the Greek islands and golfing at Pebble Beach than from driving cattle to the High Country. I'd seen this face all my life, among the top donors profiled in the programs of the Phoenix Symphony and Herberger Theater Center, smiling like a desert lord from a decorating article in *Phoenix Magazine*, discussing a huge new development or copper mine in the business section of the *Republic*. It was the face of the West's moneyed establishment. It wasn't smiling.

"I've already talked to a policeman named Hawkins," Max Yarnell said. "My brother and I agreed to help with this DNA fingerprinting. So I don't really know how I can help you."

His voice was Toastmasters, with a dash of executive-suite impatience. His athletic frame mirrored it:

practiced and toned, but a little coiled, a little tense, packed nicely into a monogrammed French blue dress shirt, and a tie with a tight pattern of gold and blue that looked a little like deranged DNA. Maybe I had DNA on the mind. I told him my job for the Sheriff's Office.

"I never did well in school," he said. "And I never lived in the past. Quickest way to waste your life away."

"I get that," I said. "Do you remember anything about the kidnapping?"

Men who reach the heights of the Yarneco Tower are accustomed to giving quick orders and moving on. Short attention spans are as important as MBAs. And they expect their minions to get the shorthand, take the hint. I pulled out a chair and sat. He really focused on me for the first time, as if a lamp had talked back to him. His eyes were a fierce light blue. "I was five years old when that happened. How much do you remember from when you were five?"

Quite a lot, actually. But I just sat there silently.

"Andy and Woodrow were my brothers. We played together. Sometimes they drove me crazy. We fought over who got to sit in the front seat with dad. I've tried not to dwell on what happened."

"You know we found them in a building that's owned by Yarneco?"

He sighed and pulled out a chair, compressing himself into it. "Yarneco owns a lot of property," he said. "Actually, no, I didn't know that."

"One of the things I'm trying to figure out is how they got into the tunnel in that old building."

"Only the man who kidnapped them would know that."

"There was never any speculation in the family about what happened?"

I could see the cords in his neck tighten, but his face and voice stayed calm. "What happened? What happened was that my father and grandfather died within a few years of that awful crime. My brother and I were raised by relatives back East. The family was nearly destroyed."

"Do you remember the night your brothers disappeared, Thanksgiving night?"

"I already told you no. My brother James is older, so maybe he does." He crossed his arms and bore those light blue eyes into me. "This is just an academic exercise for you."

"Not at all," I said. "I'm not trying to revive your pain. I am trying to wrap up an open kidnapping and homicide case, and there aren't many people still living who can give the information I need."

Whether that satisfied him or not, I don't know. He stared at the doors, maybe wishing Megan would appear in her nicely cut powder-blue suit and elegant legs. Hell, I did, too. I asked, "Did your father carry a pocket watch?"

"No, he wore wristwatches."

I showed him the photo of the pocket watch with the HY brand. "That's grandfather's brand," he said. "But I've never seen that watch. What does it mean?"

"We found it with the remains."

He shook his head a couple of millimeters. "What can any of this mean?" he said. "They caught the man and executed him. This is all history."

"They caught a woman with him, too," I said. "I talked to her yesterday."

He sat back, stared out the window toward Camelback Mountain and gave the top of his right hand a savage scratching. Then he stopped and regarded me again.

"What the hell are you talking about?"

"Frances Richie is still in prison."

He raised his hands as if to let the information slip through.

"She's nearly senile," I said. "She wasn't much help."

He was on his feet. "I have another meeting, Mapstone. I'm sure you understand. You read the paper, so you know Yarneco is involved in a very difficult project at the moment. Lots of controversy. We've received threats."

I rose, too.

"What kind of project?"

The thin executive lips pressed hard together. Then, "We're in a consortium to build a new copper mine in the state. It will be the first new mine here in decades. I'm sure you can understand, this has angered some environmental groups."

I thanked him for his time.

"This Lieutenant Hawkins said the DNA test should establish the identity. So we will finally have some closure."

Closure. Even CEOs had learned the therapeutic language of the age. "I may need to call you again if there are other questions."

"I can't imagine that would happen," he said, and saw me to the door. He didn't offer his hand.

Chapter Fourteen

I was falling into a rotten mood on a beautiful day. Within an hour of leaving Max Yarnell, I was summoned down to police headquarters for as much of an ass chewing as a lifer bureaucrat like Hawkins could muster. "Mr. Yarnell was offended by your questions and manner," Hawkins said.

I was getting offended, too. After had I left Hawkins, I went to the County Recorder's Office, where I pulled the deed records on the Triple A Storage Warehouse. It had been owned by Yarneco before the company even took that name. The original paper listed "Yarnell Land and Cattle Co., 1924"—seventeen years before the kidnapping. There was more: The recorder kept a clipboard for signing out paper deed records. It wasn't much used, what with grantor-grantee records on computer. But the occasional title company employee needed to go deeper. The records to the warehouse had been checked out just the day before, to a Megan O'Connor of Yarneco. She had to be Max Yarnell's Megan. So why did he tell me he didn't know the warehouse was owned by his company?

By the time it was five, I didn't want to stay in the office and I didn't want to go home. Earlier in the day, I sent Lindsey a dozen yellow roses, her favorites. But when I got back to the courthouse, a note was folded into my office door.

I opened it and read in Lindsey's rat-a-tat-tat handwriting:

> *Dave, I am taking Linda back to Illinois for the funeral. I know you would want to go, too, and try to save me from myself. So I will remove the temptation. You can have a nice, normal Thanksgiving with El Jefe and Sharon, and I will be with my crazy family and thinking of you. If you would look in on Pasternak from time to time, I will do unspeakable things to your body when I get back. Don't worry, History Shamus.*
> *L*

So I sat on a bench in Cesar Chavez Plaza, between the old courthouse and the municipal building, and I read and re-read the note. Then I watched the western sky gather pink and orange. The killjoys liked to say that the Phoenix sunsets were a product of smog and dust in the dry air. That was probably information that would please Lieutenant Hawkins, if he ever looked up at the sky in the first place. I didn't care. The deepening streaks of color restored me little by little. When I started to dislike Phoenix again, the sunsets reminded me of the things I had missed so much the years I had been away.

This part of downtown was utterly deserted. The government employees raced to the suburbs early on a Friday evening, and the Suns and Coyotes were out of town tonight. So you could have lain down in the middle of the five lanes of Washington Street and been completely safe. Even the panhandlers and street people were nowhere to be seen.

Then I caught movement out of the corner of my eye, and Gretchen Goodheart stepped out from between two palo verde trees. She smiled and waved and walked to me.

"I was walking up to your office when I looked out one of the stairway windows and you were out here. You looked lost in thought."

I smiled and stood. "Come join me."

She didn't have the cowboy hat today, and her auburn hair fell free in a longish pageboy, brushing the tops of her shoulders. She was wearing a denim top and print cotton skirt, looking springy in the fall as you can do in Arizona. She looked me over and sat next to me.

"You clean up nicely," she said. I still had on the blue pinstripe from my meeting with Max Yarnell.

"Thanks, I went visiting. Mr. Max Yarnell."

"What's he like?"

"He's a prick," I said. "But maybe I'm in a mood to judge harshly."

"Not everyone, I hope."

"Not Gretchen Goodheart," I said. My girlfriend's mother just committed suicide and here I was flirting. I closed up that compartment and watched the sunset.

"Max Yarnell is developing five thousand acres of pristine desert north of Scottsdale," she said. "In two years, you'll have houses and roads where there are only saguaros and empty spaces now. As if Phoenix needed more space. Then his company is trying to build a new copper mine near Superior, and they're doing everything they can to sidestep the environmental reviews." She shook her head, making the red-brown hair wave gently against her collar. "So I'm no fan of Mad Max."

"Is that what people call him?"

"I don't know, it's what I call him." She held up a file folder. "I have something for you. These are copies of plans submitted to the city over the years on your warehouse. I thought they might be useful."

We spread the sheets of paper between us.

"See, it's actually two buildings." She traced a ring-less finger across a floor plan. "This is from 1947, when a new water main was routed down Fourth Avenue to Harrison." Sure enough, the paper showed a larger building abutted by a smaller one on the corner by Union Station.

"The larger one was a hotel until 1958," Gretchen said. "Then in 1961, the new brick facade was put across both buildings and the whole thing was converted into a storage warehouse."

"I'll be damned," I said. "I used to love to come down to the station to watch the trains when I was a kid. It was a bad habit my grandmother indulged. But I never really paid attention to those old buildings."

I picked through the floor plans. "So the skeletons of the Yarnell twins were below this old hotel."

Gretchen nodded. "The plan doesn't show a tunnel running from the elevator shaft, see. But it's clearly the same building." She reached into the paperwork and pulled out a couple of dense pages. "These are out of city directories, so you can get a sense of what was around the hotel when the kidnapping happened."

"You're going to put me out of a job," I said.

She smiled that dimpled extravaganza. "It was called the Sunset Route Hotel until the late 1940s. I'm not quite sure why."

"The Southern Pacific's premier passenger train through here was the Sunset Limited."

"See, David. You've got the moves."

"I am a storehouse of useless knowledge."

"I think you're a very intelligent man." She fixed those baby browns on me, an intense connecting gaze. I invited her to have a drink at Majerle's.

Chapter Fifteen

"Now I am entranced, David Mapstone," she said. "A martini man? I don't think I've ever seen a cop drink a martini. I am shaken and stirred."

"I picked it up in another life."

"Ah, this was the life in the federal witness protection program?"

"How did you know?"

"So you lost the girl but kept the vice?"

I smiled. "Something like that."

She set aside her chardonnay and caught the barmaid's eye—not hard to do, since we were the only people in the bar. "I've decided I must have a martini, too."

"Bombay Sapphire," I instructed, and the barmaid went away, her black tennis skirt swinging saucily behind her.

Gretchen said, "When I was twenty three, I dated, well let's say he was the youngest son of one of the richest men on the West Coast. He was a total idiot, but, oh, how I loved his toys."

The crowd noise from the basketball game on TV drifted over our way and then the server did, too. Gretchen sampled the martini.

"Oh, my," she said.

"So how does one get to be the city archaeologist?" I asked and heard her story.

Gretchen Goodheart grew up in Tempe, where her dad was a teacher. She was a tomboy, and excelled at track and gymnastics in high school. She went to UCLA and then worked four years as a smoke jumper, fighting forest fires around the West. "I survived," she said. But she also loved history. "I decided archaeology was a good mix of the outdoors and the past. But it's not like you can take that degree and open an archaeology shop on Mill Avenue."

So she came home to Phoenix, worked in several dead-end jobs. Then she answered an ad for the city archaeologist's office. For fun, she rode horses and hiked in the desert. She wanted to collect Santa Clara pottery but couldn't afford it. She read Montini in the *Republic* because he made her mad and she was a Big Sister to an eleven-year-old girl in the barrio.

Gretchen was safe, pretty, athletic. She'd probably never had anything really bad happen in her life. She'd never sat up with a lover through a dark night of the soul. She had none of Lindsey's edge or surprises. She would never dig black platform heels into my back as we made love. I had that thought and then wondered why I would presume to think it. I imagined she had a pleasant-looking boyfriend who worked at Bank One.

"So what's your story?" she asked. "You don't seem like the other cops I've met."

"Oh, I'm a bona fide graduate of the Sheriff's Academy."

"David Mapstone keeps his mystery up." She smiled. "I know you left law enforcement to teach history. You were a professor. A friend of Mike Peralta. And you came back to Phoenix this year and took a job with the Sheriff's Office again."

"Gretchen, you don't miss a thing."

"I read about you in the newspaper, solving old crimes. It must be very satisfying. Who said, 'The arc of history is long but it bends toward justice'?"

"Martin Luther King, Jr. Although his words were 'arc of the moral universe' and he was quoting an abolitionist preacher named..." I let the sentence trail off. My flirty nervousness with her was turning into pedantry.

She smiled and touched the top of my hand. "I'm interested. Just from reading about you, I kind of felt like you were a kindred spirit, a refugee from the social sciences trying to make a living in the real world. I'm afraid I don't have a Ph.D. in history, though."

"Well, then you're more employable than me," I said. "I'd like to think I bring something special to all this, but mostly I think Peralta had pity on me and gave me a job."

"You seem pretty impressive to me," she said, and a flush of visceral pleasure coursed through me. "So what's he like? The famous Chief Peralta."

I shook my head. "Beats me."

We each had two martinis. Then I walked her to her truck, parked in a garage across from the new city hall at Third Avenue and Washington. I was feeling good and yet virtuous. That was until she turned at her truck door and gave me a hug.

"Thanks for the talk," she said in a voice as soft as the red-brown hair that brushed across my face. "I'm enjoying getting to know you."

"My pleasure," I said. I watched her start up the big SUV and head down the ramp, then I walked to the stairway awash in lust and guilt. It wasn't a particularly bad feeling.

The street was empty and the only sound was a distant train whistle, something that always reminded me of when I was a kid listening through the bedroom window late at night to the Santa Fe trains coming down from the main line at Williams Junction.

Sound is a funny thing here. It gets trapped in the dry air and bounced around between the mountains. So I didn't hear the old white van until it was right up on me. It crept down Fourth Avenue on the lane closest to the sidewalk, exactly matching my pace. A Ford Econoline, like ten thousand others in the city. I glanced inside and was barred by heavily tinted black windows. How many times had Peralta told me to carry a gun? Now I just looked like a guy in a suit, working late, a good target. Where the hell were those PPD bicycle patrols? I got to Jefferson and the nearest car was a pair of headlights half a mile away. The lights from the Madison Street Jail looked down like the windows of a medieval castle. Otherwise, we were all alone.

I crossed behind the van and checked the license plate. It was covered with mud and the light was out. A sudden wild gush of panic came up my legs and into my belly. I fought it down with breathing. Slow and steady. I walked easy and straight across the street, moving east down Jefferson now. Another block and I could get in the sheriff's administration building with my barcoded ID.

The van turned on Jefferson and paced me again. Now I was on the driver's side, but the windows were still opaque. I didn't want to keep looking over. I started running scenarios in my head. Wondering how much of the self-defense training I got from Peralta twenty years ago was still second nature. I knew one thing: nobody was going to get me inside a van.

"Excuse me."

The window was down now and a face peered out.

"Can you tell me where the sheriff's office is?"

He was just a guy: white, thirties, doughy face, balding into a comb-over, his eyes buried in heavy lids. I stopped and looked.

"Can you tell me where the sheriff's office is?" he asked again.

"Yeah, sorry," I said. "It's down there at Second and Madison. Park on Madison and check in with the deputy at the front counter."

"Thank you." His eyes became merry slits. "Aren't you David Mapstone?

"I am. Have we met?"

He looked at me for a moment and the window went back up. Then the van accelerated around the corner and I was alone again on the street. Just then, two bicycle cops rode by. The female officer looked like Steffi Graf.

Chapter Sixteen

Little-known fact: Mike Peralta is a fabulous cook. It makes it easy to be adopted by the Peraltas for family holidays like Thanksgiving. This year, he served the finest turkey and dressing I'd ever eaten—and I had to admit that include Grandmother's sublime cornbread dressing from my childhood. Of course, the meal didn't stop there. We had the usual array of Thanksgiving vegetables and side dishes, all fresh and delicately spiced. Plus there were Peralta's trademark carnitas, just in case our metabolism dared to process any of these excesses. And liberal amounts of quality liquor: he favored Gibsons, followed by an undiscovered Sonoma pinot noir Sharon had picked up and, after dinner, a port whose taste stayed on my tongue like a good memory. I only thought about Lindsey every few minutes.

The two daughters were home from law

school. Jamie was at Stanford and Jennifer was at Cal-Berkeley. They were luminously beautiful and very smart, and since I've known both since they were babies, seeing them now made me feel strangely old. I didn't feel forty years old—I felt like I was my early twenties. Time is a real bastard. But spirits were high and the conversation tripped from football to life in the Bay Area to the big expansion the Heard Museum was planning to some catching up on everybody's life. These people were as close to family as I had, and I was grateful for the holiday spell of belonging and well-being.

Peralta and I weren't allowed to discuss work, and that was fine. I had little new to report on the Yarnell case. Now we were just waiting for the DNA results, and that would be the end of it. Gretchen would go on to greater things and I would go back to my Philip Marlowe office in the old courthouse, writing a history of the Sheriff's Office and taking whatever forgotten workaday mysteries Peralta cared to pass my way.

I seemed to be the only one bothered about the neat bow being tied on this case, and I couldn't even tell you why. Maybe it was the pocket watch. Why had it been entombed with the little boys? Maybe it was talking to the endlessly incarcerated Frances

Richie, or the way Max Yarnell was so cagey about the ownership of the old warehouse. Or maybe it was Bobby Hamid's visit the week before—about which Peralta was strangely passive, by the way. He didn't even threaten to get the warehouse condemned and turned into a Super Fund site.

So that was Thanksgiving. Except for the strangeness of the unsaid: whatever marital battle sent Peralta to find shelter at my house that night was carefully cleaned up for the holiday. Mike and Sharon didn't even fuss at each other with their usual gusto. Sometimes my mind wandered, imagining Mike and Sharon as I didn't want to imagine them: *Bitch! Prick! Slut! Bastard!* Diminuendo for a drowning marriage. I was aware of my presence keeping a brittle peace. Or maybe I imagined that, too. For just a moment, I recalled the last Christmas Patty and I were together. We had given each other expensive gifts and no cards. Lindsey was big on cards, and I had kept every one she had given me. The dusk came up early and I declined Peralta's invitation to smoke cigars and watch the big game on TV.

The new freeway system took me from Peralta's place, nestled into the bare mountainside overlooking

Dreamy Draw, to central Phoenix in less than ten minutes. Traffic was light, traveling fast. Charlie Parker was on the BMW's CD player. I got off at Seventh Street but didn't feel like going home yet. The house would be too damned empty. I drove slowly through Margaret Hance Park, which sat atop the Papago Freeway and concealed the highway's ugly gash through several blocks north of downtown. It was once a fine old neighborhood of bungalows and period revival houses, but all that remained was my old grade school, Kenilworth, the new city library, and the nearly new park, which sprawled uninvitingly amid the empty land.

South into downtown. Bobby Hamid was right about a building boom. After years of abandonment, downtown Phoenix was coming back at least a bit. The ballpark loomed massively amid the skyscrapers. A big federal building was going up near the city and county government centers. Some nights there were even crowds on the streets. Not tonight, though. Phoenix reverted to its small-town roots on holidays. The sparse traffic cruising Central disappeared entirely as I turned down Monroe, then went south again on Fourth Avenue. I could see the pale stucco facade of Union Station at the foot of the street and I let the BMW slowly slide down the block toward it. I interrupted Charlie Parker and listened to the echoes off the buildings, the tires scraping across the old railroad tracks.

I slowed to a stop just ahead of the old Triple A Storage warehouse, which stood forlornly off to the left. A couple of homeless men looked me over and scuttled off. Preservationists wanted to make these old warehouse blocks into an entertainment district. But that would require Phoenix to show an uncharacteristic sense of its past. When these old buildings were thriving with commerce, when premier streamliners like the Sunset Limited and Golden State Limited called at Union Station, when the graceful little mission-style building was the center of life here—most of today's three million Phoenicians weren't even born and their roots were thousands of miles away. This was a new-start, tear-it-down city that gave it up for the first developer who said we were pretty.

The old brick warehouse had really been a railroad hotel, right at the foot of the street that led into town. Thanks to Gretchen, I knew it had still been a hotel in 1941 when Andrew and Woodrow Yarnell were somehow taken inside and left in a wall in a hidden basement. Franklin Roosevelt was president, Nazi tanks were rampaging through

Russia, and this street in the little farm town of Phoenix, Arizona was busy night and day with train travelers. So how did the twins get in there unnoticed? And why would Jack Talbott pick such a very public place to hide his victims? The street radiated only silence and gloom back at me.

Chapter Seventeen

On Sunday night, I dreamed a vivid dream about Lindsey in the rain. And then I realized she was really there in bed with me. We were both crying silently, big streaks of salty tears in the desert, and she was stroking my face with warm, soft hands, and I was holding onto her for dear life, and life was suddenly so precious and clear and treacherously sweet, and we didn't dare say a word.

When the alarm went off at eight, I was alone again. But I felt sore and spent in all the right places, and a single long-stemmed yellow rose sat on the bedclothes, the bud barely opened. Outside the bedroom window, the sprawling city was utterly still except for the insistent patter of early-winter rain beating on the dust of new real estate developments. Maybe someday our lives would be normal enough that I could wake up with my complicated lover in my arms. But I knew in the silence of our lovemaking last night she had really said goodbye.

The *Republic* was wet. I brought it in and tried to read it anyway. Stories on the Y2K computer worries, a multiple shooting a half-mile away, and a new leg of freeway opening out on the edge of town. Another story on a record low number of people getting married and fewer saying they were happy when they did. I pulled on some sweats and drove over to Starbucks to start my day's rituals.

By nine o'clock, I was at Phoenix Police headquarters. Little orange hoods declared the parking meters off limits today, so I parked two blocks away amid the vacant lots of an old neighborhood. Well, not a neighborhood now. Just emptiness.

Even when I left Phoenix to teach in Ohio, back in the late 1970s, these straight, wide streets that ran for ten blocks between downtown Phoenix and the Arizona state capitol had been a neighborhood. It had surely been in decline—that's why they put the ugly police headquarters out here—but it had been a neighborhood nonetheless, with people, life, *history*. That damned word again. Victorian houses and bungalows had brought the semblance of modernity to a frontier town in the 1890s. Adobe and brick apartment houses had been graced with upstairs sleeping porches for an age without air conditioning. They had stood there, along palm-lined streets, all the way to the state capitol. Now, nothing. Block upon block of leveled, grassless vacant lots. Meeting them to the west: ghastly state office buildings. *Back when. I remember.* I was starting to sound like a geezer, but I couldn't stop noticing things. Maybe that's the curse of years.

Inside police headquarters, there was Lt. Augustus Hawkins. He sat at his desk just as he had the first day I saw him, behind paperwork that looked like a besieging army of forms and reports. This time, however, two other detectives were lounging at the tiny conference table in his office. In another chair, a woman wearing a visitor's ID looked up at me and gave a little smile. Hawkins didn't look up, but he gave a hearty post-holiday hello.

"Put on your ID card."

"We have the DNA test back?" I asked, pinning the MCSO card to my pocket. It had been exactly two weeks since we found the skeletons.

"The fucking thing doesn't match," said one of the detectives. He looked eerily like O.J. Simpson, a fact that must have made for some interesting times out on the job.

I just stood there in silence. I'd heard what he said, but my mind didn't want to process it.

"Must not be your famous Yarnell twins," drawled the other detective, a white guy with the beefy looks of a second-string football player gone to seed and dark permed curly hair. The young cops favored crew cuts and shaved heads. Some older cops, from the '70s, still thought they were disco studs. Maybe I was being unkind.

I took the last empty chair and let them fill me in. The woman, who introduced herself as Deb Boswell, was a pathologist from the medical examiner's office and a national expert in these matters. She launched into a twenty-minute lecture about polymorphisms and probabilities, alleles and slotblocks, electropheresis and PCR, and how much they still couldn't determine. I was at my liberal arts most ignorant in such matters, but the cops weren't doing much better.

"Bottom line," Hawkins broke in, "the DNA fingerprints don't match."

"The preferred terms are DNA profiling, or DNA typing," she said mildly. "It's not really like fingerprinting." She faced me. "What all this means, Deputy, is that the two skeletons you found are identical twins. The DNA tells us that. While identical twins have different fingerprints, genetically they're indistinguishable. But the boys don't appear to be related to Max and James Yarnell."

She shuffled her papers and pulled out another sheet.

"This is a case where there wasn't enough nuclear DNA in the remains. So we used the mitochondrial DNA. There's many more copies of that in a cell. One big limitation is that it's passed down by the mother."

"So," I said, "these might be the Yarnell twins, but they had a different mother from Max and James Yarnell?"

Hawkins coughed loudly. "You're reaching, Mapstone. You never said this cattle baron had more than one wife."

"Actually, we're talking about the cattle baron's son. Morgan Yarnell was the father of the twins. But, yeah, he was only married once. Still…"

"You were wrong, Mapstone, admit it," O.J. Simpson said. I ignored him.

"He's right," Boswell said, "this outcome could be explained by a different mother. Otherwise, we can't say a lot with certainty, because we were able to get such a small sample from the bones. It wasn't enough for an RFLP, which would be more conclusive." She leafed through sheets of paper in her lap that looked like large bar codes.

"Hawkins," I started.

"Please don't." He held up his hands. He took a moment. The stress radiated off him like a cloud from a damaged Soviet nuclear reactor. He leaned back in the chair and it creaked loudly, even though it was the newest high-tech metal and non-allergenic upholstery. I was amazed to see such life in him.

"Gentlemen, this is a matter of case clearance. This is a matter of resources. Do you know how many new homicides we have in this city every year?"

He glanced at me with baleful pale eyes. "Excluding the county and those strangler murders. But this department has had to detach twenty detectives to help the sheriff on that. And we've got thirty more working on the Grand Avenue Sniper. Resources are too tight to be wasting time on some history project!"

It all had the ambiance of a nasty faculty meeting when someone's tenure was at stake. I mischievously recalled making love with Lindsey in a world without small men enforcing the rules of bureaucracies.

Hawkins said: "We're fucked. Do you understand that? We inconvenienced a very powerful man with friends on city council. The media is expecting this to be the bones of the Yarnell twins. Now we have nothing." *Media—are*, I thought. I couldn't stop correcting freshman papers. Nobody spoke for what seemed like a minute.

"We have a mystery," I said finally.

I swear the pathologist smiled a little.

"I've dug into some very old crimes before. And, let me tell you, it makes the clearance rate suck at first."

He exhaled dramatically. "You're a sheriff's deputy," he sputtered. "You're not really even that. We went on this very expensive snipe hunt based on your, what? Intuition? Knowledge of historical trivia? Do you have any idea how much DNA fingerprinting costs?"

He filled me with sudden malice. I wanted to say: *You pale, little badge-toting turd. I used to flunk your moron daughter when she had to take a history class to keep up her volleyball scholarship. And she would have done anything—anything, Gus—to just scoot by with a D."*

I said, "We still have to find out who the bones belong to. You can assign a new team to the case." I looked over the two detectives, who gave me sour frowns. "Or let me keep going. We know these are twins. We know they were found in a building owned by Yarneco. The pocket watch has the Yarnell brand on the cover. Maybe there is a different mother. Maybe there's something about the family we don't know, such as an adoption…"

"Maybe, maybe, Jesus!" Hawkins said. "This was supposed to be simple."

I started to speak but he cut me off. "Max Yarnell is very angry over all this, and he doesn't want to be bothered about it any more." Hawkins seemed to catch himself. In a lower voice, he said, "Of course, that won't impede our investigation. No favoritism here. But you, Mapstone, you are done now."

"Fine."

We all just sat there. He ran his hands across his paperwork, made a note, signed a form. He looked up and we were all waiting. Then he remembered some dialogue from TV cop shows. "Get the hell out of here," he moaned. "All of you!"

Chapter Eighteen

I took the back door into Peralta's office suite and sat on his sofa while he finished an interview with a blonde TV reporter.

"So it's okay for you to plant stories," I said when she and her cameraman had gone.

He walked over to his little refrigerator and pulled out a Diet Coke. He didn't offer me anything. "I didn't used to date that one. Anyway, I'm the boss. So why are you here? Progress?"

"I'd call it that. The DNA test came back. Unfortunately, it doesn't match the two living Yarnell brothers." I ran through the information from the meeting, cheating off my notes for the technical stuff. Peralta swayed back and forth in his desk chair, slurping from the soft drink.

"So it's inconclusive, but we're probably not going to get anywhere unless the Yarnell brothers cooperate, and that's not going to happen. So I'm on to the next case."

"Whoa, whoa, whoa." The chair was at a dead stop.

"Whoa, what?"

"What the hell do you mean, you're on to the next thing. You haven't fixed this goddamned thing yet."

I sank deeper into the thin cushions of the sofa. I had come into the room on the wings of liberation. I should have known it wouldn't go down that way.

"It's a city case."

"So?"

"You know, a city. This one is called Phoenix. It has a police department, a good one, despite Lieutenant Hawkins. The bodies were found in a building inside the city limits. City police departments tend to frown on interference from the sheriff's office."

"So?"

I tossed my notebook aside. "I can't believe you!"

"Chief Wilson still wants you on the case." He stood, mountainous behind the desk.

"How can he still want me on the case when the meeting just finished up five blocks from here?"

"He knows. He does. And I want you on the case. Anyway, the kidnapping happened in the county. The old geezer's hacienda was in the county back then." He sat back down, looking pleased with himself.

The idea of spending more time in Hawkins' office made my stomach hurt. "Why do you care?" I demanded. "Never mind, I know. When are you going to catch this guy?"

"That's just what little Rachel there wanted to know. And I had to be patient and diplomatic with her. I don't have to with you." After a pause, he added, "It set us back that Lindsey had to go for a few days."

"Well, it was obviously for nothing important." The mention of Lindsey's name instantly made me miss her more. I said, "Why do you need her anyway? Cut her some slack. She just lost her mother."

"She wanted this job," he said. "And she's getting along really well with Patrick Blair. Not my business, Mapstone, but she really likes him. He really likes her." My stomach manufactured a tidal wave of bile.

He looked at me mildly. "Mapstone, you used to have such a good attitude, when you were a young deputy."

"That was a long time ago."

"That was before you got your mind pickled in shit working around all those eggheads," he said. "Your case doesn't seem that hard to me."

Everything I wanted to say would have just made him angry, meaning even more determined to keep me where I was.

"We've got the skeletons, right? The DNA test proves they're twins. How many other twins went missing back then?"

"None that I know of. I could check newspaper clips and missing person's records."

"See, you're already moving ahead. And you've got that watch, right? Is that the Yarnell brand on it?" I nodded. "See, it has to be the twins."

I thought so, too. But I didn't know how to get the case off dead center if the Yarnells wouldn't cooperate. And I had been ordered away by Hawkins. None of this made any impression on Peralta.

"Hawkins doesn't matter." He was back to swinging his chair back and forth, drinking the Diet Coke. "Chief Wilson and I agreed that you will take this case alone, now. They have plenty to keep them busy, and you have special expertise for this kind of thing."

"Max Yarnell?"

"Try to be more charming, Mapstone. And go see his brother. Sharon and I met him once, at his art gallery. Seemed like a nice guy."

"I give up." I stood to go. "I'll give you some theater. Distract the media. America's Toughest Sheriff. Blah, blah, blah."

"No." His voice was like a shot. "I want you to investigate this case." He was standing and his onyx eyes were wide in his immobile face. "I want you to gather evidence. I really want it closed. Those two little boys died an awful death, and this sheriff's office will never forget the victims."

If you didn't know Peralta the way I did, you'd have thought he was just making a speech.

Chapter Nineteen

The Scottsdale night was scented with ease and pleasure, the perfect camouflage for wealth, privilege and grasping madness. Across the vast ballroom, I saw the straw-colored hair of the war-hero senator's younger wife. She was in an animated dialogue with a squadron of forty-something Republican women while her husband trolled out of state for presidential IOUs. Her mouth smiled but her eyes didn't. There in the tailored Hugo Boss suit was the chief executive of the Mayo Clinic, out checking on the highly profitable desert outpost of his empire. Beside the ice-sculpture of a saguaro cactus, the famous Indian artist, in polished silver bola tie and black jeans, nestled in a soul-talk with the skeletal Newport Beach socialite who now kept a modest, million-dollar casita on Camelback Mountain. Laughing by the bar, the owner of this season's hottest gallery in town, recently separated from wife No. Four—yes, the department store heiress—but apparently finding solace with a teenage-looking redhead in a paper-thin black minidress.

They all knew their roles in the whirl of resort-life that was just beginning a new season: the older men with their square jaws and squash-court athleticism; the newly affluent younger women on their arms, who practiced a kind of prostitution we might all do if given the chance and the beauty; the pleasant older couples with complicated lives back East, being slowly mummified by the desert sun; the aging ingénues hoping for a new meal ticket. There was the occasional oddball, like that pot-bellied Anglo with the loud voice and the greasy, gray ponytail, nursing a cause or a fading reputation. The elite from Silicon Valley and Hollywood sprinkled the crowd with celebrity. Someone said Spielberg was here tonight.

James Yarnell made his way toward me, shaking hands here and there, homing in like a handsome, benign torpedo. We'd never met, but I obviously looked out of place enough to be the deputy who called him. He owned one of the top art galleries in Scottsdale, and was the oldest of the four Yarnell brothers. It was Monday night, and he had to attend a charity event at the Hyatt Regency at Gainey Ranch, one of the new megabucks resorts off Doubletree Road.

Finally across the sea of wealthy humanity, he steered me outside, where we sat by a bonfire pit. Past the railing, Camelback Mountain brooded darkly in the perfect Arizona sunset, competing for our attention with the thousands of city lights starting to shimmer to the horizon. Yarnell wore a charcoal suit and open-collared shirt, quality but not ostentation. He looked fifteen years younger than I knew he was, and his smile was effortless, inviting you to join in the good life taking place all around. It was a game I could play, to a point.

"I'm glad to meet you, David Mapstone," he said. "I'm sorry it couldn't be under better circumstances. Are you related to Philip Mapstone?"

"He was my grandfather."

"Well, it's a small world." He sighed and clapped me warmly on the arm. "Doc Mapstone was our dentist back when I was a kid. I assume he's gone?"

"He died in 1974."

"A good man," James Yarnell said. "So how can I help Doc Mapstone's grandson?"

"I assume your brother told you about the DNA test."

"Yes, and he also told me about you. You must have made quite an impression."

"I'm afraid so."

"Oh, Max is a prick, he always has been." James Yarnell laughed from deep inside his fine suit.

"Mr. Yarnell, is there any reason the test would have turned out the way it did? Your mother was also the mother of the twins?"

"We all fell from the same tree," he said evenly. "My uncle Win, now he was the bounder in the family. Hayden Winthrop Yarnell Jr. was his given name, but everyone called him Win. His brother, my dad Morgan, he was the straight arrow."

"I wasn't trying to imply…"

"Don't worry, Mapstone," he said. "We're both old Arizonans here. We can speak frankly. Nobody wanted this crime solved more than me, believe me. Is there any chance they could have made a mistake?"

I told him it seemed unlikely, based on the DNA report that I spent the afternoon reading.

"What do you remember about the kidnapping?" I asked.

He looked out over the city lights. "I was sixteen years old, the older brother. The protector. I always looked after Andy and Woodrow. They were the sweetest, gentlest kids in the world, and I don't just think that's the treacle of sentimental memory fogging up my head.

"Anyway, we all went out to Grandpa's for

Thanksgiving. I remember how cold it was, and you know how none of us desert rats is prepared for cold weather. Grandpa had this huge fireplace at his hacienda. The hearth was made from stone quarried on his ranch in southern Arizona, Rancho del Cielo. It was framed in copper from the Yarnell Mine near Globe. And it was so wonderfully warm that night.

"I remember after dinner, all the men adjourned to Grandpa's study to smoke cigars, drink brandy and talk politics. For the first time I was invited along, and I really felt like I was a man. Max was already asleep, he was only five. Grandpa took Andy and Woodrow to bed, and sat up with them for a while. Then he came down, and joined the talk. He was convinced Japan was going to jump on us." He paused and swallowed. "I never saw Andy and Woodrow again."

"Who else was there that night?"

"My mom. My dad, Morgan, and Uncle Win."

"Any domestic help?"

James Yarnell bit his lower lip and dropped his age another five years. "Grandma died in 1936, so Grandpa had a cook. What was her name…Maria, I think? And he had a gardener named Luis. Luis Paz. He was a great guy, like a second father."

"What about Jack Talbott?"

James Yarnell shook his head. "He was trouble. I didn't know much at that age, but I knew he was trouble. He was Grandpa's driver and handyman. I don't know how he got the job. Maybe Uncle Win hired him. I don't know."

"Was he there that night?"

James Yarnell looked up into the torchlight and then shook his head. "I don't believe he was."

The sun slipped behind the mountains and the city became a vast sea of undulating blue and white and yellow diamonds.

"So what will you do?" he asked.

"I don't know," I said. "If the DNA test was correct, then I guess we have a totally different homicide case. But your brothers are still missing."

Reflected in the primal orange light of the torch and the sunset, his fine features seemed to sag.

"I guess I was hoping for some answers," he said. He groped for the word. "Some justice. But it's not going to happen, I guess. This kidnapping began the most terrible years for my family. Dad and Uncle Win were both dead before the war was out. Bad hearts, the doctor said. Grandpa died in 1942, and his hacienda burned, this lovely stone house down by South Mountain. I was overseas in the Army by then. People started talking about a Yarnell curse."

"You seem to have come out all right," I said.

"Well, I'm not Max," he said. "I've been lucky to be able to do what I want, which is collect and preserve Indian art. But I can't say there are no regrets. I wasn't there for Andy and Woodrow. And even though I was blessed with a wonderful daughter and three grandsons, I can never see little boys without thinking of Andy and Woodrow."

He stopped and I could see the slightest mist across his eyes. Or maybe it was across mine.

I stood, thanked him and offered my hand. He shook it with both of his and thanked me for coming. Even in his sadness he had more warmth than I could ever imagine from his brother.

"One more thing," I said, pulling a snapshot from my coat pocket. "Have you ever seen this before?"

He tilted the photograph into the light from one of the torches. "That's my grandfather's pocket watch." He tried to hand back the photo.

"Are you sure? Check again."

"It's his. I'd know it anywhere. Where did you get this?"

When I told him, he walked a couple of steps

away, staring out at the lingering Sonoran Desert twilight. I heard him say, "My God." Then he walked back and recomposed his fine features.

"Come by the gallery sometime."

"I'd like to," I said. "I grew up two blocks from the Heard Museum, so I come by my love of Indian art honestly."

"You would have loved Grandpa's collection," he said. "He realized the value of this art long before it became popular. In the 1920s and 1930s, he would take trips out to the reservations to buy art."

I had written a paper in grad school on Hayden Yarnell but this was new to me.

"Oh, yes," James Yarnell said. "It was an amazing collection. It would have been on the order of the Heard."

"What happened to it?"

He stopped and look at me. "Why, it disappeared during the war. When Grandpa's hacienda burned, the family was afraid it was all lost. But when they went through the ruins, there wasn't even a trace. It was gone. It's never been found."

"My God," I said. "Why?"

He rubbed his jaw as if an old ache had come back. He said, "The Yarnell curse."

Chapter Twenty

I came back to the courthouse from Scottsdale and pulled out a legal pad. I could hear Lindsey's voice telling me to use the Mac, but I needed the comfort of pen on paper. Lindsey. I was sending prayers and good thoughts to her, yet I had this feeling that some terrible breach had come upon us like a shipwreck on the unsuspecting. *Don't worry, Dave.* I was a worrier, and now I felt like something akin to a bad cold was coming over me, my heartbeat too noticeable, my brain full of dread. I shifted in the creaky old desk chair and started making notes on the case, what I knew, what I didn't know. The latter list was a hell of a lot longer. By the time I left, it was nearly midnight. I was tired and getting nowhere on a fifty-eight-year-old double-murder. The BMW's fuel gauge was nearly on empty, a little needle stuck in the festive dash display.

At the light on Roosevelt, a VW Jetta full of

Asian teenagers pulled up beside me. They flashed me clean-cut smiles and then one showed me a little machine gun, just like it was prized artwork he had bought at First Friday. I thought very clearly: am I supposed to show you mine? I smiled back stupidly. Then they drove away going the speed limit, signaled, turned right and disappeared down a side street. I didn't feel scared or brave or outraged, or even like calling PPD on the cell phone. It was time to get some sleep. All day I had been hoping I would find Lindsey waiting for me.

But Peralta was sitting in my driveway.

We walked into the kitchen in silence and I handed out beer. Sam Adams, love it or leave it. I told him about James Yarnell in Scottsdale.

"Stay on the case," he said, sipping reluctantly from my loathsome yuppie brew.

"And do what?" I was getting cranky from lack of sleep.

"What's the next step in a case like this?" Peralta the academy instructor.

I threw my hands in the air and walked out. "I'm too fucking tired to employ the Socratic method on the chief fucking deputy."

He appeared in the bathroom doorway as I was preparing to brush my teeth.

"Did you hear from your little friend today?"

"Lindsey. No."

I didn't answer beyond that.

"Sharon and I are having problems."

I just started brushing, nice circular strokes that would make Grandfather happy.

"Do you know what it's like to be in the spotlight all the time." he said. "No, you don't. It's not like I can just go check into a hotel, without this showing up in *New Times* next week." That was the alternative paper that had waged war with the sheriff for years.

He went on, "They've already got me as the next sheriff. Shit, I haven't even decided to run. Anyway, my personal life is none of their business."

I would leave the First Amendment arguments to Lorie Pope. I just kept brushing. Circular strokes. Rinse. Spit. Floss.

"I guess I should get a place of my own, quietly," he went on. "I just…Hell, it seems like such an irrevocable step. I can't figure out what she wants. How the hell can any man figure that out nowdays?"

I was a silent poster boy for dental diligence.

"Goddamn it, Mapstone. This isn't easy for me. You know what I mean?"

I looked at him. His face seemed heavier and

more careworn than I could remember. I looked back in the mirror for some vain reassurance.

"No, I don't know what you mean," I said. "It's fine for you and Sharon to fuss over my personal life for fifteen years, and I don't get to be let in to yours?" I wanted to say: *You demand to know other people's weaknesses but never show yours.* But I was just dragging. I said, "Stay here when you want, for as long as you need."

I cleaned up and turned out the light. "You know where the guest bedroom is. There's an extra door key in the black pot on the kitchen counter. I'll buy some Coors and try to keep the noise down from my reading."

"Fuck you," he called after me as I went in my bedroom. Then, very quietly: "Thanks."

◇◇◇

So began the strange life we fell into that season. Peralta and I acted like two bachelors sharing an old house. Most of the time, we barely saw each other. He was in no mood to cook grand dinners. One night we got takeout from Hong Kong Gourmet and rented two Dirty Harry movies—Peralta was contentedly critical of the actors' combat shooting stances. We didn't talk about love and women. He was neat and nearly invisible as a roommate, but a steady beachhead of Peralta's clothes and county reports built up in the guest room.

I was grateful for the company. As the days went by without word from Lindsey, I grew tired of leaving clever, unanswered messages in her voice mail. The conviction grew on me that I might never see her again, at least as a lover. Or maybe I knew that at an instant when the phone rang at midnight, when she told me of her mother's suicide. I put the copy of Dante back in the bookshelf. I kept the rose she left me in a little vase on the bedside table as the leaves turned black.

I grieved to myself, without the poleaxed pain that lived in my middle for the first year after Patty said she was leaving. That first time Lindsey made joyous love with me, I saw her as such a miraculous appearance in my life that I vowed not to jump into the vortex of hope and fear that breeds possessiveness. I just let her and us unfold, and I would never regret that. Maybe I always knew it was temporary, and if she didn't run away first, well, maybe I would. So I grieved to myself and tried to create a world of small forward motion.

For the next few days, the Phoenix Police went away. I was the sole investigator on the Yarnell case, a sign that they saw me as both incompetent and harmless—not a bad place to be in a large bureaucracy. The only stipulation: I check in with Hawkins once a week. The skeletons case quickly departed from the minute-long attention span of the Phoenix media. Christmas was coming and a new Nordstrom was open in Scottsdale.

I did what I could.

I spent hours looking over old missing-persons reports from the 1930s and early 1940s. I hooked up with an FBI cold-case expert in Washington. I went through reams of old police logs. Anything to figure out whether twins other than the Yarnell brothers could have ended up walled into the basement passage beneath the Sunset Route Hotel.

James Yarnell gave me permission to examine the Yarnell family papers that were boxed up in the archives of the Arizona Historical Foundation and the Arizona Collection at the Burton Barr Central Library. So every morning I stopped off at my office, made myself not look for an e-mail or voice message from Lindsey, and then drove to the library for at least two solid hours' work. It was like grad school all over again.

The papers told me that the Yarnell family enterprises were complicated even back in the 1940s. The Yarnell Land and Cattle Co. included ranches around the state, citrus, cotton, mining, even development of a "new subdivision outside Phoenix," which was about half a mile from where my neighborhood sat in the inner-city today. Hayden Yarnell had been about seventy-five years old in 1941, but he had still managed his empire with precise notes and direct orders: when to move a herd to the High Country, how much to price some land near Bisbee, why he thought the company's offices in the Luhr's Tower were too expensive. His scrawl across yellowing memos and creaky ledgers was loopy with age and carried the flats and edges of an old fountain pen.

Yarneco was very much a family business back then. Morgan Yarnell, Hayden's son and James and Max's father, was a regular cast member in the corporate records. In the 1930s, it looked like he took over the cattle business. Then in 1939, Morgan was named vice president, putting him directly below the old man. Loan documents for farm land around the Valley and railroad shipping contracts were routinely signed by Morgan after 1939. Occasionally in a board document I saw the name Emma Yarnell Tully, Hayden's daughter, but she seemed to have little to do with the company.

Those same documents might name Hayden

Winthrop Yarnell, Jr., Morgan's brother. His nephew, James Yarnell, called him the "bounder of the family." But he was a cipher in the corporate records, and appeared little more in the family photos. I looked at a man with a long, weak face, hardly the face of a bounder. He was two years older than Morgan, and as far as I could tell he never married, had no children, and lived off the family fortune.

One afternoon, I came across a slender, vanity-press volume to commemorate Hayden Yarnell's seventy-fifth birthday. He'd come a long way from the gunfight at Gila City. My finger slid across grainy black-and-white images of the patriarch with the snowy, full head of hair. The fierceness was still in his eyes, undimmed by the stiff white collar and heavy wool suit and decades of comfortable wealth. He looked so out of place, standing in the foyer of his mansion, fingering his watch chain. I wanted to see him as my mind's eye did—the cowboy, the miner, the quintessence of pioneer Arizona.

The watch chain. My eye lingered.

Here was a family photo, with a caption identifying Morgan Yarnell and his sons, Andrew, Woodrow, Max, and James. It put me back in my chair for a moment, to see the actual faces. The twins were dressed in Western shirts, boots, toy guns, staring menacingly at the camera. Innocent little faces with that long Yarnell nose. Disappeared for half a century, little boys lost.

I'm not particularly good with numbers; that's one reason I never made it big in the history business, which today emphasizes statistics and social science. But it didn't seem that Yarneco was doing well in the 1930s. No surprise there, considering the Great Depression was dragging on and the towns and rural areas of the West suffered longer and deeper downturns than many places. Still, a string of tense letters from bankers indicated that even businesses that should have been doing all right were suffering. I had written my Ph.D. dissertation on the Depression in the West, and I knew the dude ranches and fledgling resorts actually helped prop up the Phoenix economy during that time. That was not the case of the resort owned by Yarneco. It was sold in 1939 under threat of foreclosure.

I saw more of Gretchen Goodheart. Every couple of days, she dropped by my office, delivered a new insight, if not a new blueprint, to the underground passages where the twins were walled up. Gradually on the cork bulletin board that sat on an easel in my office we built a little collage of facts. One day she asked if I would go horseback riding with her, and we spent a Saturday out in the desert. She had a quality of depth that was appealing and rare. It was the holidays and I was needy. But I wanted to believe I would have appreciated her in any season.

Chapter Twenty-one

It was nearly nine on Friday night and I stood at the office window, listening to carolers down in a nearly deserted Patriots Square. They sang "Hark! The Herald Angels Sing" and then "Jingle Bells" before a fire truck went by with siren screaming. I picked up the phone on the second ring, but there was only a light buzz in the background. I was about to put it down when a voice said my name.

"You know who this is?"

"I don't."

"Everybody knows my voice. The damned president knows my voice. It's Max Yarnell."

I sat down in the wooden swivel chair. "How may I help you, Mr. Yarnell?" He sounded very drunk.

"I need to talk to you," he said. "I need to see you. Tonight. Can you come out here?"

"Where is 'out here'?"

He started into directions heading me into the McDowell Mountain foothills in the far north of Scottsdale. I scribbled them onto a sheriff's office memo pad.

"Mr. Yarnell," I said. "It's late, it'll take me an hour to get out there."

"Goddamn it, Mapstone, you could do it in thirty minutes. I do. I really need to talk to you."

"What about?"

"Not on the phone," he slurred. "Out here, where it's safe."

"Safe from what?" I could hear "Frosty the Snowman" wafting through the open window.

"Never mind," he said. "I'll call you back." The line clicked off.

It reminded me of an eccentric old professor at a university where I had taught. At work, he was distinguished and aloof, a giant in his field of research. But he drank alone at home and after the first few glasses, he reached for the telephone—sometimes he called female students he had a crush on, sometimes colleagues he was peeved at. He was quietly pushed into retirement after he made an obscene call to a dean's wife. I made a note to call Max Yarnell the next day.

When I got the car out of the garage to head home, though, I felt differently. It was nothing as formed or sophisticated as a premonition. Just a murky anxiety. I pulled out the address and drove toward Scottsdale. I slipped onto the Red Mountain Freeway at Seventh Street and shot through the older neighborhoods of east Phoenix, cruising at seventy-five at treetop level. Then the freeway jogged southeast into Tempe, past Rural Road, and I took the connection to the Pima Freeway. That took me north into Scottsdale, the city off to my left, the Indian reservation off to the right. I got onto surface streets at McDonald, put the top down, and drove through north Scottsdale. The night was crisp but I was warm inside my leather jacket.

You couldn't touch a house out here for less than a half-a-million dollars, and it was the older part of Scottsdale. I went through McCormick Ranch into the horse properties. Past Shea Boulevard, across the Central Arizona Project Canal, and into the estates running up to the McDowell Mountains. A discreet sign promised "gated canyon living." Twenty years before, this had all been empty desert.

Before I got into Fountain Hills, the developments thinned out as the road climbed. I reached the scenic lookout for the city lights—we used to come up here in high school to make out. Then off to the left was a road named Cheryl. I took it and climbed deeper into the foothills until I reached a gate of black steel.

I slipped the car into park and it purred at idle, just the way the engineers in Munich intended. All around me, hills and mountains stood out black against the night sky, and beyond them the city glowed with a ghostly sheen. A small black communications box stood by the gate. I pressed a glowing red button. I waited and nothing happened. I shut the car off and listened. The hum of traffic on Shea, and farther away on Beeline Highway coming down from the Mogollon Rim. Closer in, the desert sounds: the breeze in the palo verde leaves, a rustling in the mesquite, the indescribable but very real sound of the emptiness. You could even see the stars out here. But I couldn't see what was on the other side of the gate, and the communications box failed to return my affections. I gave another couple of tries and turned back toward the city. Apparently the booze had answered whatever questions Max Yarnell had for me.

He was right: It took about half an hour at this time of night. I exited off the Red Mountain at Third Street and turned toward home. It was around eleven-thirty, and I was suddenly feeling jumpy. The vastness of the city felt claustrophobic. I was too aware of every breath. I raised the top and didn't feel better. When I turned onto Third Avenue and headed into Willo, I swear I saw that damned Ford Econoline van again, making the turn with me, on my tail. When I checked the mirror again, crossing Palm Lane, the street was empty behind me. Time to call it a day.

Back at home, Peralta was snoring contentedly in the guest bedroom. I closed his door, got undressed for bed and slid in the sheets naked to read. That's when the phone rang.

I thought it might be Max Yarnell. But it was Gretchen.

"Did I wake you?" she asked.

"Nope, I was just reading."

"I'm glad I didn't wake you. How is your quest going?"

"Oh, not so good. There don't seem to be any answers."

"There are always answers, David. You just have to know where to look."

"Well, you have the patience of the archaeologist," I said.

"I'm not always patient," she said. "In fact, I can be very impulsive." She paused and I was very aware of the softness of the sheets against my body. "In, fact, I was calling to ask you if I could come over and be with you."

"I would like that very much," I said.

"I hoped you'd say that. That's why I took the chance."

Chapter Twenty-two

When I came awake, Gretchen was lightly stroking my hair and staring at me intently.

"You have the softest hair. Just like a baby's hair."

Then the pounding on the door resumed. I sat up a little and groaned. My head ached like I'd finished off a bottle of red wine, but I hadn't sipped a drop. My shoulders and arms, legs and back ached, too, but I knew what that was from.

"Who could that be at this hour?" I whispered through a cotton mouth. The clock on the bedside table said one but it was bright sunny outside.

"Jesus," I said, and sat up. Gretchen just watched me. She was wearing one of my white dress shirts and nothing else. I looked back longingly at her, slipped on my robe and limped out into the house. Peralta's bed was made and he was nowhere to be seen. Out the window was an unmarked police unit. Something bad.

"Quit screwing around," came a voice through the little grille in the heavy wood door. The voice went to the body of Sheriff's Detective Patrick Blair.

"What the hell, Mapstone?" he said. "I've been pounding on the door for fifteen minutes."

"What's going on?" I demanded, suddenly wide awake. I was instantly worried about Lindsey, so worried that I momentarily forgot who had been in my bed last night. Then I felt immediately guilty.

"Can I come in?"

"The house is a pit," I said. "What do you need, Blair?"

He was as tall as me, and several light years more handsome. Just about thirty, he had luxurious black hair, merry Irish blue eyes, a perfect central casting face, a robust body. He had on a denim shirt, chinos and a Glock in a cross-draw holster, but he still looked like he just stepped out of a fashion magazine.

"What do I need?" he demanded. "What did you have going with Max Yarnell?"

I opened the door, suddenly angry. "Quit giving me the cop fuck-around," I said. "I was doing that when you were in grade school. Give me some straight talk." It brought out all the adolescent jerk in me, but it worked. His gorgeous face registered surprise and he said simply, "Max Yarnell has been murdered."

We drove out to Scottsdale in silence, Blair at the wheel of a department Ford Crown Victoria, and me sitting in the passenger seat cloaked in a feeling of oppressive strangeness. Sometime after Max Yarnell had called me at the courthouse last night, he had been killed. Blair didn't know the details; he had simply been sent by Peralta to fetch me. And Blair was the guy who was seeing Lindsey every day. Jealousy is the most irrational and destructive of emotions, and I let it take a run through my mind all the way out to Max Yarnell's gated canyon living. Lindsey and Patrick Blair. Lindsey who didn't return my calls anymore. So this was why.

But almost as a backbeat was my memory of Gretchen from last night. When I had met her at the door, we had fallen hungrily into each other's arms with the telepathy of lonely people. Every centimeter on my body had been electrified as her mouth explored my lips, my ears and my neck, and then her hands had worked their way around me. I had kissed her greedily, wrestling her tongue gently with mine, stroking that miraculously lovely reddish brown hair. I had felt so lucky that she wanted me.

Gretchen Goodheart. She was very different in bed than I would have imagined. I loved aggressive women, but she had surprised me. The kind of gentle foreplay that Lindsey craved had just made Gretchen more demanding. We shouldn't make comparisons among lovers, but we all do, don't we? Lindsey had that little oscillating move when we made love in the missionary position—it was the most amazing sensation and when she started it, I could never last long. Gretchen—Gretchen had her own moves, but they were all so different. I learned quickly that Gretchen's favorite position was from behind. There's no polite, romantic way to put it. This was pure fucking, as she had clenched the sheets and screamed into the pillow and pushed back to me for more. Gretchen was a screamer. I had trusted the thick walls of the house for our privacy. I hoped she'd still be at home when I got back.

The deliciousness of the memory lost some of its taste as we pulled up into the desert cul de sac, past half a dozen sheriff's cruisers, Scottsdale Police units and unmarked Crown Vics. A TV van pulled in after us and started setting up. Blair shifted into park and said, "You're Lindsey's friend, right?"

"That's right," I said, mindful of any ironic inflection in either of our voices. We slipped our badges onto our belts and walked through the gate.

The house was long and low, hugging the side of a hill with lots of glass and modern adobe. From one side, the McDowells towered above. From the other, the city fell off through an arroyo, the view going all the way to the Estrellas, which today were cloaked in yellow-brown smog.

I walked through the double doors into the home and Peralta met me.

"What are you doing here?" I asked.

"Just watching your ass," he said. "Yarnell's house is in a little piece of county land. So technically, it's our case, although we'll cooperate with Scottsdale. I want every constituent served, even the dead ones."

I followed him into a large room where evidence technicians were taking still and video photographs. The room was sparsely but expensively furnished with the kind of modern pieces you see in decorating articles in the *New York Times Magazine*. One wall was entirely glass, facing toward the city. The light show must be breathtaking. Then there was an airy chrome and wood desk, and beside that I could see a man's head on the floor.

I didn't understand what had happened until I walked carefully to the other side of the desk. Yarnell was on his back and a milky-colored stake was jutting out of the mashed bones and tissue where his breastbone used to be. There wasn't much blood dirtying up the spotless hardwood floor. His eyes stared up with the peculiar glaze of the dead.

"God," I said in spite of myself.

"It's petrified wood," Peralta said. "Looks like it came from over there." He indicated a minimalist bookshelf off to the left. "A good Arizona kind of murder."

"Somebody must have been strong as hell," I said.

"This thing looks pretty heavy, so all you'd need is gravity," said an evidence technician named Hernandez. "Especially after you cracked him on the jaw. Look at this." He knelt and ran a gloved finger over the bottom of Yarnell's face, which was discolored but not quite bruised. "Somebody hit him good," Hernandez said. "You'd see a hell of a strawberry if he still had a heart beating."

"Maybe he was a vampire," said a uniform and everybody laughed.

"That's enough," Peralta said. He caught me by the shoulder and steered me out on the broad stone terrace.

"Tell me why your phone number is on the note pad on the dead man's desk."

"He called me last night and said he wanted to talk. He sounded like he'd had a few too many."

"What did he want to talk about?"

"Beats the hell out of me. I told him I'd call today. Then I thought about it—he hasn't been cooperative and now he wanted to talk—so I drove out here. No answer at the gate. So I drove home. You were already asleep."

"This was what time?"

"Maybe ten-thirty."

"Did he want to talk about the skeletons, or what?"

"He didn't say. He said he'd only talk in person, not on the phone."

Peralta shoved his hands into his pants pockets and stared down at the brown cloud enveloping the city.

"He had enough enemies," he said. "You've heard about this new copper mine? He had the environmental whackos on his ass."

"I don't get the sense there are very many environmentalists in Arizona, much less whacko…"

"Well, the neighboring property owners aren't too happy, either. They wanted to develop subdivisions."

"When I first interviewed him, he said the company had received threats. He had some major-league bodyguards in the office."

Peralta crooked his mouth down as he mulled it over. "Well, he was all alone out here last night. But he had a state-of-the-art alarm system, and a .38 in his desk drawer. When the housekeeper showed up this morning he was like this."

"Maybe it's the Yarnell curse."

"I only worry about bad luck that shoots back, Mapstone. I want to know what progress you've been making on this case."

"Not much," I said. "The pocket watch belonged to Hayden Yarnell, according to his son, James. I can't find any other twins who would have been missing and buried in a basement in downtown Phoenix during that same time. Yarnell's businesses were having cash problems…"

"That's not good enough," he said harshly. I felt a flush spread up my face, angry and embarrassed to be brought up short by him. He went on: "Max Yarnell had a stake driven through his damned chest last night right after he told you he needed to talk to you. Doesn't that raise your curiosity a bit, professor?"

I looked at the smog. "I'll get you some answers."

"I want to know if this homicide had anything to do with what you're working on. This isn't just a little Phoenix Police matinee anymore, Mapstone. It's a real case. Try not to fuck up."

"I'll see if I can measure up." I turned and strode to the door.

"Mapstone," he called. When I turned, a mischievous grin momentarily played across over his dark features. "Hope you got a good night's rest."

I shrugged and walked back into the big room. I wanted out of Max Yarnell's big house, back into my big bed with Gretchen where all the violence of the world couldn't reach us. I sidestepped a Scottsdale cop making a diagram and an evidence technician setting up some high-tech contraption. I made my own mental notes. The room was neatly arranged considering the physical violence that had occurred. Whoever attacked Max Yarnell did it with suddenness and precision. He was probably someone Yarnell knew and let into the house. Yarnell was dressed in slacks and golf shirt. I looked around for a glass that might have held his libations, and sure enough one sat on a table by two leather chairs on the other side of the room. A cordless phone sat nearby. The evidence technician was preparing to bag them up.

Then I saw it.

Something cold crawled up my shoulders and slithered slowly up the back of my neck. I didn't say a word. But Hernandez, the evidence tech, was watching me, and he followed my eyes.

"Christ!" he said, and then all the cops were looking, too.

It was on one of the shelves behind Max Yarnell's desk. You might have missed it in the sheer size of the room and the distraction of a man sprawled on the floor with a piece of petrified wood sticking out of his chest. But I knew what it was instantly. A doll. Just like the one that had been delivered to my office a week ago, only this one didn't have a little sheriff's star. Instead, its hands were smeared bloody red.

I sensed Peralta behind me. "What the hell is that goddamned thing?"

That was when I realized how long it had been since I took a breath.

Chapter Twenty-three

Patrick Blair dropped me off at home a little after five. Gretchen was gone and the house felt huge and forlorn and freighted with the knowledge of how quickly life turns against human beings. I wanted to call her, but I realized I didn't even have her phone number. And for a long moment, I was relieved that I didn't. I couldn't say exactly why. Then I didn't want to be alone. Even Peralta would have been welcome.

The dusk gathered outside the picture window, a fading, unfocused, weightless part of the day. Even the winter lawns looked dead. The lights hadn't come on in the neighboring houses and it looked as if the neighborhood had been abandoned a long time ago. I sat on the living room staircase and thumbed through the books on the tall shelves. *The Price of Admiralty* by John Keegan, one of my books. *The House by the Buckeye Road*, one of Grandfather's. A heavily thumbed *Modern Researcher* by Barzun and Graff, a classic when I was being trained as a historian. Inside lurked a five-by-seven color photo of Lindsey, the desert wind whipping her dark hair. Back in the days when she was smiling at me with lust and joy.

The phone cut into the silence like a scream.

"David? Are you okay?"

"I'm fine," I said.

"You don't sound fine." It was Lorie Pope. I told her I was okay, and, carrying the cordless phone, walked into the kitchen. I peered into the refrigerator, which held leftovers from half a dozen ethnic restaurants, and a fresh case of Coors for Peralta. I got out ice and started making a martini.

"Max Yarnell," Lorie declared, as if she had spoken a whole paragraph.

I sighed and started mixing the drink.

"Are you making martinis?" Lorie demanded. "Why don't you make one for me?"

"Because martinis blur judgment," I said. "You told me that years ago."

"So? It would do you good."

"I would bore you. I was never dangerous enough."

"Yeah, but we could have fun while I was reaching that self-destructive conclusion." She gave a deep, sensual giggle. I imagined her too-wide smile and the toss of her short dark hair. I sealed up the gin and ice in Grandfather's deco cocktail shaker and I gave the concoction a good workout.

I took out one of the Neiman Marcus martini glasses my colleagues had given me as a going-away present from San Diego State University when I lost the tenure sweepstakes. I had a lot of going-away presents. The clear fluid slipped delightfully into the glass, little frigates of ice cruising the surface.

"Max Yarnell," Lorie said again.

"I honestly don't know much. I'm as baffled as everybody else. You know, 'police are baffled.' That's me."

"David!" Her voice was suddenly taut. "He's one of the richest and most prominent men in the state, and he's been murdered less than three weeks after it seemed like the Yarnell kidnapping had been solved? This whole thing stinks."

"I don't doubt it, but how?"

"You're the one with the Ph.D., my love."

"Fat lot of good it's done me."

"Look, I'd love to play career one-downmanship, but I've got a deadline. What's Peralta holding back?"

"Don't put me in that position, Lorie."

She sighed and said, "I'd like to put you in a position all right, but I guess you've got to go drink martinis out of Leslie's navel."

I dropped an olive into the martini like making a green wish. "Lindsey."

"Whatever," Lorie said. "Give me something, David. How was Max Yarnell killed? Gun? Knife? Sunday edition of the *Arizona Republic*? The PIO won't tell me a goddamned thing."

"You know the cops always hold back details, stuff the suspect alone knows. And you know I can't tell you that. "We'll talk."

"Hey," she said. "Be careful, David. I don't know what you've gotten yourself into but it's pretty heavy-duty. Watch that sweet melancholy-intellectual ass of yours."

She could always make me smile.

I put Count Basie on the stereo and went back to the staircase. From the perch of the carpeted steps, I savored the martini. Gotten myself into something heavy-duty, but what? What could a 58-year-old kidnapping have to do with a murder that happened yesterday? Hadn't the DNA test said those skeletons weren't even the Yarnells? Then what had Max Yarnell wanted to talk about with me? This same Max Yarnell who had his assistant pull the property records on the Triple A Storage Warehouse and then pretended to be surprised to learn his company owned it. Was he already dead as I was sitting at the gate, pushing the little red button on the communications box? Would it have made a difference if I had immediately agreed to a meeting? What was I missing?

It could all be a coincidence. Maybe he just surprised a burglar; maybe he only wanted to complain to me again about my lack of respectful behavior toward him, only this time with the liberating influence of alcohol; maybe he pissed off some environmental activists who decided to return him to the soil a little early.

That all could make sense, until you had to figure in that damned doll.

I went back to scanning book titles. All that history. The only problem was the history I didn't know. Out the picture window, the world appeared dark and profound, my valley of low ranch house rooftops and big sky, where stranglers, snipers and killers of rich men with secrets did their restless trades. I thought about what Philip Roth said: "the terror of the unforeseen is what the science of history hides." Then I heard James Yarnell's voice in my head and I jumped to my feet.

The garage-apartment behind the house was where I was building an HO-scale model railroad, a scene of Phoenix in the 1950s. It was a place to store boxes of books, old clothes and things headed for Goodwill. I guess I could have rented out the upstairs to a boarder if I wanted to clean out about forty years of records stored from Grandfather's dental practice.

I opened up the musty apartment and stared at the boxes and filing cabinets. Old patient records from my grandfather, the dentist. James Yarnell had said Grandfather had been their dentist way back when. Could it really be this easy? I started looking through files, getting a sense of how things were organized, or not. For decades, it seemed, Grandfather had an assistant named Mrs. Hill. I could barely remember a large woman with steel-wire stiff gray hair and thick fingers. Now I detected her steadfast handwriting on files before the 1950s, when typewritten labels took over. Her filing was quirky, made more so by the move of the records from Grandfather's old office on McDowell after he had finally retired. It took some time. I mixed another martini, came back to the garage apartment and dug in again.

In about an hour, I heard the door from the

house open and Peralta's heavy tread came over the walkway to the apartment.

"What are you doing, Mapstone?" He stuck his head in the door.

I held up the files.

"Finding the Yarnell twins," I said.

Chapter Twenty-four

"I don't hate all men," Gretchen was saying. "Maybe I'm wary of the species in abstract. When your name is Gretchen Goodheart, it brings out the predator in some men."

When she spoke, her mouth animated those double lines that became dimples when she smiled. They were like double parentheses etched into the smooth skin around her mouth.

"A good heart is good to find," I said.

"I like a few individuals of the species very much." She touched my arm.

It was Monday night. We were sitting in a booth at Los Olivos, the oldest Mexican restaurant in Scottsdale and one of my favorites. It was our first real date and the place was overflowing with winter visitors. Max Yarnell had been dead for a little more than two days.

We had been talking about Frances Richie, about

the bad sense and bad luck to fall in with somebody like Jack Talbott. Gretchen had said he represented a type of man that made women hate all men.

Philosophy and enchiladas. I was glad for a break. Sunday had been nonstop for fourteen hours, as I trailed along with sheriff's and police detectives as they interviewed people in the homicide of Max Yarnell.

He had been one of the richest men in the Southwest, and one of the loneliest. He had divorced his wife of thirty years back in the early 1990s and then had gone through a string of pretty young trophies, none of the women in the picture recently. His children lived out of state; one lived in London. He and his brother, James, hadn't spoken in seven months. His assistant, the lovely Megan, was on vacation in San Diego. So apparently on Friday night, Max Yarnell had worked in the midtown skyscraper until around four, then had driven home. He lived alone, with a housekeeper and cook who only worked as needed. With business dinners and travel, Max Yarnell didn't seem to have much time to enjoy his sweeping views.

All that work had produced enemies. The defense company owned by Yarneco had faced government investigations into alleged contracting fraud. Another Yarneco subsidiary had terminated an employee who had vowed to come to Phoenix and personally kill Max Yarnell. It was a promising lead until the man was found with a new job and a tight alibi in Seattle. But the biggest trouble came with the company's ambition to open the first new copper mine in Arizona in years.

Yarneco was not only being sued by environmental groups, but also by its erstwhile partner, a giant mining conglomerate from Australia. The Aussies' lawsuit claimed Yarneco had misrepresented key geologists' reports about the site. Yarneco counter-sued for breach of contract. Only thirty million bucks were at stake.

And that was the gentlemanly part of the troubles. Earlier this year, the Gila County sheriff had investigated two arsons at the site office of Yarneco near the Arizona town of Superior. Then Yarneco headquarters started getting phone calls threatening worse if the project wasn't stopped. The most recent phone call came the previous week. Unfortunately, with the too-smart-by-half mentality of corporations, Yarneco didn't report this call to the cops. It just hired more bodyguards. On Sunday afternoon, I had listened to the tape on the twentieth floor of the Yarneco Tower.

"This is your last warning." The voice had sounded strangely altered, like putting Harry Connick's voice track through a blender. "If the mine isn't stopped within a week, the criminal Max Yarnell will be executed."

"That's it?" Peralta had asked. One of the tough boys I first noticed in the oversized suit coats had nodded. Peralta had nearly spat on the carpet.

"And you didn't think this was worth telling us about?"

He had just stared, slightly cross-eyed. "I was following orders, sir."

How many times had we heard that in this bloody century?

I had thought the voice sounded male. Peralta had been sure it was a woman. He had it sent off to the FBI to be analyzed.

Yet outside of the security boys at his office, Max Yarnell wasn't acting like someone who was afraid. Alarm company records showed the system at his house was not armed the night he was killed. Yarnell only armed it each night around midnight when he turned in, and while he was away. He left work early that day, saying he was going to work from home, but no, he hadn't mentioned that he expected visitors that night.

All these thoughts kept replaying themselves as we sat in the restaurant.

"In a way," Gretchen said, "it sounds like Frances had bad luck with men all her life."

I savored a mouthful of cheese crisp.

"I mean, after Jack Talbott, she was kept in prison her entire life by the Yarnell brothers. That's what you're saying."

"I guess so," I said. "I guess one might take it personally if somebody kidnapped his brothers and they were never seen again."

"We don't even know they did it!" Gretchen shouted, holding my wrist tightly enough that it hurt.

"Sorry." She let go. "When I drink, I get passionate."

She was on her second margarita.

"Do you doubt they did it?"

"I don't know, David. I don't know."

"The newspaper articles made it sound pretty open-and-shut."

"The newspapers," she said, her tone neutral. Then, "So what do you think happened with Max? Are you allowed to tell me?" The rich brown eyes fixed on me intensely. "Do you trust me, David?"

"You're helping me on the kidnapping, so of course I trust you. On Max, we just don't know much."

"He sounded so powerful. So much money."

"Didn't do him much good in the end."

Gretchen sipped her drink. "Do you wish you could have that kind of world? All that money? And you didn't even have to work for it. It just seems like a madness nowadays. Twenty-five-year-old kids with millions in stock options. And here we are, two civil servants."

"I envy the rich their options," I said.

The waitress brought our check. One other couple came in and sat at the opposite end of the room. They weren't talking to each other.

Gretchen said, "My dad's a teacher, so I'll never inherit much money."

"Well, my grandfather was a dentist before dentists made big money."

"And your parents?"

"They died in a small-plane crash. I was just a baby. Dad was a lawyer for the state. Mom was a music teacher. I didn't really know them."

"Oh, baby…"

"I was very fortunate with my grandparents. And who knows about great wealth. There's that whole business about the rich man passing through the eye of a needle."

She rolled her eyes. "Please, no religion during the holidays."

I couldn't tell if she was being ironic. How could you know these days?

Just then my cell phone rang. The number was unfamiliar.

I excused myself and went to the little alcove off the Los Olivos bar to return the call. A mariachi band was playing Christmas tunes in the sound system.

"Deb Boswell."

"It's David Mapstone with the Sheriff's Office," I said.

"Mapstone, you're quite something." Her voice was brighter than the dour academic I remembered from Hawkins' office. "Your grandfather was a dentist?"

"That's right."

"And he treated these boys? Andrew and Woodrow Yarnell?"

"Apparently."

"Why would that be? Why would he have treated them?"

Suddenly I felt like I was in an interview room

with the cops, on the bad luck side of the table.

"He was a dentist," I said. "Phoenix was smaller then. It probably had 40,000 people during the Depression, and not that many dentists. I don't know."

"Oh," she said. "I'm from Detroit, so it's hard for me to have a sense of this place."

"I found the records stored among Grandfather's files. I immediately logged them into evidence."

"It was pretty unusual to see dental X-rays in 1940," she said.

"These were rich people," I said. "And Grandfather loved gadgets."

I was bursting with anticipation, but something told me not to rush her.

"Well," she said, "it's the jackpot. Based on the dental records, the skeletons you guys found are indeed the remains of Andrew and Woodrow Yarnell. Each little boy had a silver filling in a molar."

"And the DNA profile?"

"Both tests are telling us accurate information," Boswell said. "Deputy, you have a mystery on your hands."

Chapter Twenty-five

I walked Gretchen to her truck, reveling in the cool, dry evening. She wore a lightweight leather jacket over a dark blouse and tight blue jeans. The leather felt soft and supple as I slipped my hand around her. She leaned into me. The Christmas lights were up in downtown Scottsdale, and tourists sauntered along window-shopping, pairs of shadows down the street.

"Do you want some company?"

She put her hand in my back pocket. "That would mean I would have to give you my address."

"Do you trust me, Gretchen?"

"If you came to my place, you'd fuck me," she whispered, her voice husky. "You might just fuck me crazy."

I ran my hands down her sweet, denim-encased hips, pulled her closer.

"That would be the idea."

She checked her watch. "Why don't I come to your place later? Will your high-powered roomie be put out?"

For a moment I wondered if she were married. That might be one reason to not give me her address, to not ride out here with me. We stood beside her big white SUV. I caressed her face and she leaned in, kissing me deeply. As we were parting, I told her the latest news on the twins.

"It is definitely them," I said. "Either the DNA test was inconclusive, or they had a different mother from Max and James."

She turned her head away and I could see her eyes were full of tears. They gleamed off the street-lights like new stars.

"Gotta go, David. Thank you for a nice evening." She gently but firmly pushed me away, and soon the Ford's taillights disappeared around the corner. I was left alone on the street.

I drove slowly down Main Street, past the rows of tony galleries. The car was a warm haven for a man mellowed by two Negra Modelos and aroused by Gretchen's kisses. Clots of white-haired tourists milled along the street. Then, past the traffic circle with the bronze of the bucking bronco, Main Street emptied out. I was just about to accelerate over to

Goldwater Boulevard when another white head caught my eye. A man in a checked shirt and khaki pants, sitting on a bench. It was James Yarnell.

"I'm seeing you more often than I see my wife," he said after I stopped and got out. We had interviewed him on Sunday.

"Are you all right?"

He looked me over in an unfocused way. I could smell booze on him.

"I'm just closing up for the night." He gestured over his shoulder to the Yarnell Gallery's large, well-lit windows. I sat on the bench beside him, and for a long time we just listened to the night noises in a city of cars.

"Eventually you lose everybody," he said.

"I'm very sorry about your brother."

"I didn't love him," he said. "I won't pretend that." I thought of Lindsey's anguished words about her mother. "It's just he was family. We were the last of the famous Yarnell brothers."

James stared into the sidewalk. "Max wasn't always the man he became, the man you met. He was a link to my parents and my grandpa and my little twin brothers."

A little group of tourists speaking German walked behind us, wowed by a large painting visible in the gallery.

"What do you think happened to Andrew and Woodrow?"

He shook his head, his handsome face a mask.

"Deep inside, I always knew they had to be dead. But when you never have a resolution, you never really know. So you always hold out hope. Grandfather hoped nearly to the end. He'd been able to do so much in his life out of sheer will. Then, he just seemed to give up one day. This great life force went out of the man."

The tourists moved down the street and we were alone again. I said, "You don't talk about your father much."

He leaned back on the bench and sighed. "Morgan Yarnell had the misfortune to be the son of a larger-than-life man, and the husband of a very strong woman, my mother. Even his brother, Uncle Win, was colorful and loud. Dad wasn't a bad person. He was just so…" he searched for the word, "…eclipsed. I guess he deserves more memory than that from his son. But, you see, when you're a boy, those big personalities stay with you. By the time I came back from the war, Dad was dead. I guess I never really knew him."

I hunched down, feeling suddenly cold. "How

much did you know about your family's affairs back then?"

"How much does a kid know?" he said. "We weren't the happiest family in the world, but we weren't the unhappiest either."

"The records you let me see, they show a company that was in trouble."

"It was the Depression."

"Morgan took more of a role in the company."

"Yes, Dad was the reliable son."

"What about Win?"

"Win wasn't in the business."

"So no problems with the Yarnell Land & Cattle Co. other than the general economy?"

James shook his head. "Mapstone, I had my head more on horses and girls, not necessarily in that order, than the family business. In fact, I couldn't wait to get away from it. Max was the businessman, always was. Let's walk down the street and get a drink."

"I've got to go," I said. "One more question. Are you sure your brothers were blood kin?"

For just a moment, he looked remarkably like Max: the piercing, impatient glare. "What are you talking about?"

I told him about the dental records.

"That's impossible." He stood and started to walk away.

I followed him. "Why would it be impossible?" I demanded. "People are adopted all the time."

"You're crazy," he shouted, in a breathy, drunken voice. I was surprised by his reaction. Gone was the easy-going demeanor of that night at Gainey Ranch, when I had first asked about the adoption issue.

"Those remains are your brothers. But they're not your mother's children. Help me solve this!"

"Leave me alone!" He walked faster, his gait turning oddly effeminate. Then he ran, a sad little-old-man run, back toward the gallery.

That's when the air behind me exploded with a single whip-crack.

Ahead of me a shop window shattered into a thousand shards of plate glass. A woman screamed. James Yarnell gaped at me, his eyes overtaken by terror. I ran and jumped on him, throwing him roughly to the ground behind a little wall that separated the shop fronts from the sidewalk. My handgun was in the bedside table at home and my cell phone was in the car. Some Boy Scout I was: Be prepared, hell.

He was whimpering beneath me. "Are you

hit?" I whispered. He shook his head.

Then everything was silent again. Even the traffic over on Scottsdale Road seemed to have disappeared. We were safe behind the wall—unless whoever shot at us was mobile, and coming our way. "We've got to move," I said.

I scuttled down the sidewalk, keeping the wall between us and the street. *Come on,* I motioned, and James crawled after me. But after about ten feet the low wall ended, and the next protection was a dark breezeway in the next building, an additional, eternal ten feet away.

"What is going on?" James gasped.

"You tell me. Have you received any threats, anything at all?"

"No, no, nothing!"

"Can you run?"

"I don't know," he whispered.

"You've got to try," I said viciously. "We can't stay here." The streetlights burned down on us, the bright, dry air emphasizing our vulnerability.

James looked at me.

"Ready?"

He nodded. His eyes were wide and bloodshot.

I grabbed him by the arm and hauled him

up. My knee and ankle were hurting again, but I felt every muscle in my legs tense and pulse with energy. We bolted to the breezeway, our shoes echoing loudly off the concrete.

I heard that whip-crack sound, louder now, and I knew we were dead. But I was too hyped to be scared. A wooden post shattered just ahead of us. I felt the splinters against my face. I dragged Yarnell and made us keep running. Then I threw us down into the darkness of the breezeway as another shot snapped behind us. The bullet ricocheted violently off the walls, adding in a weird tuning-fork kind of sound.

"Go!" I whispered and pulled him along. We ran through the breezeway and through a gate into an alley.

Turning right, I pounded toward Scottsdale Road. Yarnell fell onto the dirty asphalt. I picked him up and pulled him by his arm and his belt until he was running again. We kept to the backs of the buildings and the sheltering darkness. Then we burst onto Scottsdale Road and the beloved sight of people and traffic.

Chapter Twenty-six

I needed to get out of the city, so the next day I followed Lorie's notepad-sheet full of directions to the outskirts of Black Canyon City, a village loosely spread across the foothills along the interstate north of Phoenix. I was on business. Peralta was getting testy, the Yarnell case distracting him from the Harquahala Strangler. That morning, he had presided over a meeting downtown. Two detectives named Kimbrough and Mitchell—I'd worked with them before and we'd established something like mutual respect—would do the traditional cop work on the Max Yarnell murder. They would also handle liaison with Scottsdale PD on the attempt on James Yarnell's life. I was to focus on the kidnapping of the twins, and find out how, or if, it connected to the other crimes. I was happy to be working back in the past, where you were shot at less frequently. Still, I had the Colt Python .357 magnum on my belt now, the black nylon holster feeling uncomfortable and comforting at the same time.

The directions led me to a sun-beaten, single-wide trailer perched on the edge of a squat mesa. Scrub-covered hills and blown-apart rock formations swept away in every direction. The purple mass of the Bradshaw Mountains piled up to the northwest, and off to the east a ten-story-high rock prism sprouted out of a butte. Down below, Interstate 17 emitted a steady moan and I could smell the exhaust fumes this far away. To the south, the mountains were obscured in a brown soup: Phoenix. I parked the BMW next to a Harley, grabbed a satchel of file folders and stepped out onto the hard ground.

"I got a twelve-gauge and you're way lost, mister," a woman's voice came from the trailer. Another day, another gun aimed at me.

"I'm looking for Zelda Chain," I called.

"Who the hell are you?"

"David Mapstone. Lorie Pope sent me."

A screen door flew open and a large, pear-shaped woman, poured into a brown house dress, scrambled out. "Why the hell didn't you say so, honey? You almost gave me my morning target practice. My, you're a tall one. No wonder Lorie likes you."

I knew she was pushing eighty, but her face had a youthful animation. Her hair was long and colorless, falling back over her shoulders. Her eyes were large and full of fun.

"Things have gotten too dangerous," she said. "That damned city." She gestured toward Phoenix.

"We have Major League Baseball," I volunteered.

She gave me a vinegar look. "When I moved out here years ago, it was a half-hour drive before you even got to the outskirts. Now, I hear they're doing one of these goddamned 'planned communities' right across the wash from me." She gestured across the dry creek bed. "It will have forty thousand people. Hope I'm dead by then."

She saw me eyeing the Harley. "Don't worry, honey. That hog doesn't belong to some big drunken boyfriend who's going to come home and catch us." She laughed until she drowned in a phlegmy cough. "That's my bike. Don't ride as much as I once did. Fell too damned many times. It's a credo for life: don't ride if you're afraid to lay the bike down."

Zelda Chain invited me into a living room crowded with books and furniture, and insisted on serving iced tea. It was in a mason jar and smelled of bourbon. She pulled a Marlboro and lit up.

"I always used to joke that I'd end up in a trailer outside Gallup, New Mexico," she said, dropping across from me on an ancient stuffed sofa. "Hell, I couldn't even get that far away from Phoenix. But, as Lorie probably told you, I was the librarian at *The Republic* for forty-seven years. I'm damned proud of that. I retired in 1985. Well, they retired me. Now I don't even read newspapers anymore. I don't want to know how awful the world is. Never watched television. I'm tempted to tear out the phone."

I asked about Hayden Yarnell and the history of the kidnapping, but she leaned back, rearranged her long, dry hair like a shawl over her shoulders and smiled like a young girl. "Lorie tells me you're a history professor and a deputy sheriff."

"That's true."

"That's like being a gas company and an Internet company all in one," she laughed. "I own stock in one like that. Bastards. Never gets above nineteen dollars a share."

"Kind of like me, I guess."

She crushed out the cigarette and lit another. "Young people aren't taught history any more," she said. "They haven't been for thirty years or more. It's one reason the world's so insane." She waved the cigarette around like a smoky wand. "My uncle fought in the Spanish-American War," she went on. "And he lived to see Americans walk on the moon. We don't have that sense of connection to our past now. But that doesn't mean it's not there. What did Faulkner say? 'The past isn't even past.' We just have to rediscover every truth the hard way. Such arrogance."

She stopped and looked at me. "Ah, Mapstone, you are in the clutches of an old lady with too many crotchets and grudges against the world. What did you specialize in, in graduate school?"

I hadn't been asked that question in a while. "America in the Progressive era and the Depression."

"To each his own," she said. "Pardon my sexist language. I specialized in eighteenth-century England." The merry eyes reasserted themselves. "But my dad also made me learn to type. So you're lucky you have a skill to fall back on."

She waddled over to a bookshelf filled with file boxes labeled in old-lady-scrawl. "Can you believe the newspaper wanted to throw all this out?

"So," she said, "which one of you wants to

know about Hayden Yarnell? The history teacher, or the lawman?"

She pulled out a large file box, blew the dust off and set it on a Formica table. "The year was 1941. Pearl Harbor hadn't happened yet. Phoenix was still a small farming town, with some dude ranches and tuberculosis sanitariums—they called the patients 'lungers' then. Hayden Yarnell was the richest man in the state. He had a big house on South Mountain. It burned in 1942, not long after the kidnapping. He died soon after that. Talk about a string of bad luck. The ruins of the foundation are probably still out there. He also kept an apartment at the Hotel Westward Ho, like the rest of the Phoenix elite. Rumor had it he kept a mistress there, too. Back then, they called the big men in town the 'summer bachelors.' When it turned hot, they'd ship their wives off to someplace cool, and their summer girls would show up."

All this was before she even looked into the files.

"What if I told you we found the skeletons of two children, entombed in a basement wall in a downtown warehouse owned by the Yarnell family? And somebody is now killing off the remaining Yarnell brothers."

She exhaled from somewhere in her ankles. "I'd say I need a drink." She took my mason jar and banged into the small kitchen. "You need one, too. Bourbon is the house specialty."

"Easy on the dose for me."

She returned and leaned on the table, watching me intently. "You found the Yarnell twins? Holy crap. Maybe I'll have to subscribe to the newspaper again."

"What do you remember about the time of the kidnapping?"

"Well," she eased herself into a chair, "everything. It was Thanksgiving, an unusually cold autumn. Do you know we used to get hard frosts in Phoenix before they paved everything over? Anyway, I'd been at the paper for about three years. We all had our eyes on the war in Europe, and we knew it was just a matter of time before Japan jumped on us. But Phoenix was so isolated then, and things were very quiet."

"Morgan Yarnell waited a week before reporting the kidnapping to the police."

She nodded. "Strange, huh? He was the father of the twins. But the fact that they waited to call the cops was never very widely reported. The family had pull with the newspaper publishers, so no surprise there. I assume they figured they could handle it themselves, and any publicity might make the kidnapper kill the twins. Remember, the Lindbergh kidnapping was still very fresh in everyone's minds. Talk about a media circus. The Yarnells were very well known, much more so than today."

"But did Morgan get a ransom note, or what? It's not clear from the record."

She opened the file box and leafed through some yellowed papers. She produced some reading glasses from her pocket and angled them on her nose. "He told the police that the twins were taken from their rooms at the Yarnell mansion on South Mountain on the night of November 27, and their nanny discovered them missing the next day. He received a telephone call that day demanding a hundred thousand dollars be put in a locker at Union Station. He complied, but after a week the boys still weren't returned, so he went to the police. No mention of a note or any communication beyond the call."

"Did they have direct dial in town then? Maybe an operator helped the kidnapper place the call. I wish somebody had tried to find where that call came from."

"Honey, I wish I was twenty years old with

a cheerleader's body, still with my IQ, of course. Nobody was asking these questions. When Jack Talbott was caught, everyone was convinced justice was done. Wait." She leafed through a file of yellowed newspaper clippings and paper. "Maybe not everyone. Here, look at this."

It was newspaper copy paper, flimsy and brittle with age. It was datelined Florence, Arizona, July 20, 1942. I read the lead aloud:

"'Convicted kidnapper John Henry "Jack" Talbott was executed in Arizona's gas chamber early this morning, but not before his last words accused Hayden "Win" Yarnell Jr. of masterminding the kidnapping of his four-year-old nephews.'"

I sat up straight. "I never saw this story."

"That's because it didn't run in the newspaper. The publisher himself spiked it. The publisher was a good friend of the Yarnells, remember, and this Talbott character was hardly the most reliable witness. So the account of his last words never ran."

Another Marlboro flamed to life. She swept away the smoke with an incantatory wave of her bony hand.

"As I said, Mapstone, it was a small town. People talked. They knew Win Yarnell—that's the name Hayden Jr. went by—they knew he was the black sheep. He drank, womanized. His wife left him. He had a terrible gambling habit. Used to gamble in the old Duece—they bulldozed it in the '70s to make that horrible Civic Plaza. He gambled with Bravo Juan."

"Great name."

"Bravo Juan ran the numbers in the Deuce. He had an arrangement with the sheriff and the police chief, and kept everything in order. But the story went that Win Yarnell was deeply in debt to him. How do you like that, Mapstone? A loser named Win? Anyway, it all made the old man so mad, he disowned him, cut him right out of the business and the will."

I asked when that happened. "The late 1930s," she replied. "Everybody talked about it. It was a little town. People felt sorry for Mr. Yarnell, ending up with the sons he did. I guess Morgan was okay, but never that bright. And Win was a lost cause."

I gingerly sampled the bourbon. "So was Win enough of a lost cause to kidnap his nephews?"

"Maybe." Her voice became momentarily precise and delicate. "People are capable of anything. Didn't Solzhenitsyn say that the line separating good from evil doesn't run between nations or parties but through every human heart? Maybe it was Dostoevsky."

"Solzhenitsyn, I think." I thought of Lindsey, my Russian literature expert.

Zelda exhaled a plume of smoke. "What if Win stole Morgan's children to get a ransom to pay Bravo Juan and something went wrong? Nobody thought Win was a killer, much less of his own nephews."

I thought about that. "On the other hand, it might make more sense that Bravo Juan or somebody like him snatched the kids to put pressure on Win or the family to repay the gambling debts. Why didn't the police ever do any checking?"

"Oh, even a college professor can't be that naive. This was the most powerful family in the state. Phoenix was a corrupt little town where the elite got what they wanted. Look at the way they had railroaded Winnie Ruth Judd just a few years before that. Anyway, in this case the cops had a man caught red-handed with the ransom money, or part of it at least, and with the pajamas. Why would they need to do more?"

I just let the bourbon and information burn my throat.

She fished out a brown file folder and handed

it to me. Yellowed papers bulged out from the sides. "Here's Jack Talbott's police record. Do you have it?" I shook my head. "You can add it to your collection."

I slipped off the rubber band and leafed through the papers. Talbott had received a suspended sentence for burglary back in Elwood, Indiana. In Phoenix, he served a month in the county jail for assaulting a fellow drunk. That was in June 1940. Another arrest came in November 1941 for public drunkenness. I slowed down my reading. I read it again.

"This is strange. Jack Talbott was arrested for public drunkenness outside a bar on Second Street on November 27."

She reached for the report. "Let me see that. I never noticed that before." She stubbed out the Marlboro and scanned the page with her finger.

"Mapstone, that was the day of the kidnapping. Could he really have been set up, just like he claimed?"

"Maybe not." Peralta's skeptical voice was in my head. "The booking record shows he was arrested at one-ten a.m. that day. He could have been released in a few hours. The kidnapping was later that night. Maybe he got just sober enough to steal those little boys. It's impossible to know without the jail release record. What about the art collection that disappeared? Could that have played into this?"

"Oh, you know about that. It was another thing the newspaper never reported. Supposed to have been quite a collection. But it disappeared after the kidnapping. Let me think…after the kidnapping, and before the old man died."

"Maybe you *can* take it with you."

She gave a wheezy laugh and slugged down the remains of the bourbon.

◇◇◇

She walked me out to the rocky drive and we talked again of Hayden Yarnell.

"I met him, you know. It was around 1938. He came by the newspaper one day. He was very formidable. I'll never forget his handshake—firm and honest, and for a nobody like me, a young girl working as a clerk. He was a legend, and it was a more innocent time. We were taught to venerate men like Hayden Yarnell."

The wind had come up and I couldn't help a little shiver. "What do you think from the perspective of a less innocent time?"

She put her hands on her ample hips and stared

out toward the High Country. "The republic is founded on a noble lie," she said. "Plato, as you know. When Hayden Yarnell came to Arizona, it was a wilderness. Men like him made it a state. They dug the mines and took the wealth out of the earth. They killed the outlaws and forced the Apache to make peace. Then they mortgaged their land to build the dams that allowed that city down there…" She gestured angrily toward the dirty air. "All in all, I think it was a mighty achievement. They created a civilization so comfortable and safe that now they can be portrayed as exploiters and oppressors. Isn't that the history you teach now, Mapstone?"

"I…"

She really didn't want an answer. "But they were only men, and they had their flaws. Hayden Yarnell was a builder, but he was greedy, too. He was this engine that never stopped. You could see that even when he was an old man. Maybe the qualities go together. And he wanted to build a family that would carry on everything he built. Make his name immortal, if you will. He was an orphan, you know."

"I didn't know."

"He wanted sons of strong character more than

anything, more than the Copper Queen Mine or the largest ranch in the state. And it was the one thing that was out of his grasp."

I thanked her and started the BMW.

"Cops must make a lot more money now." She eyed the car.

"It's a long story."

"That's what they all say," she said. "Did you find anything else in that building with the skeletons?"

Damn. I had nearly forgotten. "A pocket watch was with them. Does that mean anything to you."

She narrowed her eyes and shook her head. "Anything else down there?"

I shook my head. "There were tunnels under the building, but they didn't seem to lead anywhere. Why?"

She stared toward the brown metropolitan cloud.

"I don't know. Just thinking. Sometimes I think too much."

Chapter Twenty-seven

I drove back to the city against the outbound afternoon rush, but the traffic was still miserable. The city limits went nearly to New River now, a good twenty miles north of where they sat when I had been in high school. I played the Heather Nova CD Lindsey had given me last summer. Now I was pricked by the lyrics of longing, love and regret. I had to stop midway through *Avalanche*. So I took it off and slipped in Sinatra. He got to "One More for the Road" as I blew over the Stack and into downtown. I shut the music off. I would rather have been thinking of Gretchen again, wondering about her next appearance.

I stopped off at the courthouse, where a plain envelope was sitting on the floor in front of the door. At least it wasn't one of those damned dolls. I took it in, put it on the desk as the phone was ringing. It was James Yarnell.

"How are you?"

I told him how I was.

"I'm no worse for wear," he said, his voice a little raspy. "The good ladies and gentlemen of the Scottsdale Police are keeping a twenty-four-hour watch on me."

"No problems?"

"No, everything's fine," he said. "I should thank you for saving my life. I was three sheets to the wind last night."

"Not a problem."

"We'll talk more," he said and hung up.

The phone again. I was suddenly a popular guy.

"They didn't find another doll." It was Peralta. I muttered an obscenity.

"They checked two blocks around the Yarnell Gallery, even where the shooter probably stood."

"Maybe he didn't have time to leave the doll."

"Maybe this attack isn't connected to the Max Yarnell murder," Peralta countered.

My own hands were shaking when he hung up. My heart was hammering in my chest. What the hell was wrong with me? I was alone in the room with my heartbeat and worries. It made me wonder why I had come into the office at all. I took out a legal pad and made more notes from my visit with Zelda Chain. Then I turned out the lights and locked up.

I drove through Ramiro's, where you can eat like a king for five dollars, and ordered a chorizo burrito and a Diet Coke. Then I went over to Encanto Park and walked to the lagoon. In the distance, the late-afternoon sun was painting gold into the folds of the South Mountains.

Encanto was the classic city park, green and lovingly manicured, built when Phoenix was smaller. It was about half a mile from my house, and as a kid, I had fished in the lagoon on lazy, lost spring afternoons, watched the sky from the empty old bandshell, and ridden the little train in the miniature amusement park. Encanto was still a beautiful oasis, but most days now it was largely Latino. Maybe the sounds of Spanish frightened away my yuppie neighbors. Today, with a cool wind whipping in from the west and only an hour's sun left, the place was nearly deserted.

I wanted to eat my burrito and try to clear my head of murder. I was about halfway through dinner when I heard lovely Castilian Spanish behind me. Then I turned and saw Bobby Hamid.

"I said, 'History is a sacred thing, so far as it contains truth…'"

"I have a few phrases in Spanish for you, Bobby," I said.

He ignored me. "Have you ever read Cervantes in his native language, Dr. Mapstone? It is a true epiphany. Rather like the difference between learning Shakespeare in Farsi, and then learning him in English. Or discovering for the first time the real Dante in Italian…"

I set aside my burrito. "Why are you here?"

"It is a public park. I actually bring my children here sometimes. They love riding the little train." He pointed across the lagoon.

He studied me carefully. "Does it surprise you that I have children, David? Make it a little harder to see me as evil incarnate, as Chief Peralta believes?"

"Stalin had children," I said. "Anybody can reproduce."

"Not you, apparently," he said. "You and Patty had no children, as I recall. Maybe she instinctively knew something." For a moment I felt strangely stung by this man who mattered nothing to me at all, except as a threat to the community.

He sat next to me on the bench. His gray slacks draped perfectly. I wished I knew his tailor, or maybe not.

"You had an adventure last night," Bobby said.

"Have your goons been monitoring the police radio?" I looked around for hired muscle with automatic weapons, but only saw the light fading on the greenish water. I wished that would just make him disappear, too.

"Businessmen do have to think about security nowadays, David," he said. "Anyway, I get my news off the Internet." Just two guys talking in the park.

"Do you think this murder of Max Yarnell and the attempted murder of his brother are related to the skeletons you found?"

"You know I can't discuss that."

"So you don't know."

"Do you know? Are you the man who killed Max Yarnell, Bobby?"

He smiled indulgently, then said, "All over the world there is violence. The violence of the murdered. The death squad. The secret wars. The violence against people who merely vanish. Political prisoners. Refugees from wars. My parents disappeared in the revolution, back in 1979. My sister, too. None of us is safe in the world, I suppose."

I had heard one of Bobby's favorite methods for dealing with informants was to stuff them in oil drums and toss them overboard into the Sea of Cortez. But when I said that to him, he just gazed away and sighed.

"I hope you find your answers," he said finally. Then, "I also read that you failed to positively identify the bodies found in the old warehouse. A frustrating week for my friends at the sheriff's department."

"The DNA profiling was no help," I admitted. It would be interesting to see how current his intelligence was.

"And what do you think that means?"

I suddenly wanted to strangle him. I understood Peralta's Ahab-like obsession. "Bobby, this is none of your goddamned business."

"You don't have to shout and use profanity, Dr. Mapstone," he said. "Actually, as I told you, buying that warehouse is my business. Do you realize the costs that even a week's fluctuations in interest rates can add to the bridge loans?"

"So, sell more cocaine," I said, and went back to the burrito.

"Have you looked at the will of Hayden Winthrop Yarnell?"

The chorizo became a tasteless lump in my mouth. I was tempted to lie, but I said nothing. I could feel my facing turning red. Damn it.

"It is actually in the probate records," he said.

"You might find it interesting."

So much for David Mapstone, expert researcher of historical mysteries.

I said, "And tell me again why this case interests you?"

"Just as I said, Dr. Mapstone, I have an interest in purchasing the building. I hope I can save our city's vanishing warehouse district before it is too late. Surely you won't begrudge me a desire for historical preservation."

He smiled and looked at me with dark eyes encased in long lashes, eyes that seemed to reflect no light.

I said, "Okay, Bobby, what does the will say?"

"It has a codicil that states if any new evidence emerges that a Yarnell family member was involved in the kidnapping, then his entire estate and all its subsequent earnings will be passed on to charities, mainly the Yarnell Foundation."

I let his words sink in, still not sure about his game. "So the old man didn't believe Jack Talbott kidnapped his grandsons?"

"At the least, he believed the kidnapping was more complex than it appeared."

"Based on what evidence?"

Bobby spread his manicured fingers and shrugged.

"I'll look at the will. Anyway, this Yarnell case will be solved fast, we've got so many cops working on it. So I'm sure you can get the building at a fire-sale price from Yarneco."

"Buy low and sell high," he said. "In Phoenix, we buy high and hope we can sell higher. But Yarneco, they are difficult people. A very complicated company. So many shell corporations and obscure relationships. Almost the way an illegal enterprise would be structured, or so I have read in books."

"It's not a good day for a mind fuck, Bobby." I tossed the remains of the Mexican food in a trash can and rose to leave. My stomach felt like it was getting an acid bath. My life was descending into permanent weirdness. The biggest drug dealer in the Southwest was becoming a fixture in it.

I was about halfway across the grass when he called to me.

"David," he said. "You know that he stalks them over the Internet? The Harquahala Strangler. That's how he gets his girls."

"You're yesterday's news," I called.

"So you know Peralta is using your pretty friend Lindsey as bait."

"I know." I kept walking away from him.

"Very well. I can imagine she probably likes

the change—being out there on the streets as a detective. And with that handsome partner, I hear they are an item now…"

I ignored him.

"I thought the newspaper took a lovely photo of her for that article."

I stopped and turned back. He was holding out a page from the *Republic*. I stalked back and tore it from his hand. Sure enough, a large photo showed Lindsey and Patrick Blair, standing outside the doorway to the detective bureau, and yes, she looked radiant.

"What the…?" I read the paper every day, and somehow I hadn't seen it. Then I checked the date: it was the morning after Lindsey's mother died. I had missed the paper that day. Now I skimmed the article, but soon I was rereading it closely, squinting in the gathering dusk.

"A nice feature story about the lead team on the Harquahala Strangler case," Bobby chirped. "I have to say, the local newspaper is not enterprising enough to just go out and profile the detectives investigating a sensitive case, and I doubt the sheriff would cooperate."

I finished reading it and looked at him. "What's your point?"

"Only that the sheriff wanted everyone to know that Miss Lindsey is on this case. And I do mean everyone."

"Okay, so he likes publicity."

"I see Chief Peralta's shrewd hand here, Dr. Mapstone. You see, this monster stopped killing prostitutes last year. He's killed college students. The most recent victim was a housewife. And they all have straight dark hair and pale skin…"

Chapter Twenty-eight

I drove to Sunnyslope in a fog of urgent anxiety that was unrelieved by the rivers of car lights on the busy streets. It had been weeks since Lindsey's mother had killed herself. It had been weeks since we had last made love, since I had last seen her. I was suddenly not in a mood to be a good, docile post-modern man. I didn't even think about my new affair with Gretchen. And it was only as I bounded up the outside stairway to her second-floor apartment that I realized I might well find her with a new lover. Suddenly I had a pornographic image of Patrick Blair impaling Lindsey as she writhed and moaned.

Instead, I found nothing but a locked, dark apartment and Pasternak nosing at me through the window. I waved at him with my finger. I folded one of my Sheriff's Office business cards into the door and walked slowly away, down the stairs, past the pool, through the breezeway, all the time wishing she would appear at the door and invite me back inside. Then I walked back up and retrieved my card. What the hell.

I drove home alone, feeling aloneness all around me as the SUVs and low-riders sped past me on Seventh Street. At Thomas Road, I was overcome by a feeling I was being followed. But when I tacked over to Fifth Avenue, nobody was in the rear-view mirror but my momentary paranoia.

Somebody was killing the Yarnell family.

The Harquahala Strangler was stalking Lindsey.

◇◇◇

"Where did you hear that?" Peralta demanded, sitting up in the leather chair and nearly upsetting his Gibson. "I swear I'm gonna shut down your pipeline to Lorie Pope once and for all."

Controlling my rage as best I could, I told him I heard it from Bobby Hamid. Peralta expelled a mulish breath. "I think he has a mole in the department."

"Maybe he's the killer," I said.

"God doesn't like me that much," Peralta said. Then, "So you're gonna get all territorial on me about Adams? Anyway, I thought you had something new going with that tall redhead. Or are you doing both of them—damn, I always wanted to do that, but it seemed like a lot of trouble."

I was still standing in the entryway at home. I needed a drink. "You didn't tell me you were using Lindsey as bait. I just thought she was working on the tech side of it, hacking the strangler's computer. Something safe. Why the hell is she working with Patrick Blair…?" I called all this over my shoulder as I mixed an angry Bombay Sapphire martini.

When I came back in the living room, he said mildly, "Are you going to get a Christmas tree?"

He was knocking my anger off stride. "I haven't even thought about it."

"She volunteered for the job," he said. "And she's a deputy sheriff, same as you, and she took an oath to protect and serve, even if it means personal danger, same as you."

"Spare me the damned academy graduating class speech!"

He made a purring sound and set the Gibson aside. "What did you find out today on your case?"

I drank a big slug of gin and told him about Zelda Chain. His eyes became slits as he listened. Then he said, "Preliminary lab work on Max Yarnell says he was knocked down by a serious blow to the chin, maybe a kick. Then the petrified wood was driven into his heart. Nothing unusual in the trace evidence, fibers, blood, chemical workup."

"What about that doll?"

"It's the same brand as the one delivered to your office. You can buy 'em at any Toys 'R' Us. No prints, no unusual fibers or chemicals. The blood was painted on, a common, water-based art-store paint. Made in China."

"So we're nowhere!" I said a little too vehemently, plopping down in the other leather chair.

"Look," he said, leaning his bulk forward. "There's a whole subculture out there of escorts working on the Web. You have heard of the Internet, right Mapstone?"

"Fuck you."

"I never can be sure with you and pop culture," he went on. "Anyway, they cruise chat rooms and set up profiles to let guys know they're available for business. It's hard as hell to police, because they can hide their identity and screen potential customers."

"Apparently not well enough," I said.

He nodded. "All these girls were involved with meeting people online. The early victims were escorts. But the last two haven't been, although they did frequent chat rooms or dating sites. One was a college student. The other was a housewife. So the bastard has upped the stakes. He's broken out into the general population." He made the killer sound like a disease.

"Lindsey's team was initially working with the Internet service providers to track the guy, but I guess it's so easy to hide your trail if you know what you're doing. So we felt we had to do something more."

"Why her?" I demanded.

"She volunteered," he said. "And, she looks kinda racy and cute. The other deputies I could call on look like East German swimmers."

"It's not just that, and you know it! She fits his profile, right? Straight, dark hair, and pale skin. You wanted him to come after her. You put her photo in the paper!"

Peralta started to say something and stopped. He finished his drink and held it out to me to refill. I ignored him.

"Look, Mapstone, this is complicated, and very confidential. This guy is a risk-taker, always pushing the envelope. We think his first victim was a street hooker that he just picked up. Then, this whole Internet thing starts, and, believe me, not all these victims are crack whores. He kept moving more upscale. In some cases, these were party girls who made a little cash on the side with freelance prostitution. But now we've had two victims with no known ties to prostitution. He meets them online—he can pretend to be anybody. Then they meet for real, and sayonara. This city's on the verge of panic."

I took pity on him and made a new Gibson. When I came back he continued, haltingly, hating to give up so much information.

"We heard from this guy. He sent a note, dropped it on the sidewalk in front of headquarters. He wrote that he was so powerful now he would kidnap and kill a female detective, just to show us he could. Nobody knows this outside the key investigators."

"So you planted the story in the paper profiling the detectives. And, wow, one of them is Lindsey, looking just the way he wants his victims. Why didn't you just give him her address, too?"

Peralta just stared at me.

"Any luck?" I asked quietly.

He shook his head. "Not yet."

"You could have told me." Too many ten-ton rocks had fallen on me for one day.

"I did tell you."

"You ought to run for sheriff," I snarled.

"You're starting to lie like a politician."

He just sipped his Gibson calmly. "Mapstone, are you one of these knuckle-draggers who doesn't believe in women deputies? Anyway, you told me she's not yours. So what right do you have to interfere in her life?"

Trumped by the notorious liberal, Mike Peralta. I went to make myself another drink. When I came back I told him about my encounter with the man in the white van.

Chapter Twenty-nine

I drove east on Camelback in the heavy clots of traffic, vaguely going to Scottsdale. It was Thursday and I had Ellington's tribute to Strayhorn in the CD player with the volume up and the top of the car down.

I imagined a stroke of luck that might let me slip into Scottsdale Fashion Square, find a parking place and do a little Christmas shopping. I didn't want Christmas coming so soon. Time was moving too fast. It was 1999 and the decade, the century, the millennium were slipping away. The change was too big for me to get my mind around. I couldn't even get my mind around the Yarnell mess. I was feeling stymied, feeling every insecurity about being a make-believe cop in over his head. Peralta had even dismissed my information about a possible encounter with the Harquahala Strangler.

"How would he know you had anything to do with Lindsey?" Peralta had asked.

I tried to parse that out. The newspaper article with Lindsey's photo had come out before Thanksgiving. I saw the man in the Econoline several days later. So he could have followed Lindsey and seen us together.

"So how did he know your name?"

This piece of detail that chilled me simply deflated my case to Peralta.

I did my best. "I've been in the paper. The guy pays attention. He wants to know about his victims, her boyfriends, where she works. He asked for directions to the Sheriff's Office, and he asked if I was David Mapstone." But in the end, even I couldn't be sure. I let it drop.

"Maybe he was one of your old students, Mapstone. He recognized you. Anyway, if I arrested every weirdo asking for directions, we'd have to build a hundred Tent Jails."

Now I was behind on my shopping list, especially for friends back east. Patty always gave gifts that were elaborate in their imagination and the attention they paid to the recipient's tastes and enthusiasms. I gave too many books and CDs; it was a failing. Peralta, I could buy some cigars. Sharon, she was a book reader, thank goodness. Lorie liked jazz and I knew just what to get her.

I needed something for Gretchen, something not too intimate, but intimate enough. Lindsey, well, Lindsey was out of my life.

When I got back to the old courthouse and climbed the four flights of stairs to my corner nook, I found the door open and Sharon Peralta sitting in one of the old straightback wooden chairs.

"The security guard said it would be okay if I waited for you," she said, standing. I gave her a hug and we both sat down. "I also brought that in, it was in front of your door." I opened the FedEx box and loose files cascaded out across my increasingly messy desk. It was from a graduate school friend who now taught environmental law at the University of Arizona, and he had promised to send me copies of his files on the battle over the Yarnell mine in Superior.

"Sorry this place is kind of a mess," I said. "I'm behind."

"It has real charm," she smiled. "I do love the big windows."

"I bought you a Christmas present," I said. "But I have to wrap it."

We sat enveloped in the long silence of high-ceilinged rooms. I hadn't seen Sharon since Thanksgiving. Today, she was turned out smartly in a charcoal pinstripe pant suit, set off with a simple, crew-neck white blouse. Phoenicians don't know how to dress. Sharon is an exception.

"So how is he?"

I leaned back in my chair and told her he was all right. How could you tell with Peralta?

"I assumed he'd come to you," she said, clasping her hands over a slender knee.

That silence again. I started to say something about not wanting to be caught in the middle of a battle between my two oldest friends in the world. But she beat me to the verbal draw.

"So how's your mystery?"

Was this how she relaxed her patients? "Getting better," I lied. "We know now those skeletons we found were Andrew and Woodrow Yarnell."

"Seems like a long time ago," she said, her voice different, losing a little of its high sheen. She sighed. "How's Lindsey?"

"She left me," I said, then wished I hadn't. Overshare.

"Maybe it's the season. She was probably a transitional affair, anyway, David. Nothing wrong with that, as long as you know."

I looked into the desktop. "How are you?"

She made a stretching move with her head,

making her lustrous black hair wave about. Sharon never touched her hair when she was nervous.

"Do you have any idea what it's like to live with him?" she said, speaking quickly. "I mean, really live with him. It's not like he beats me or is really emotionally abusive. But he's just like this supernova of a personality, and underneath it's really needy, incredibly needy. But it's not like the need can ever be met."

Then she suddenly stopped. "Sorry."

"It's all right."

"I'm not trying to involve you in our troubles."

"It's delicate. I care about you both."

She watched me with large, dark eyes. "I'm not seeking your approval."

Bam! That one landed in my lap. Later, I would think of all sorts of witty comebacks for this conversation, but for now all I could manage was a mute awkwardness.

"Do you know how long we've known each other?" she asked. "You and I?"

"Twenty years?"

"Twenty years, David Mapstone. In that time, I put myself through school, raised two daughters, who turned into people I admire. I built a practice, learned to appreciate jazz from you, taught myself

Navajo sand painting. I wrote a book. I faced down my fears."

She was off on the kind of riff that marital discord breeds; I'd been there. But it's true that Sharon had made the most amazing transformation from the first time I met her as Mike's shy, working-class wife to the role model she is today.

She stopped, then added. "He hasn't changed at all."

I let it lie in the silence between us like a wounded soldier in no-man's land. It was true.

Then she said, in a voice merry with ironic self-knowledge, "How does it feel to be ad hoc counselor to Dr. Sharon?"

"I wouldn't presume," I ventured gallantly, failing.

"No, I guess you wouldn't." She looked at me with something unreadable and incendiary in the large, dark eyes.

So I told her about the Yarnells, the family curse and the secret covenant. Then I told her about Max Yarnell. I told her about the attempt on James Yarnell. I told her about Jack Talbott's death row statement that never made it into the newspapers.

"This family is hiding so much," Sharon said.

"From you, from each other."

"Is that a professional opinion?"

"It's my opinion," she said. "There's something dangerous, something treacherous hiding in all this."

"I know," I said, but I didn't know. "Why would somebody leave a doll at a murder scene, with his hands bloody?"

"The message isn't subtle. The killer thinks the victim has bloody hands. It's vengeance. Or maybe it's a childhood issue out of the killer's life. I'm not a criminal psychologist."

"And an identical doll was left here in my office, without the bloody hands."

"David, good lord. This is a disturbed person, if the murder itself wasn't enough to tell you that."

I asked her not to tell anyone about the dolls, which was information held back from the press. Then I realized I might be sounding like her husband.

"So tell me how David is doing. Just working?"

"I'm fine, Sharon. I don't know what I want to do with my life. Everything is kind of chaotic right now."

"New love interest?"

"I don't know." Why was I hedging? Was I afraid she would tell Lindsey? Why would I be afraid of that? She never would even run into Lindsey. What did it matter if Lindsey found out?

"So is this the life you're going to live?" she asked, in another tone of voice, higher, more detached. "David among his old paper records and his old cases, living his life between his ears."

"Between my ears?"

"You have your nice house in Willo, and your little twenty-something sex machine—or you'll find another one. You'll cruise through your forties having affairs and witty friendships, reading books and working for the sheriff as a media celebrity."

"I'm not…" I protested, but the words didn't follow.

"You don't want to venture anything," she said. "Not after Patty. And you think you've found a little island of emotional safety where you won't have to."

"What is this about?"

"What do you want?"

I stammered the stammer of the invaded.

"No, dammit," she said. "Don't give some politically correct answer. What do you, David Mapstone, want? David Mapstone who has no family, no offspring, and is all alone in the world?"

We stared at each other. She went on, "You're at the age where if you don't know that answer, you're going to ruin the lives of a lot of women." The last word echoed through the old sheriff's office and dissipated in the ceiling.

Then, she said, "Sorry, David. I'm all wound up. Mike always found me too intense, so he worked all the time so he wouldn't have to deal with me."

"God, I don't know, Sharon," I said finally. "I want to keep you both in my life. You know very well I can't fix whatever's wrong between you…"

"Like the fact that he hasn't touched me in five years."

"I don't need to know this," I said reflexively.

"What are you afraid of?"

I thought about that, wrestled down the words flying through my mind, then, "I'm afraid I'll lose you both."

She looked at me a long time in silence, an expression on her face I had never seen before.

"I hope that doesn't happen," she said quietly and rose to leave. "Please make sure he takes his medicine," she went on. "He has diabetes, you know."

I didn't know.

"He controls it orally," she said. "Don't let him cook too much. He cooks bad things for himself."

I followed her as she walked to the office door, her heels snapping precisely against the old hardwood floor.

"May I ask you something?" She wheeled to face me. "Why is it, all these years, you never made a pass at me?"

"Well, you were married."

"That never stops men," she said. "I thought you guys wanted to sleep with every woman you saw."

"We think about it," I said quietly.

"So?"

"So," I said, "some fantasies you shouldn't act out."

"That's my line," the doctor said, and she suddenly took my face in her hands and gave me a long, prosperous kiss on the lips. Then she slipped through the door like an apparition, leaving me leaning against the wall as the electricity coursing from my brain to my groin subsided.

Chapter Thirty

At nine o'clock Friday morning, twenty cops from three law enforcement agencies sardined themselves into a conference room at the sheriff's office to compare notes on the Yarnell case: Phoenix cops, Scottsdale cops, sheriff's detectives, and me. Being here made me uneasy for a lot of reasons. For one thing, I didn't want to run into Lindsey and Patrick Blair. I had a big mocha from Starbucks; they all had plain joe in Styrofoam from the museum-vintage coffee machine down the hall. I sat in the back, committed to keeping my mouth shut.

"Our part of this can be short and sweet," said Hawkins. He leaned against a wall, wearing a rumpled, short-sleeved dress shirt and a tie that looked like it came from Sears in the 1970s. "The dental records identify the Yarnell twins. The case is closed. We're prepared to hold a news conference and go public with that fact."

"We wish you'd hold off," said one of the Scottsdale detectives, an older guy in a polo shirt and black jeans. He had a droopy mustache like an old West gunfighter and had slung one leg up on an unoccupied chair.

"Why?" Hawkins asked. "The Yarnell kidnapper was executed in 1942. We now have the bodies. The case is closed."

I tried to focus, but my mind kept wandering to my increasingly chaotic personal life. It wasn't like me, none of it. I had never considered myself any kind of babe magnet, had gone for years without a date in my twenties. *My God, the chief's wife had kissed me.*

"What if the kidnapping is related to the murder of Max Yarnell and the attack this week on James Yarnell?" This from Kimbrough, the sheriff's detective. He was a thirty-three-year-old buppie on the department's fast track. Peralta expected him to make captain soon and then go into politics. He dressed the part: stylish three-button coat, worsted wool slacks, bow tie, all in colors that complemented the rich cocoa color of his skin.

Hawkins sighed and sat down. "Whatever. I'm just telling you we're done looking at this unless something new comes along."

Kimbrough said, "What about it, Mapstone?" Hard cop eyes all bored into me—and I was dressed more like Kimbrough than Hawkins. I needed the comfort of nice clothes: Brooks Brothers blazer, J. Crew white dress shirt, rep tie from Ben Silver, and pleated chinos from Banana Republic. A brand slut. All those cops knew was that I was the outsider.

"Hayden Yarnell believed someone in the family was involved in the kidnapping," I said. "He put a covenant in his will that's still binding."

I passed around copies of the relevant page from Yarnell's will.

"It's like a doomsday bomb for the Yarnell heirs if any new evidence ever implicates the family. As he was being led to the gas chamber, Jack Talbott said that the boys' uncle put him up to the kidnapping. This uncle was in debt from his gambling, and the Yarnell company wasn't doing great, either. So there are lots of questions."

"But no evidence we can take to court," Hawkins said.

"Right," I admitted. "But this whole thing is hinky. The man charged in the kidnapping was booked into the city jail the day of the crime." I wished I could find a record of his release, but I kept running into the chaos of old files. "He claimed he was set up. A reporter witnessed this before he was executed."

"They all say that," said Hawkins.

"Nice job saving James Yarnell the other night," Kimbrough said, and the cops looked at me again, curious now.

"There is one other thing," I said. "We know Andrew and Woodrow Yarnell didn't have the same mother as James and Max. Maybe they were adopted. Maybe Morgan Yarnell had them with another woman. We don't know yet. It just makes me wonder…"

"The kidnapper was convicted and executed," Hawkins said in a low monotone. "This isn't complicated."

One detective said, "My parents are getting very old. And it's not like they're rich or anything. But you can already see the children lining up to influence their cut of the will. I just wonder if something like that was at work here. If these twins were a factor…"

There was a collective chair shuffling and coffee slurping, then a Scottsdale detective, a blond, lanky woman named Carrie somebody, gave the report on the James Yarnell attack. No suspects, no arrests. There were no witnesses in the area that night. The bullets recovered looked like .357 rounds, but they were badly deformed. No shell casings found. It appeared the shots came from some bushes across the street.

"I'm not seeing any connections," Hawkins sing-songed.

Kimbrough sighed. "Well, you've got the report on Max Yarnell, what we know so far."

"Roust some burglars," Hawkins said. "It was probably a burglary gone wrong." He pointed at me. "The professor over here has got everybody paranoid. We just need to do some basic police work."

"Nothing appears missing from the home," Kimbrough said.

"So the burglar got scared and ran!" Hawkins shouted.

"Look, Gus," I said, "the alarm was disengaged. What if Max let somebody in, somebody he knew? He called me that night and said he needed to talk to me, in person, about something urgent. Before that, the guy didn't want to give me the time of day."

Hawkins' mouth became a lipless line of exasperation.

"And what about the attempt on James Yarnell?" I said. "That wasn't a burglar."

"So maybe it was unrelated, Mapstone. A husband of some woman this Yarnell is banging. Maybe some artist he screwed over. I dunno. Hell, you don't have one scrap of evidence these are related."

"We're checking out Yarnell's business acquaintances and old girlfriends," said one of the Scottsdale detectives.

"The dolls!" I was shouting by this time.

"There was no doll at the Yarnell Gallery," Hawkins said. "There was one at Max Yarnell's house, and one delivered to your office. Maybe we ought to consider you a suspect, Mapstone." If it was meant as a joke, nobody laughed. Then the cops started arguing over resources with two other high-profile crimes going on. It continued until Kimbrough got up to refill his coffee.

"I'm inclined to very here-and-now theories," said Carrie, the Scottsdale detective. "We have threats from an environmental terrorist group over this mine in Superior. That's a profitable avenue. It could explain the attacks on both Yarnells. The FBI is getting very interested in eco-terrorism."

She flipped through a spiral notebook and went on, "You also need to be aware that Yarneco is having major trouble right now. We talked at length with their chief financial officer. Their real estate holdings are in trouble. They made some bad bets on developments up in Colorado. And the banks were about a month away from pulling the plug on the mining venture."

"Jesus Christ!" Hawkins said. "You're making everything too complicated. I gotta go." He sidled his way out of the room, taking a pair of minions with him.

"What if it's a family member?" a Phoenix cop asked. The room erupted with opinions. "No, I mean it," he went on. "If this crime happened in an ordinary neighborhood, we'd arrest a wife or a brother-in-law before sundown."

"I'd do it," Kimbrough said, "if we had a scrap of evidence."

"We don't have any fingerprints? Nothing?" demanded a voice from off to the left.

"Not on the petrified wood," Kimbrough said. "It was wiped clean. Family fingerprints in a family member's house don't mean squat. Can you say 'reasonable doubt'? Ask the county attorney."

We were getting nowhere. I wondered if Bobby Hamid would solve the case before three police agencies.

"Look," Carrie said, a new edge to her voice.

"We have one of the most prominent men in the state murdered. I don't know about you, but I'm feeling major heat to get some damned results, and soon. And I'm also feeling heat to treat the Yarnell family with tender loving care."

Everybody stared at Kimbrough. He adjusted his bow tie and looked at me.

"Hawkins may be getting at one thing," I said. "There's something simple and straightforward in all this. We're just not seeing it yet."

◇◇◇

That night, Peralta came home and announced we were going to get a Christmas tree. So we drove over to a little lot on Seventh Street and wrestled a six-foot-tall spruce into the back of his Blazer. Back at home, Peralta cooked steaks—I avoided the urge to fuss over him about his diet—while I dug out old Christmas lights and ornaments from the garage. We put the tree in the center of the picture window, just where the trees stood when I was growing up. And we trimmed it while the Mormon Tabernacle Choir sang carols—Peralta vetoed my *Blues Christmas* CD. He restrained his bossiness. I restrained my guilt, and my memories of Sharon's lips, fingers and lustrous black hair. I had allowed something secret and scary into my life.

After dinner, we lit the tree and, armed with scotch and cigars, we carried lawn chairs out by the street so we could sit and enjoy our handiwork. The night was suitably cool, almost crisp.

Peralta luxuriated in the lawn chair. "Want to come on a raid of a skinhead organization tomorrow? You haven't been in a good gunfight for a few hours."

"I'll pass." I lit the cigar and watched the tip glow festively in the night.

"C'mon, Mapstone. Drop your socks and grab your Glock."

"I saw Sharon today."

"How is she?"

"She's okay. She's worried about you."

I am the most loathsome man on the planet.

"Well, that was nice of her."

"I think she was reaching out to you."

I am unworthy of any friendship.

"Well, she could try picking up the phone. That would be a first."

"I know it's not my business…"

Your wife kissed me. Your wife, who I have tried for 20 years to view like a sister and a friend, kissed me. And I kissed her back. And I liked it. I am lower than a worm.

"Mapstone," Peralta said mildly, "you're right. It's not your business. Hell, she probably just came to see you."

I started to say something but he held up a finger. Shhh.

Up and down Cypress Street, we could see Christmas lights coming on, festive little reds, blues, and greens from windows, self-conscious whites wrapping the orange tree two houses down. Our tree was traditional and comforting, filling the picture window with a poignant magic. The year had gone by too fast. There were too many people I was missing.

Chapter Thirty-one

The address Gretchen gave me went to a four-story, red-brick apartment building on the corner of Twelfth Avenue and Adams. The place was eighty years old if it was a day—big windows closely spaced together, sleeping porches on the upper floors. She surprised me every time. At first, I imagined her in a single-family house in Ahwatukee, then maybe in a condo up around the Biltmore. It was that pleasant sensibility she carried around with no urban edge.

But her real home was in one of the toughest parts of the inner city—or it would have been if much were left. These old buildings from Phoenix's early days once decorated the neighborhoods between downtown and the capitol. Brick replaced adobe as a sign of the frontier town's progress. Now adobe was the sign of progress and Gretchen's building was alone on the block, with a row of thick-trunk palm trees at the curb, half of them lacking tops. I parked, set the car alarm and went inside.

Her place was on the top floor, and she met me as I stepped onto the old hardwood of the hallway. She was wearing a white robe and maybe nothing else underneath.

"This is an amazing building. Something in Phoenix older than 1975."

"An architect bought it and she's restoring it floor by floor," Gretchen said, coming into my arms and giving me a gentle, brush-across-the-lips kiss, then something deep, wet and lingering. "I love it here. Come in."

The big front room was dominated by an Edward Hopper print. I'd seen it before, but it wasn't one of his popular ones. It shows a woman sitting on a train. She has a dark hat, dark suit, fair hair. She's reading and you can't see her eyes. Out the train window is a stone bridge.

"It's called *Compartment C, Car 193*," Gretchen said, putting her arm around me. "I've always loved Hopper, once you get past seeing *Night Owls* everywhere."

"We both like trains, I see."

"I love trains," she said. "One of the pleasures

of living this close in is I can hear the whistles at night. I can even hear the cars banging together sometimes."

She watched me as I walked over to a framed portrait on a table. It showed a young woman in bulky coveralls with a pack in front and holding a helmet. She was smiling broadly. Gretchen.

"I've read that smoke jumpers are the elite," I said.

"It's true, and there still aren't many women who do it. I was very proud to get to be one of 'the bros.' Then I lost my passion for it. My youthful adventure."

"Jumping into fire."

"I've been known to do that."

Her lips again came up. She was a woman who knew just how to tilt her head to meet the kiss from a taller man. "I was worried about you," she said. "After you told me what happened the other night after we had dinner. Am I allowed to worry?"

"I want to be cared about," I said. "I want to care in return." She nuzzled my neck.

"Maybe you'll come meet my parents sometime. I've told them about you. Don't be nervous."

"I'm not nervous."

"Come on, I'll give you the tour."

She showed me around: a spacious workroom with a wooden table serving as desk; big bathroom with a claw-footed bathtub; a sleeping porch with wicker furniture and plants, and the bedroom set off with a comfy-looking queen-size bed beneath a curvy, wrought-iron headboard. Another Hopper on the wall, this one I hadn't seen: a nude woman with reddish-brown hair, alone in a room and staring out a window, the sun bathing her skin in an alabaster glow. The woman wore black shoes and nothing else. Plants were everywhere, filling the space with a cheery greenery. I started to ease Gretchen toward the bed, but she said, "I have plans for you."

She took my hand and led me through to the bathroom again. She started water in the tub. Then she turned and did that melting thing in my arms, where we totally merged. I reached inside the robe and caressed her warm skin.

"Thank you for trusting me to tell me where you live," I said.

She kissed me, gently bit my lower lip, unbuttoned my shirt and ran her hands over my chest. "I do trust you," she said. "But I want you very relaxed."

She dropped to her knees in one fluid move and

undid my jeans. They fell in a heap at my feet. The floor was small tiles of black-and-white ceramic.

"Boxer man," she whispered, burying her face in my shorts, running a finger around the band, up inside the legs. She nibbled and licked around my belly as she eased the boxers off, too.

She took me in her mouth. She had the moves. Not every woman does, in fact few do, but Gretchen did. I stroked and clenched that silky reddish-brown hair and she expertly worked me over. In a few minutes I would have done anything for her.

She kissed me and our tongues exchanged the taste of me. She pulled back slowly and let her robe fall on the floor. She leaned into the medicine cabinet and pulled out some shaving cream, put it into a stainless steel cup with water and started mixing it with one of those blond brushes you see in old-men's barber shops. She reached back in the cabinet and pulled out something that looked antique and covered with tortoise shell.

It had a blade.

"Ever use one of these?" she smiled, her lips still glistening.

I must have visibly stepped back. She gently took my hand and pulled me closer. "Take it in your hand."

I grasped the straight razor. The handle was smooth from years of handling, but the blade was so tacitly charged it felt sharp even inches away from my fingers.

Gretchen wrapped herself against my back, nibbling on my ears, and said, "I want you to shave my legs."

◇◇◇

"See, it's easy," she said. She was in the tub now, and I sat on the edge, holding a soapy leg in one hand and the straight razor in the other. Her legs were appealingly long, with slim ankles, shapely calves and lovely thighs comprised of just the right proportions—not chunky but not anorexic, either. I made easy, straight strokes, then shook the blade in the water to get the soap off. It was a move like driving over one of those barriers that says "Do not back up, severe tire damage!"

"Don't be afraid," she said. "You're doing great. I have very stubborn leg hair. Once, on a dig in Peru, I lost my Lady Bics and there was only this crusty old professor with a straight razor. So I tried it."

It took a gentle, sure touch. No hesitation. But I could see the sensual appeal: danger and pleasure in one basic human tool in your hand. Something to do with the nearness of the unencumbered blade, with the discipline of strokes to cut close—but not too close.

"You have a natural talent for it," she said as I moved along the muscles of her right calf. "What happened to your friend Lindsey?"

I shook the blade in the water and cut against the stubble. "She left. Before you and I got together."

"I'm sorry," Gretchen said, "if you're sorry."

"She was going through a lot. Her mother killed herself. But she didn't want anybody close, didn't want me close at least." I felt like I was betraying Lindsey. I shifted my grip on the heavy, smooth handle.

"Do you worry about a woman with the suicide bug?"

I hadn't even thought of it. The thought of it—the thought of relief from Lindsey's leaving— made me feel small.

"I don't think we're a prisoner of our genes," I said finally.

"I do," Gretchen said firmly. "Lindsey is a deputy?"

"Yes. She mostly does computer work."

"Did you worry about her getting hurt?"

"Yes."

"The thighs are very tender," Gretchen said.

"That's where the real loving care takes place." I moved above the knee. "Did you love her?"

Her words rattled around in my head, and the answer wouldn't have mattered. I shaved for a few minutes. "I'm very glad I met you."

She reached a finger out of the water and touched my nose. "Me, too," she said.

"What about you? Ever been married?"

"No," she said quietly. "It just never worked out."

She fell into silence and we listened to the scrape of the razor across her flesh, then the watery sound of the blade being cleaned. The razor felt heavier than it looked. Then I told her more about the Yarnell case.

"I feel like there's something fundamental I'm missing," I said. She had a dark brown freckle just above her left knee.

"It's a lot of strands," she said. "Maybe you have to choose one and pull it, see where it leads."

"Why would someone be killing the Yarnells now, over something that happened more than half a century ago?"

Gretchen leaned back and the tips of her hair brushed into the water. "You know the past is never past, David."

Then it was my turn in the tub. She brought us both glasses of chardonnay as I slipped down into the near-scalding water of the big old tub. It had been years since I'd taken a bath instead of a shower. My muscles yawned and stretched in the hot water.

"Now it's my turn," she said. She mixed new shaving cream and dabbed it on my face. Then she pulled a little strap out of the medicine cabinet and ran the razor against it several times. The blade shimmered in the light.

"Relax," she said, kissing me and gently easing my head down against the lip of the tub. "After legs, this is a breeze."

I barely felt the pressure against my neck, but I could hear the sound of blade against beard like it was on loudspeaker. "You have nice, taut skin," she said. "Did you ever think about growing a beard?"

"I had one when I was teaching."

"I love beards. But they take a lot of work to keep neat."

I didn't say anything. I just gave in to the experience: the pressure of her stroke, the muted grating-ripping sound of the stubble falling before the sharpness of the blade.

"My first lover had a beard," she said. "His name was Will."

I could hear a train whistle out the window, long and mournful.

"I really loved him. We were both smoke jumpers. We thought we were invincible. I guess everybody does when they're young. Anyway, we had this romantic notion of living out in some national forest for the rest of our lives."

She swept on fresh shaving cream, the soft bristles of the barber's brush the very opposite sensation of the blade. I closed my eyes. I felt her fine hair brush my cheek as she leaned down to resume shaving me.

"We went on a fire in northern California. It was outside Susanville. Just a little lightning strike that got out of hand. I went down a ridge with some fusees—those are ignition flares—to start a backfire. And when I turned around there was just this wave of fire rolling down the mountainside. It looked like it was ten stories tall. There wasn't any time to run, to do anything. I pulled out my Shake 'N Bake—they issued us these little individual tents made of aluminum, but we didn't really believe they'd work. And I got under it and just drove myself into the ground. God, I can still taste those pine needles."

I didn't open my eyes. I just listened to the alto

melody of her voice, felt the confident rhythm of the razor in her hand.

"Well, the fire jumped over me. It was an amazing feeling of being in the stomach of this *thing*, but I was alive. I couldn't believe it. But when I went back up the hill, I found Will."

She stopped shaving and I opened my eyes.

"He had fireproof boots." She spoke more slowly now. "And that's about all there was."

She had the razor poised in front of me, and then there was a drop of water on the blade. Just big enough for a tear.

Chapter Thirty-two

Monday. Exactly a month had passed since I had fallen into the elevator shaft of the Triple A Storage Warehouse. The Yarnell twins had been identified. But otherwise, as my friend Lorie might say, police were baffled. I didn't care. I had shaved a beautiful woman's legs with a straight razor.

The phone was ringing as I walked down the hall to my office. I unlocked the door, bounded to the desk and grabbed the receiver.

"Mapstone." It was Hawkins: "It's all over. You got something to write on?"

Twenty minutes later, I pulled into an old gas station, where Buckeye Road crossed Nineteenth Avenue. Buckeye was the old highway west. Today it was populated with the ruins of small motels, coffee shops, and filling stations, most encoded with gang graffiti. Some forlorn street vendors operated from vacant gashes of land where a crack house had been bulldozed. Bleak concrete ware-houses intruded every few blocks. It was a rough neighborhood.

Peralta was sitting with Hawkins in an unmarked car. Both of them were wearing flak jackets. I parked the BMW and climbed in the back seat of the cop car.

"Hey, Mapstone," Hawkins greeted me like his best friend in the world. "Just thought you'd want to be in on the bust."

"Bust?"

"The guy who did Max Yarnell," Peralta said, sounding subdued.

I sat back on the slick vinyl of the seat. "How do we know?"

"Confidential informant," Hawkins said. "You guys at the S.O. ought to try it on the Strangler case."

"Eat shit," Peralta growled. "Suspect is Hector Gonzalez, age twenty. Has a long record for bur-glary and assault. He was in county jail Wednesday night for beating up his girlfriend. He started talk-ing shit in jail, and the informant heard him talk about killing somebody named Yarnell."

Hawkins crowed, "A burglar, Mapstone. 'Yar-nell curse,' my ass."

Peralta went on, "He's apparently crashing with some friends at one of these scummy little motels that has been turned into apartments. It's about two blocks west of here."

"In the city of Phoenix," Hawkins added.

Peralta passed back a jail mugshot of a young man with exotic eyes and a sullen, small mouth.

Hawkins smiled. "When the cavalry comes, we're going after him." He eyed me. "Stay back and don't get in the way."

Peralta winked and handed me a vest. I strapped it on and wished I had brought Speedloaders for the Python. I was supposed to stay back. Six rounds should be enough.

The cavalry came in the form of four more unmarked police cars. We formed up in the lot, listened to some redundant instructions from Hawkins, then drove leisurely two blocks to where Hector Gonzales, age twenty, was supposedly waiting for us.

Behind a faded neon sign that proclaimed "Thunderbird Auto Court" stood two long, low brick buildings overlooking a concrete parking lot that had been patched too many times. We bumped over cracked pavement and deep chug holes, coming to a halt in front of a door labeled

1-A. Instantly, half a dozen cops in flak jackets jogged to the sides of the door and headed around to the rear of the building. Peralta and Hawkins took up positions right by the door, guns drawn. I stayed behind the car, maybe ten feet away, and knelt down behind the fender.

We were too late. A dozen young Hispanic men dashed out of the back and scattered across Buckeye, bringing shrieks of tires and car horns from the traffic. Hawkins rose and kicked in the door, shouting commands in English and Spanish. He was knocked backward suddenly and landed face up on the pavement just as the roar of a shotgun blast reached my ears. I hit the ground and drew the magnum. A spray of machine-gun fire erupted out of the room, echoing weirdly under the eaves of the little motel. Then there was silence.

From under the car, I saw Hawkins roll to the side and then be pulled away by other cops.

"I'm fine, goddamnit!" he rasped. They had him off to the side of the door, sitting upright in the dirt. He had a tight little pattern of birdshot in the middle of his vest. I leaned in the car door, grabbed the microphone and gave the radio code for "officer down, needs assistance."

Then it was over, just as suddenly as it started.

I heard some voices calling out in Spanish, then some guns were tossed out. Two guys who looked no older than fourteen swaggered out, all cheap machismo. They were dragged to the ground and handcuffed by the cops. Peralta planted a knee in one suspect's back and his Glock at the base of his head. Neither kid looked like Gonzales.

"Secure. Code four," a male voice called from the motel room.

I got on my feet, dusted myself off and walked over to Hawkins. He had the air knocked out of him, at the least. I pulled the flak vest off, and he moved his head in a little circle, looking around. The shot hadn't penetrated the vest, but raising his T-shirt, I could see an ugly purple bruise on his chest from the impact of the round. Like mom always said, never go out without your bulletproof vest.

"We get the little bastard?" he demanded in a slurry voice.

"Not yet."

"What do you mean not yet?" He focused on me. "I told you to stay out of the way."

I leaned him against the wall again and stood.

I walked south along the building to work a charley horse out of my calf. Behind me, I could hear sirens coming down Buckeye. In about three minutes, half the cops in the district would be here, along with paramedics, firefighters, and the TV stations.

The Thunderbird Auto Court was still and silent now. But I could feel eyes watching us from behind the dirty window screens. One partly opened door was carefully closed again. The place was oppressive in its layers of age and dirt and despair. Then I passed a little carport marked by a large pool of ancient grease and Hector Gonzales was standing just inside.

I drew down on him. "Deputy sheriff," I said in a shaky voice. "Policia!"

But he already had the drop on me. As my eyes adjusted to the relative shade of the carport, I could see he held a silver-plated revolver in his right hand, and the barrel was on a disconcerting trajectory to my head.

"Fuck you," he said. "I ain't goin' back to jail."

"Nobody's dead or hurt yet," I said, hearing the sirens getting louder, wondering if anybody even knew I was back here.

"Oh, yeah?" The exotic eyes were bright. "Well, put down your gun, then." He wore filthy cargo pants and he had no shoes on.

"That's not going to happen." It was Peralta's first rule: You never give up your piece. Never.

"Why did you have to walk back here?" he demanded, his eyes turning sleepy.

"Just bad luck," I said, doing a quick calculus of armed standoff: with my heavy-grain, hollow-point .357 rounds, I could drop him with one shot. With luck, it would have enough force to keep his finger from squeezing a round into me. I needed to do it now. The longer I waited, the more things fell to my disadvantage. A huge lake of sweat opened up down my back. The precise, twin sights of the Python were aligned on his heart. I didn't take the shot.

"What do you know about the Yarnell killing?"

"What the fuck?" he said. "I didn't kill nobody. Yarnell, he…"

"Drop your weapon!" It was Peralta. "Drop your weapon!"

"Back off, Mike," I shouted, keeping the drop on the kid, who took a harder aim at me. "What do you mean?" I shouted at him. "What do you mean you didn't kill anybody?"

"Don't make us kill you, kid!" It was another cop, off to my right. I couldn't see anything but that silver-plated barrel. I had to take the shot.

"Tell me!" I shouted.

He shook his head slowly, his front teeth biting into his lower lip, a tear falling down his cheek. He raised the revolver.

"Drop it now!" More cops.

"Do it now, son!"

"Put the gun down!"

Just as I took in a breath, they opened fire. I expected a bullet in return but it never came. He did an absurd little dance, and a spray of dark blood ejaculated from his back, and the exotic eyes were still staring at me as his body crumpled backward onto the dingy concrete.

Chapter Thirty-three

I swam in the ocean at night. Me, a desert rat who refused to swim in places where I couldn't see the bottom. But I had lived seven years in San Diego, where the ocean was always in your sight or your nostrils. One night, on a first date luminous with connection, conversation, and laughter, my new friend and I had gone for a walk along the beach. When we came to a little cove, she had stripped off her clothes and run straight into the surf until only her blond head had been visible in the blackness of the waves. Then I had waded into the blackness, too, casting aside my native caution, letting the seaweed sweep against my legs and the fish bump me. I am a strong swimmer, so I had no trouble keeping up with her as we swam against the sea until finally we had become part of the swell and tide ourselves. When we were maybe a mile out, she had pointed back toward the land. I had turned to see, from our vast solitude, a dazzling necklace of lights on the horizon.

After I had married her and we had moved into a little house a block from the beach in La Jolla, I often swam out at night, often alone. The Pacific off San Diego is usually so calm that you can get careless. I always remembered that first night of revelation, when I had swum to catch her, fighting my own fear of being consumed by this world-making thing, and then finding myself a part of it. And I had always tried to remember the terrible power waiting in the gentle waves.

One night, angry over some now-forgotten academic feud, I had driven home from the university, changed into my trunks, and plunged recklessly into water that looked as calm as black glass. I had swum until every muscle burned with pain and I had ejected the argument from my mind. I recall very clearly thinking how much simpler it had been being a deputy. And then I had felt the current change beneath me.

A cold, black wave had hit me full on, then it pulled me straight down into the swell. Salty water had forced its way into my nose. I had felt as if I did a somersault and didn't know the way to the surface. My lungs had ached for new breath. But the cold had kept my head straight, so I just let the wave carry me out to sea. In a few seconds, that seemed like something less than a year, I had popped to the surface again. Then I had swum as best I could parallel to the lights, feeling a current insistently bearing me south. By the time the ocean let me go, I had been carried a mile away, down to Pacific Beach.

Treading water, exhausted, feeling the ocean say, *Don't mess with me. I will kill you,* my mind had calmly rested on things I didn't think of much on land. Things like God and family and the measure of a man's life. A sense that I had let too many sunny weekend afternoons slip on by, and now maybe I wouldn't make it back to shore before I froze to death or that rip current came back. When I walked across the rough sand, safe, I had promised myself I wouldn't lose that clarity.

I wasn't making promises Monday. I was shaky and nauseated. My ears rang from gunfire in a confined space. The only lucky break was that the elevator at the courthouse was working again. I went up to my office, closed the door and locked it. I sat at the desk and just stared into the bright Arizona sky and thought of swimming at night in the ocean. Still, I couldn't stop shaking, couldn't tone down the metronome in my chest.

I sat long enough that my eyes focused on the edge of an unmarked brown envelope. It had been set up against the door last week. I had brought it in and forgotten it. Now I pulled it out of the new pile of files that partially obscured it, pulled it across the desk. It didn't even have my name on the outside. I ran a letter opener through it. Two sheets of papers were inside. They were Photostats. The quality was rotten—but good enough to make out. I read them and set them aside, staring up at the old high ceiling. Then I read them again. By that time I wasn't shaking.

"Talbott. He wasn't…" I realized I was talking to myself. Grandmother had done that when she was older, and now I wondered if it was hardwired in the family. The first Photostat was the same booking record Zelda Chain had shown me. John Henry Talbott, also known as Jack Talbott, was arrested for misdemeanor drunk and disorderly at 1:10 on the morning of Nov. 27, 1941. The second record was new: it was a Phoenix City Jail prisoner release for Talbott, two days later.

Maybe a burglar had murdered Max Yarnell. Maybe the attack on James Yarnell had been completely unrelated. But Jack Talbott couldn't have been at Hayden Yarnell's hacienda on the night of the twins' disappearance.

I had the phone in my hand with the first two numbers of Peralta's extension dialed, but I stopped. There wasn't enough information yet. I knew that Talbott claimed he was framed for the kidnapping, that Win Yarnell had done it. The Photostat before me showed Talbott couldn't have done it. That Thanksgiving night he was in the city jail one floor above my office. I also knew that Hayden Yarnell had a codicil in his will that implied he had doubts about who had taken his grandsons. But why had Talbott gone to Nogales, and why was he carrying part of the ransom money and children's pajamas when he was arrested? And what had gone wrong in the kidnapping that had led to the deaths of Andrew and Woodrow Yarnell?

And who had dug up the release record that seemed to clear Talbott of at least direct involvement, then put it in a plain envelope and placed it before my door? Someone who was interested that I make progress on this investigation. It couldn't have been Zelda Chain; it was delivered the day I was visiting her. Not Peralta: he would have lorded it over me that he had found a record that had eluded my searches of the city and county records. Bobby Hamid? More likely. It seemed like a lot of trouble just to consummate a real-estate deal. But this was Phoenix, after all.

I must have visibly jumped when the door opened, and then Gretchen was running across the room to embrace me, saying how worried she had been after hearing about the shooting. Suddenly it felt so damned good to be alive. It felt so good to be alive to hold and kiss this beautiful woman, who looked at me with adoring eyes. The other feeling that kicked me was guilt, for momentarily thinking about Lindsey and missing her.

Chapter Thirty-four

That night the rain came, watery inflections on the pavement. Seven inches of rain water this desert in an entire year, so every drop is memorable. Every streak from a seldom-used windshield wiper. Every patter on the bedroom window. Every misty sprinkle on my face on a cool December evening.

When the winter rains come, the sidewalk restaurants move inside. The Fiesta Bowl promoters worry. The resorts cover up the pool furniture, and the snowbirds grumble. But we Phoenicians quietly exult—that after all the punishing months of sun and heat, the sky brings back the healing water. That, after all, the desert is God's chosen, sacred place.

More secular thoughts were on my mind as I cruised the parking lot at Biltmore Fashion Park for ten minutes before finding a parking place anywhere close to the Coffee Plantation. I had reluctantly turned down Gretchen's offer of company tonight. Maybe it was the post-shooting jitters, or maybe it was the fact that the Yarnell kidnapping was still unsolved, and these loose ends, forgotten for decades, were still my loose ends. So I worked. The buildings were draped with white holiday lights and steam came out of the car exhausts. The cars glided across the wet parking lot like a dream. By the time I got inside, a familiar blonde in a smart suit with a high hemline was waiting for me. This time the suit was pink. She was sipping from a tiny espresso cup.

"I told you on the phone I shouldn't even be speaking to you," said Megan O'Connor, looking around as if bulky Yarneco security guards might spring from under the empty tables nearby. "I thought the crime had been solved. That awful young man, they ran his mug shot on the news tonight. Of course, it's terrible you had to kill him, but I understand you were doing your job. In any case, I'm meeting my fiancé in just a few minutes. We need to do our Christmas shopping."

I sat down with her. Taking time to get anything to drink seemed too risky. This skittish bird might fly.

"I didn't shoot the kid." Why was I making

that point? "There are still a few things we need to clear up. I'm interested in a codicil to Hayden Yarnell's 1942 will. Are you familiar with it?"

You would have thought I had caressed her fine inner thighs. Her eyes grew wide and she pulled back.

"You know of it?" I asked again.

She gave a slight nod and looked around again.

"Is someone following you?"

She laughed. She had a big, fun laugh and it made me smile. She said, "I'm sorry, Deputy Mapstone. I know this seems absurd. You work around a company like Yarneco for enough years and you get paranoid. Yes, I know about the codicil. Working for Max meant that I did a good deal of work with the Yarnell Trust."

I asked her about that. She ran a long finger around the rim of the cup in front of her.

"The trust supports twenty-seven heirs of Hayden Yarnell and his sister. I know, must be nice. Few of them live in Arizona any longer. Anyway, the trust is entirely funded by the wealth that Hayden Yarnell left, plus the investments made since then by the bank, advised by an independent board. Not even Max or James Yarnell were given seats on the board."

"It doesn't sound like Hayden Yarnell trusted his family."

"He was a self-made man," Megan said. "And I guess he saw what a little money and leisure time did to his son, Hayden Jr."

"The one they called Win."

"Right. Anyway, this always struck me as strange. But when I started dealing with trust business, I heard about this codicil. I thought it was just a family legend. But one day I was researching something, and there it was. If it turned out that any family member had conspired or participated in the abduction of his grandsons, the conditions of his bequests would change. Among other things, the trust would be liquidated and given to charity."

"That sounds extreme."

"It's very odd," she said. "Before I went to work at Yarneco, I had worked at a big law firm that did a lot of estate planning. I never saw anything like it before. Kind of like vengeance beyond the grave."

"Did Max ever talk about this?"

"Never. The one time I asked, he got really flustered."

"Did he talk about the kidnapping?"

"No. It was understood that we didn't discuss it."

"You were close to him?"

She flashed angry eyes at me; they were green. "Not what you think, deputy."

"I didn't think anything. I'm just trying to understand."

She kept sipping the espresso, but the level of the liquid never seemed to go down. I needed to develop that technique with liquor. After a moment, "Max said his grandfather died a bitter, crazy old man. He said the codicil was a result of that. He also doubted it could even be enforced by a court."

If that were true, it made me wonder why he became flustered, to use her word.

"Max wasn't close to his brother?"

"You could say that. Or you could say they just despised each other. James still controlled a share of Yarneco—within the parameters of the trust, of course—and he would vote against Max, just for spite, it seemed to me. James lives in this art world. He's very connected and handsome, charming in a way his brother never is. Was, I mean. He doesn't know anything about business."

By this time a tall, boy-faced man was hovering. He was dressed in an over-long T-shirt, baggy jeans and expensive sneakers. Megan excused herself without introducing me, and walked away with the fiancé. There was no time to ask why she felt paranoid working for Yarneco, or whether her boss had felt the same. There was barely time to appreciate her elegant beauty as she walked out with her slob boyfriend. I unconsciously straightened my suit coat and headed to the rain-anointed parking lot.

Chapter Thirty-five

Choose a strand and pull it, follow where it led. That had been Gretchen's advice. So on Tuesday I drove down Central into the south Phoenix barrio, across the Salt River that stayed dry despite the rain, past the brightly colored storefronts with signs in Spanish. A brave ice-cream man patrolled the corner of Southern Avenue with his pushcart, even though it was fifty degrees outside. Shops covered their wares in plastic against the rain. Working people huddled on the muddy, broken concrete of city bus stops.

Every face I saw was Hispanic, and it made me think of the kid in the old motel, Hector Gonzales. Just before Peralta arrived, when I had asked him if he had killed Yarnell, he said something odd. He said, "Yarnell, he…" I had forgotten about it in the mayhem that followed. Now I remembered it. "Yarnell, he…" He said it as if he knew whom I was talking about, and yet it wasn't necessarily the way you'd begin a sentence of denial, or confession. "Yarnell, he…" Nothing about these cases seemed right. I was thinking too much, or so Peralta had said. So I drove on, but didn't stop thinking.

The Phoenix I had grown up in had been little removed from its roots as a largely Southern town, and south Phoenix was the segregated wrong side of the tracks. It was a very Anglo city, with a relatively large African-American population, and Mexican-American families that had lived here for generations. All this had been swept away by the past ten or fifteen years, as hundreds of thousands of first-generation Latino migrants had crowded into a city whose population had tripled since 1960. The historic Golden Gate barrio had been bulldozed for Sky Harbor expansion. The new-comers had turned everything from the onetime white-bread suburb of Maryvale to many of the formerly black neighborhoods of south Phoenix into new barrios. Now the Midwesterners were coming, too. The citrus groves and Japanese Flower Gardens that had encircled the south edge of the city like a cooling, green necklace were falling to subdivisions, shopping strips, and gated properties. There were hard feelings and tensions on all sides.

I was after different history: a man who had been at the Yarnell hacienda the night of the kidnapping. Finding people was easier than when I had been a young patrol deputy. Now the department had a software program called AutoTrack that allowed us to search through public records using as little as a name. I had more than that, because Luis Paz's Social Security number was still in the Yarneco records from 1941, and the Department of Motor Vehicles had issued him a driver's license in 1988. But his old phone number had been disconnected. With AutoTrack I found he was still alive, and living with his son. I tried to keep my heart from leaping into my throat in excitement.

Luis Paz, Hayden Yarnell's gardener, would be the only person left alive who had been an adult at the hacienda when the kidnapping took place. Although the case files showed that Paz was there that Thanksgiving night, there was no evidence he had been interviewed. Another case of lost paperwork, I was sure. But what if he had seen something that escaped the attention of young James or Max Yarnell? Maybe he could tell me what happened on the night when Jack Talbott was sleeping off a drunk, not committing a kidnapping. Or maybe Paz was in diapers with his memory gone. I had to try.

I parked the BMW in front of a single-story cinder block house on a street without curbs or gutters. Around me was a poor neighborhood hunched in the shadow of some kind of industrial operation. The air smelled of an unknown chemical. But this house was neat, freshly painted and lushly landscaped. I counted four pickup trucks in the driveway. At the door, I showed my star and asked for Luis Paz.

"He's not here. Who the hell are you?"

A big man around my age pushed out the screen door. I backed away instinctively. He was taller than me, broad shouldered, and carried his arms in the way of weight lifters. Resentment shone on him like sweat. I didn't know what flavor of resentment, but it didn't take a Ph.D. to know it involved cops. I told him who I was.

"I'm investigating the kidnapping and murder of Andrew and Woodrow Yarnell. I know that happened a long time ago. But our information is that your…grandfather?…was there the night it happened."

"He's my grandfather. He doesn't know anything." His voice was low and decidedly unfriendly.

"I'd like to talk to him."

"What if he doesn't want to talk to you, huh?

Look around, you think cops are welcome in this 'hood? They only come when they bring trouble. Like that kid who was murdered over on Buckeye yesterday. Sounds like he never had a chance. The TV said he had a gun, but you know that's bullshit. You cops carry guns to plant on the people you shoot."

I let that go on by. My ears were still ringing from the shooting.

"And what kind of a cop has a ride like that?" He nodded toward the BMW.

"You probably don't know that we recovered the remains of the Yarnell twins…"

"What? Do you think I'm stupid? I read it in the newspaper." My charm was obviously working on him. "I thought that was solved. They caught the guy way back when. He was an Anglo."

"He might not have done it. There's new information. That's why I was hoping…"

His eyes bore into me and the rain sprinkled on us. "You don't know anything about my dad. You think you're going find some dumb old Mexican. He's a retired small-business man. He took the money he saved while he was young, while he was working for the Yarnells, and he started a lawn service. By the time he retired, he had more than a hundred men working for him."

As he lectured me, I could see the glow of a television screen beyond the doorway, but it was impossible to see who was inside. Then someone was watching me, a little girl with luxurious black hair and a nose pressed against the screen.

"I learned all about the police as the arm of the dominant power establishment when I was a student at Princeton," he went on, watching me closely. "Does it surprise you a homeboy went to the Ivy League?"

"No."

"Bullshit! I come back here and there's no work except in real estate, and there's a cop on my doorstep. Class and race and power, man. If this house were in Paradise Valley, you wouldn't dare come here. You'd be dealing with some lawyer."

"I just want to ask Mr. Paz if..."

"Hey, Pablo!" I turned to see a low-rider Honda stopped on the street. Four heads with close-cropped haircuts were staring at me. "This guy giving you trouble?"

My stomach tightened. Suddenly this seemed like a really bad idea. The little girl kept watching me.

"Look. I'm not here to hassle you or your

grandfather. I saw the bones of the two little boys. It's all that's left. Andrew and Woodrow. They were four years old. I've seen a photo of them in cowboy outfits. I bet they were like any kids that age. Then somebody took them. They were sealed into a wall, and they probably suffocated in there. I don't care whether they were rich kids or poor kids, they didn't need to die that way. And we've gone for fifty-eight years without knowing what really happened. I think your grandfather could help. I can't imagine he wouldn't want to try."

Pablo's mouth turned down. Almost involuntarily he looked back into the house, at the little girl, and in a voice of unbelievable tenderness, "Go back in now. Go be with Lito. I'll be right there." Then he cocked his head. "It's okay," he called out, and gave a meaty wave to the occupants of the Honda. "We're glad you're back in town," they yelled and rolled off.

"At least consider it." I held out my card, and after a long moment Pablo took it.

Chapter Thirty-six

Pull a strand and it breaks. There was as much chance of talking to Luis Paz as there was that Phoenix would become a city of rain like Seattle. It put me in a rotten mood for the shooting board, which met all afternoon. I had been a bit player in the incident on Buckeye Road, but that didn't prevent the usual savaging by internal affairs, an assistant county attorney and a board of senior officers. "Why didn't you fire?" they kept demanding. "Why did you hesitate?" The kid seemed pretty dead without my assistance.

Back in the courthouse, I was arranging neat piles of work on the big counsel's table that sat beside the white board when the phone rang. It was James Yarnell.

"We're home free, Mapstone."

"Oh, sorry I didn't tell you about the suspect in Max's homicide. I just assumed the other detectives…"

"I'm not talking about that. Didn't you hear? Scottsdale PD made an arrest this morning."

I sat in my chair, letting the creak echo off the high ceiling.

"It was this woman, she was obsessed with me," he went on. "She was on the art scene in Santa Fe, and I thought she had a little talent. It turned into an affair. Bad judgment on my part. That was a year ago, and after we broke up she moved to Scottsdale. She would come by the gallery. Then she started getting nasty, making threats. But I thought she was harmless."

I stopped him. "Are you telling me this woman has been arrested for taking the shot at us?"

"Yes, yes! Lisa showed up outside my house, screaming at me. The cops were watching me, of course, and they arrested her. They told me she had a pistol in her car, the same caliber as the one that was used on me. Right now they're calling her a 'person of interest,' whatever that means. I guess they have to run tests."

Why wasn't I happy for him? Another neat bow was being tied around the case, and all my fears about a link to the kidnapping were just so much paranoia. So what if the same kind of doll that had been delivered to my office door was also found in Max Yarnell's house, with the charming addition of bloody doll hands? Calm down, Mapstone. Get in the holiday spirit. So I told him it was great news. Then I was about to tell him that Jack Talbott couldn't have been at the hacienda the night of the kidnapping, but he was in a hurry.

"Let's catch up after the first of the year, Mapstone. I'll call you."

My next call was to Gretchen. I told her I had to work for the next few nights. Believe me, I didn't want it that way. But the Yarnell kidnapping was still unsolved. In my mind, it was more unsolved than it had been when I fell into the freight elevator in the dark a month before.

I finally had to settle down to the hundred small disciplines that separate the historian from the cop. We live in a state of incomplete and contradictory knowledge. It's what keeps historians arguing and publishing. That wasn't much comfort now, because I lacked the scholar's critical distance from this piece of history. But I would try. And if I were lucky, I would live with a little less uncertainty. I discussed my theories with no one.

I needed the comfort of research, informed by technique and imagination. I wanted evidence.

I wanted contrary evidence even more. Reconstruction. What happened? Interpretation. Why? Pattern and bias. What was I missing? It was solitary work.

I mined archives scattered across the city: the state archives, the library at Arizona State University, the Arizona Room at the Phoenix Public Library, the state historical society, the Arizona Historical Foundation. I returned to the old files of the Phoenix Police, and added data from the county assessor and recorder. I spent half a day at the state vital statistics department. I tore apart ten boxes of court transcripts that had been boxed up longer than I had been alive. Dusty pages and decaying volumes. Each one said, "I was there"…"I have something to tell you."

I sat in on the monthly breakfast held by some retired Phoenix cops at Bill Johnson's Big Apple, and each one had an opinion about the case. Unfortunately, none had firsthand knowledge of it. I pored over maps and blueprints of the warehouse district, old plans from the city water department, and a survey of the area by the Salt River Project. At the Phoenix Police Museum, amid the display of a real police motorcycle and a mockup of the city jail in frontier times, the curator showed me

Joe Fisher's memoirs. He let me borrow a desk and I settled in to read it.

It was a hardcover book, but it looked self-published. *My Years on the Phoenix Force*, by Joe Fisher. Using the skimming technique familiar to any former graduate student, I leafed through. It was badly written, although, hell, throw in some statistics and you could probably get it published in a professional history journal today. Fisher wrote about his role in the 1931 case of Winnie Ruth Judd, the trunk murderess. There he was again helping the Tucson cops arrest John Dillinger and his gang in 1934. If the writing hadn't been so dry, I would have been tempted to linger. I knew that Fisher had been repeatedly decorated for bravery. He brought the most modern techniques to the force. And he had amazing success in coaxing confessions. Unfortunately the book seemed to offer no insights on these things, and I didn't have the time. I moved forward, looking for the Yarnell kidnapping.

It wasn't there. No index, damn. I went back through, but it still wasn't there, and the book was nothing if not chronological. One of the most famous cases of his career, and he didn't write about it. The book ended with a murder in 1943, and a typewritten insert in the back gave Fisher's bio, including the fact that he had died in 1947.

I gave the book back to the curator, explained my dilemma, bought a museum membership, and lingered over a photo of the detective bureau, circa 1940. Fisher was identified, a short man in a fedora and suit with a broad, forgettable face. He didn't look like a tough guy at all.

I spoke to him under my breath. "What the hell were you up to?"

"Deputy," the curator called out and I walked over.

"I have one other idea for you," he said.

Chapter Thirty-seven

"What do you mean Frances is dead?"

"She had a stroke the afternoon after your visit, Deputy." Heather Amis' voice was raw as sunstroke. "She slipped into a coma, and she died last night."

It was Thursday morning and I was back at my office in the old courthouse, and suddenly the cavernous room felt claustrophobic. My travel plans for that day were evaporating.

"So now she's finally free. Fifty-seven years she spent in here. I just can't believe the cruelty. This poor, poor woman. And please spare me your speech about the rights of the victims."

"I wasn't going to make a speech. What happened to her sounds rotten."

"You have no idea."

I felt all my theories crashing into the wall of silence that developed on the phone. Finally, I asked, "Did you get a chance to ask her any of the questions I left for you?"

"No. You got her to talk more than I had ever seen. And she never said another word before she had the stroke."

"Do you know about the crime?"

"I learned everything I could," she said. "I also went back in her medical records."

"I've learned a few things." I shouldn't have been discussing the case with a civilian, but how could my luck get any worse? "I learned that Jack Talbott couldn't have been there the night of the kidnapping."

Heather gasped, and I told her more.

"Oh, my God," she said. "So old Hayden Yarnell must have suspected his son Hayden Jr. had done it. My God, that explains everything."

"I can't go that far," I said. "I don't know Talbott's involvement. He was found with some of the ransom money in Nogales and the boys' pajamas. That would still sway a jury today."

"But Frances!" she nearly yelled. "My God, Frances was just caught up in this."

"Maybe. She was an accessory. She went to Nogales with Talbott. Why?"

"I don't know!" Heather's voice was taut with

frustration. "But I believed in her! It's not like she had any family or even a lawyer. Nobody was fighting for her. And don't think I'm a pushover, David. I know every inmate says she's innocent. I think Frances really was."

"Did she ever say so?"

"No. But have you found anything new that implicates her?"

I had to grant her that I had not. But if Frances had explained her innocence at the trial, told how she was caught up in something with which she had nothing to do, it was on pages of lost court transcripts. That was possible, but the newspaper accounts had no mention of it. She also never took the stand.

Heather started talking even before I was finished. "Maybe she was covering up for someone!"

"But then to not talk for all those years in prison? Why? Why still be covering up in the sixties, even the nineties, for God's sake."

"You're dealing with the Yarnell family. Anything is possible when money and power are involved."

"So why didn't they have her killed, or have her released and buy her off?" I said. "Her silence was an act of her power, when you think about it. She made this choice. Most of the ransom money was never recovered. Maybe Frances knew where it was hidden, and she thought she would get out someday and retrieve it. That's a powerful motive to keep silence."

"God, I'm sick of men talking about power and women living without it! Do you believe what you just said?"

After a pause I had to admit I didn't.

"I've been reading some of the notes the lead detective made in the case," I said. "Joe Fisher. I just found some of his files. He had reservations about whether Frances was involved in the kidnapping. He testified at her trial for leniency."

"My God…"

"But he couldn't get past the fact that she was found with Talbott, with some of the ransom money and the pajamas. I have no idea whether he knew that Talbott was in jail the night of the kidnapping, but he did interview a lot of people about the possibility that others were involved."

"Why didn't he…?"

"I don't know. Maybe he wanted to do the right thing, but he could never make the case."

"You cops," Heather said. "Always sticking together. Can't you do anything, Mapstone? This woman was a victim! She never got justice. Don't you care?"

I just listened. Anything I said would seem insincere.

"Mapstone?"

"I'm here. I do care, Heather. That's why I'm asking these questions. I just can't figure out what would have caused Frances to keep silent."

Heather said, "I can think of one thing."

Chapter Thirty-eight

The rap on the door was tentative, almost like someone made a mistake. Still absorbing the news from Heather Amis, I wanted to let them walk on. Whoever it was couldn't want me that bad. But I set aside my notes and went to the door.

Before me stood a small, dark man in a starched white shirt and a bola tie. His face looked as lined and cracked as the desert itself, but his hair was vividly black and slicked back on his scalp. He carried a Stetson in one hand, a large, powerful-looking hand for such a small man.

"I am Luis Paz."

I invited him in and sent Carl down to the marriage license bureau to get him a cup of coffee. Carl wouldn't like it, but I was afraid the old man might walk out if I kept him waiting. Or he might just disappear like the apparition he seemed to be. I led him to one of the straight-back wooden chairs and invited him to sit. He put the Stetson on my desk.

"My son gave me your card."

I told him that I appreciated that.

"He didn't want me to come here. To open up things that should have been closed so long ago."

"But you came anyway," I said. I sat cautiously behind my desk. He regarded me in a long appraising glare.

"You work for Chief Peralta?"

I said I did.

"He's a good man. I knew his father, the judge."

"Mr. Paz, you worked as gardener..."

"I worked for Mr. Yarnell for nearly twenty years."

"Hayden Yarnell?" I coaxed.

Paz stiffened. "There is only one Mr. Yarnell," he said. "His older sons were..." He let the sentence hang between us, as if only a fool would not understand.

"After he died, I started my own lawn business." He relaxed a millimeter, no more.

"Sir, may I ask how old you are?"

"Ninety-three," he said.

"You don't look it."

He smiled a little. "I feel every year," he said. "But I am not here about me." He sighed and looked across the desk, then met my eyes. "What happened in 1941, all those years ago, I've carried it in my heart."

We fell into quiet that seemed endless. It was a taste of the silence the Yarnell twins must have felt, an absence more frightening than their cries for help, the silence of Jack Talbott before the executioner did his job, or the endless years for Frances Richie. But I didn't dare break it. Finally, Paz did.

"At first I could tell myself stories, that maybe I was mistaken about what I had seen and heard. And then it didn't seem to matter, so much had gone wrong it couldn't be made right."

I spoke into the next long gap. "What couldn't be made right?"

"You don't understand. They were so power-ful…"

"The Yarnell family?"

He nodded slowly. "First they told me to keep my mouth shut, that Mr. Yarnell wanted it that way. I couldn't believe that, but he became so sick, and I couldn't talk to him." He sighed heavily. "I was afraid. I had my own family, and I was afraid.

Later, when the Yarnells offered me money to start my own business, I took it."

His hands bunched into gnarled, hard-time fists that sat on his knees like holstered weapons. "Do you know what it is like to hold something terrible in your heart for so many years?" he asked. "Do you know how heavy it becomes?"

Carl stepped in and put the coffee on the desk. He started to say something. Then he saw Paz's face, and walked quietly out, closing the door without a sound.

Paz sipped the coffee. "They tell me I should not have caffeine, or anything else I love. Am I going to live another twenty years? I hope not. A man can live too long."

I didn't try to guide him. I just sat and listened.

"Mr. Yarnell could have lived forever but he died of a broken heart," Paz said. "I was so young and stupid then, I would not have believed such a thing. But I watched it happen."

"When his grandsons were kidnapped."

"Yes!" Paz erupted. "Yes, it killed Mr. Yarnell."

"You were there the Thanksgiving they were kidnapped?"

He nodded.

"And you stayed with Mr. Yarnell until he died?"

"I was there the entire time," he said. "I didn't understand all that was happening. I didn't know how to help Mr. Yarnell. There was no straight course that I could see."

"You cared about Mr. Yarnell."

Paz stared at his fists, opened them and stared inside, as if the lifelines on his palms could translate for him.

"Do you understand what I am trying to say?" he demanded.

"I think I do," I said. "But I need you to tell me in your own words, from the beginning."

He sat for a long time in that death silence, the big room swallowing up even the sound of our breathing. Then he set the coffee cup carefully on my desk and began to talk in a strong voice.

Chapter Thirty-nine

The rain stayed all week, under a sky that looked like boiling lead. On Friday morning, I walked across Jefferson Street to the sheriff's administration building, showed my ID at the deputy's entrance and used the back hallway to reach the private entrance to Peralta's office suite. His space held the comfort of the familiar: the big Arizona flag furled in its coppery sunset behind his desk; the framed photos of a storied career on the wall; a bulletin board on wheels with the latest case reports; a wall-sized map of Maricopa County; the contrast of his credenza piled high with files, law books, and used legal pads with the utter emptiness of his big modern desktop. He was leaning back in his chair, black cowboy boots on his blotter, sipping a caffeine-free Diet Coke.

"Where have you been? I've eaten all your leftovers at home."

I dropped a two-inch-thick file folder beside his boots. I said: "Progress."

He lifted his dark brow a quarter of an inch. I sat down and gave my report.

In the end, he wanted to talk to Luis Paz himself. All the way down, Peralta quizzed me rapid-fire. Turned my ideas on their head. Turned my words against me. Questioned the sequence. Questioned the motives. He could demolish the careless truth-seeker in one sentence, and I needed that. He reminded me we would face tougher questions from the county attorney—and from Superior Court Judge Arthur C. "ACLU" Lu, if we were to get the court order we must have.

But after spending an hour with Paz in the living room of the modest, well-kept home, Peralta was uncharacteristically silent. All the way back downtown he was as pensive as Mike Peralta can get. Only when we got to a dark booth in a deserted corner of Majerle's did he speak.

"I'll go to Judge Lu for a court order this afternoon," he said. "How do you want to play this?"

I laid it out and he listened with his eyes closed and his hands folded, a massive tent of fingers on the tabletop. He asked a couple of questions. Made a couple of changes. Finally, he gave a sniff, set his face and hardened the dark eyes.

"You'd better fucking be right."

I just shut up and sipped my beer.

Chapter Forty

Gretchen's apartment was dark except for the yellow-blue flame in the fireplace. It was just cold enough outside, otherwise she would have had to use the air conditioning. I came in at the sound of her voice, closed the door behind me and locked it—it had one of those old deadbolts, turned by a delicate T-shaped latch in the hardware. Then there was Gretchen, standing in the archway, backlit by a gentle lamp in the kitchen and the remnants of a scarlet sunset, wearing a short black cocktail dress and carrying martinis. Was that Coleman Hawkins on the stereo?

"I know you like these," she said, holding out a drink.

"Definitely the whole package," I said. I crossed the room and kissed her passionately, toasted her, and then felt the gin on my lips, cold and warm at the same time. She smelled vaguely of old rose petals and clean bedsheets.

She had a body made for the look: long and leggy. Right down to the expensive black pumps. I'd never seen her in a short skirt before, and as much as I appreciated the rough-gentle denim she wore like a uniform, this was something else again. Gretchen!

"Are you close to solving your case, deputy?" she asked, sipping her drink, animating those lips and dimples.

"I think so," I said.

"I'm very proud of you," she said. "I'm very honored to know you."

"I couldn't have done anything without the help of the city archaeologist's office. Specifically, one archaeologist…"

She started unbuttoning my shirt with one hand. She was good with one hand: long, elegant fingers dominating the buttons of a man's shirt. She should have played the piano. Instead, she dug up the remains of ancient civilizations.

"I don't want to know more," she said. "I won't put you on the spot. I can read about it in the newspaper, and then I can smile to myself and say, 'I know that man.'"

She slipped her hand in my shirt and caressed my chest, teased my nipples.

"I have more plans for you," she said, taking another ounce of gin.

I set my glass down and took hers, too. "Maybe I have plans for you," I said.

I lightly kissed her lips. Her tongue came out to meet me, but my mouth moved on to her high, aristocratic cheekbones, to her long, warm neck, to the loamy-smelling province where her neck met her shoulders. She pressed herself against me and gasped. I could feel her nipples harden like pebbles under the dress.

Men underestimate the sensual power of kissing. For a long time, I just kissed her—long and deep, short and teasing and anticipatory. Using the tongue, a circle and a thrust. The subtle turns and tenses of the lips. Gentle bites on her lower lip. Nothing much else. Not much caressing or hugging, yet. The room felt ten degrees hotter. Then she let me push her to the sofa, and slowly ease her down. She smiled a far-away smile. Her pupils were black and wide. I knelt down and used my tongue.

"Oh, my," she gasped.

This was my show. Starting at the ankles—the exquisite planes and facets of the ankles of a woman gifted with athleticism and good DNA. Moving up to the smooth, taut surfaces of the calves. Behind the knees…The intimate, dangerous, tender skin of the inner thighs. Then starting all over again on the other leg, slowly moving up.…

◇◇◇

She came awake with a start. We were on the rug in front of the fire. It had cooked to embers, like a little burned village. I pulled her back down to me, smoothed her mussed hair, and pulled the comforter back up.

"That wasn't like me…" she whispered.

"You were wonderful."

"I have a hard time giving up control."

"You sounded like you had fun."

"I'm very loud," she said. "My previous boyfriend didn't like that."

"I love it," I said, wondering about this previous boyfriend. So much I didn't know about Gretchen Goodheart.

"I had a dream about you," she said. "About you and those two little boys trapped in the wall." She shivered against me.

"What was it about?"

"It's bad luck to tell a bad dream. You'll make it come true."

She stood and put on a Lucinda Williams CD, the volume low. The fireplace snapped and sizzled.

Then she came back and nuzzled against me. I held her tight. The old building creaked. A train whistle sailed through the window.

"Why did they put that woman in prison and keep her there her whole life?"

"I don't know," I said quietly.

"The Yarnells had all the power. Frances had no power at all."

"They didn't have enough power to stop the kidnapping," I said. "I guess none of us is safe." I thought of Bobby Hamid: *None of us in the world...*

"Do you believe in justice, David?" She raised up and looked at me. Her eyes were bright with imagined starlight.

"I wouldn't do this if I didn't." Women were asking me about justice this week.

"I mean real justice."

I thought about that. I said something lame. Something egghead-stupid about fallible human institutions, the rule of law, and the razor edge between justice and vengeance.

"I believe in vengeance," she said, a catch in her throat. "Don't you, really?"

Before I could answer, she had me on my back and was pulling my clothes off. Then she straddled me, guiding me inside her with one sure move.

"Come here, my cactus heart."

"What?" I was into more than hearing at that moment.

"You know what I mean."

She rode me gently, an achingly tight sensation coursing up from my groin. She still had on the cocktail dress. I moaned and stroked her smooth knees and forgot about thinking.

"Could you ever love me like you do Lindsey?" she whispered.

"I..." She slid down on me with a twisting motion.

"Don't lie to me, David."

"You feel so goddamned good," I gasped.

"That's better." She kissed my chest, circled my nipples with her tongue.

"You have just the right amount of chest hair," she said. She rode me slowly, then fast and deep, tossing back her head, brushing that straight, fine hair against her shoulder blades.

"I love to play with you," she said, slowing down again.

"I love to play with you."

"I believe you," she smiled, her white teeth gleaming in the half-dark.

She moved up and down, met my stroke,

tensed and released. I grasped her hips, syncopated our movements.

"I want you to love me, David," she said, quickening her pace a bit. I reached up and caressed her breasts through the fabric of the dress.

"Don't be afraid. Don't you see what kind of life we could have together?" She put her hands hard against my chest for purchase and moved against me with more urgency. *My God, what a feeling!*

The fire popped. "I want your heart." She was breathing faster. "The heart you hide behind all those books and thoughts. You keep it from me right now." She gasped and shuddered. Then, "It has thorns around it because you've been hurt before, and you are very conflicted now. I can feel that. You hold back.

"But I know it's a good heart, like mine is a good heart…" She giggled. "Goodheart."

She moved faster, an irresistible rhythm. Lucinda Williams sang "Right in Time."

"I want you to come back to me when this is all over, and let me in David's cactus heart…"

"Gretchen…"

"I love the way you say my name!" A moaned anthem. "I love you, David!"

I knew I was too far gone. I was ready to say anything. And I did.

Chapter Forty-one

Saturday the sun returned to a sky scrubbed flaw-lessly blue by the rain. It would take Phoenix at least a day to dirty up the air again. Downtown was deserted as usual on a non-sports weekend. I was sitting on the old broken curb in front of the Triple A Storage Warehouse when a gleaming new silver Mercedes drove past, parked and disgorged a tall, snowy-haired driver.

James Yarnell walked up. "I could be through nine holes by now, Mapstone. On the other hand, it's good to know I can be out in the world and nobody's trying to kill me. What's this all about?"

"I think you'll agree it's worth your time," I said. "Let's go inside."

I led him through the side door into the old building. It smelled different after the rain: dust stirred on bricks, ashes tamped into mud, a vague scent of rot and disuse. Our footsteps echoed in outsized sounds. Inside, the big room was once again visible thanks to bare bulbs, far overhead. A strand of temporary lighting followed a heavy orange cord down into the elevator shaft.

"This is where you found them?" Yarnell said, putting his hands on the hips of his tan chinos and looking around. His eyes followed the orange cord to the frame of the freight elevator and to the square hole in the concrete.

"Come down," I said.

He hesitated.

"It's not far," I said, walking to the ladder. I started down, and after a minute James Yarnell followed me.

Then we were down in the passages. It was noticeably colder, the cold of a violated grave. Every six feet, a small fluorescent light attached to a spindly aluminum stand beat back the blackness. We tramped down the main tunnel, made the now-familiar turn, came to where the bricks had fallen away. Yarnell stepped around me and just stared at the opening. The only sound was a slight hum from the lights.

"Is this how you spend your weekends, Mapstone?"

"Actually, I've been spending my time trying to figure out this case."

"I didn't think that was in doubt. The handyman was tried and convicted."

"That's what everybody keeps telling me," I said. "But the more I looked, the less made sense. Talbott couldn't have kidnapped the twins. He was in jail that night."

"He was? How do you know that?"

I told him about the booking and release records. "I'm not saying he wasn't involved somehow. He just couldn't have been the initial kidnapper. Then I heard about Bravo Juan, who ran the numbers in the Deuce. It seems your uncle Win was in debt to him."

"My God, do you think he was the one?" Yarnell was absently scratching his forearm. "Let's get out of here. You can tell me more upstairs."

I just let the dusty creepiness of the place be. "Bravo Juan's real name was Juan Alvarez. I spent a lot of time finding out about him. You see, Mr. Yarnell, there weren't a lot of records left about this case. So I've had to run a lot of stuff down. And I thought I had hit a brick wall." I said it without irony. "I thought I'd never get the information I needed."

"So? Did this Juan kidnap my brothers?"

"No. There was a very good Phoenix detective on this case named Joe Fisher. He ran down several suspects, including Juan Alvarez, who had an alibi and was also a good police informer. I didn't know that."

"Can we leave now?"

"Just a sec," I said. "You see, Fisher's notes had disappeared from the case files. But I learned that detectives in his era dictated their notes to a stenographer, and they were sent to the old I Bureau." Yarnell sighed impatiently, rested his hand against the bricks and drew it back. He stared into the burial chamber as I continued. "The point is, there was a duplicate set. Fisher was running down other suspects because he never believed Talbott acted alone. He didn't believe Frances Richie was involved at all."

Yarnell turned back to me, a stream of sweat dropping down onto his fine temple. He started back out but I barred the way.

"What?"

"You've been here before, haven't you, Mr. Yarnell?"

"What are you talking about?" He pushed around me and walked quickly back to the main passage, where he could stand up straight again.

"Thanksgiving night didn't happen the way you told me," I said, following him.

"Joe Fisher didn't believe you, either. In his notes of your interview, he wrote that you seemed to be covering up something, that you made contradictory statements about your whereabouts that night. That's because you were here. After the house had turned in, you and Uncle Win took the twins out to the car and drove away and brought them here."

"You don't know what you're talking about," he said. "Jack Talbott took those boys! Your dead detective didn't know anything but that."

"What did you tell your brothers? That they were going on an adventure with you and Uncle Win?"

"Jack Talbott!"

"Jack Talbott was in the city jail sleeping off a drunk. He was nowhere near the house that night. The boys were taken out by you and your Uncle Win."

"That was more than fifty years ago," Yarnell spat.

"And the man who saw it is still alive," I said, watching the words register on his face. "He's already signed a statement."

Yarnell's mouth opened, a dry paste clinging to his lips. He said, "Paz."

"Paz saw you and your uncle carry Andrew and Woodrow out to a car and drive away that night."

"I…"

"How did it go down?" My voice was quiet but still echoed off the walls.

Yarnell found his poise again, folded his arms and looked at me contemptuously. All the Scottsdale charm was gone. I wouldn't be invited back to the gallery.

"You're the history professor," he said. "Tell me a story. I bet it will be a good one. Then I'm going to get the best law firm in Phoenix to sue Maricopa County and you personally for harassment."

The closeness of the underground chambers seemed to advance on us as I started talking. "How's this story? Win Yarnell had been thrown out of his father's company because he couldn't keep his gambling under control. Then he was thrown out of the will. He staged the kidnapping to get enough money to repay Bravo Juan. Or maybe as leverage to get back into the will. Either way, the twins were the only assets he could grab."

I stared hard at James Yarnell. "Where does a sixteen-year-old snot-nose kid come in?" I asked. "Maybe you liked to come down here and gamble with your uncle. It must have been very forbidden and exotic to hang out with gangsters, even the small-timers Phoenix was growing then."

"Jack Talbott…"

"Jack Talbott was an accomplice," I said. "Nothing more. He was your uncle's gambling buddy. My guess is that the plan was for Talbott to hold the twins until the money was paid. Maybe he was just the bagman. Either way, somebody screwed up. Talbott implicated your uncle as he was being led to the gas chamber. Only your grandfather's influence kept it out of the newspapers."

Yarnell smiled with a perfect set of teeth. "Is that the best you can do?"

"Isn't that good enough?"

"No," he said. "To hell with you." He started up the ladder.

I said quickly, "Maybe you didn't care about Andy and Woodrow because they weren't really your brothers."

He took a hand off the rung and faced me with fury in his blue eyes.

"I have the birth certificates. It names twin boys born on Andy and Woodrow's birthday in 1937." A muscle in his neck started throbbing. "The mother is named as Frances Ruth Richie, age twenty. The father is listed as H. W. Yarnell. Senior. Your grandfather. Andy and Woodrow weren't your brothers. They were your uncles."

"Those records were sealed!" Yarnell hissed. "No one was supposed to…"

"Frances Richie was Hayden Yarnell's mistress," I said. "When I met her, she kept talking about this man she loved, and I assumed it was Jack Talbott. She meant your grandfather."

"He was an old fool, a dangerous old fool." He shook his head violently. "And that little whore."

"Nothing new under the sun," I said. "Families have been killing each other since Cain and Abel."

Before he could turn to climb out, I fired my right fist at him, a nasty hook. If it had connected, it would have broken his nose, easy. I was counting on something else.

He caught my fist with his hand, a fast, graceful motion. He was strong, damned strong.

"Appearances are deceiving," I said. "You're a lot tougher than you look."

He pushed my hand away, then drove the flats of his palms into my chest to push me back. "Leave me alone!" he shouted. It hurt like hell, but I wouldn't let him see it. I cuffed his wrists away with an outward swing of my arms, then I shoved him roughly against the ladder. It clattered but stayed in place.

"You think we're talking history here, Yarnell? You seem strong enough to drive a stake into a man's chest. I think you killed your brother. Max started asking questions after we found the remains. You couldn't have that, could you?"

A new expression rippled across his face, almost like a weather front changing from hot to cold. Something like fear appeared. Then he quickly pushed it down deep.

"A punk named Hector gave you up," I said.

"You don't…"

"Oh, I do. I was in a motel carport with him alone, just him and me with guns on each other. He told me all about you. That shooting at the art gallery was just an act."

"You're bluffing."

"I checked Hector's cell phone records. He made a dozen calls to your gallery in November. He made five in October."

He cursed under his breath. Then: "So why the hell aren't I under arrest?"

"Because nobody else knows yet," I said. "The cops came bursting in and shot Hector to death, and you must have seen that on TV and thought you were home free. They think Hector did it. Or some environmental terrorist. Or both. But, see, Hector told me before they got there. Only I heard it. And if you fuck with me, everybody will know it."

Yarnell stepped back and smiled. He shook his head and chuckled. "So this is what this is about."

I was silent for a long time. Neither of us moved. Finally, I said, "It's a fifteen-year bull market and the only people who haven't gotten rich are teachers who didn't buy Microsoft stock and honest cops."

His face relaxed a notch. He shook his head. "You have to think about your future. You're probably sick of shits like me living an easy life while you live paycheck-to-paycheck. You didn't make any money as a historian, and now you can't make any as a cop."

I didn't answer.

Yarnell rubbed his shoulders. "And what if I don't go along?"

"You go down for your brother's murder."

"That's bunk," he said. "I didn't kill Max."

He started up the ladder and I let him go.

I heard his voice from the top. "You're just a dirty cop who made a big mistake." Then I heard his footsteps echo through the big room and the heavy door clanged shut.

I waited five minutes, then climbed up the ladder. The place was empty as a looted tomb. A layer of dust hung in the air at eye level. I reached down in my shirt, pulled up the little microphone and spoke into it.

"He's gone. I don't know if he went for it or not. I'll meet you over at Madison Street in a few minutes."

I unbuttoned my shirt and pulled the rig off, a little strand of fiber optic held by surgical tape and a battery down by my belt. I wrapped it up and slid it into my pocket. Then I shut down the lights, listened for a moment to the silence of the awful place, and quickly stepped outside.

Chapter Forty-two

The two men rounded the corner from the street as I stepped out the door. For just a nanosecond, I stood and stared in disorientation. But the guns they were carrying got my attention. I slipped back in the building just as they saw me and started running after me.

The door wouldn't lock from the inside. I moved as quickly as I dared through the dark room, panic starting to jelly the muscles in my legs. I dropped to the floor at the far end of the building just as sunlight spilled into the passageway and footsteps pounded toward me. Then the door closed and the world was utterly black again. I could hear footsteps scuttling across the concrete. I connected where I had seen those two bulked-up goons before: in the reception area of Yarneco, wearing oversized suits.

I called out: "I'm a deputy sheriff and I'm armed!"

Suddenly the whole room seemed to shatter into fragments. I realized someone was shooting, an automatic weapon with a silencer and a muzzle flash suppresser. Pieces of masonry rained down as I slid the Python out of its nylon holster. Its heaviness filled my hand. There was a little spark across the room, and some wooden pallets came apart behind me. His flash suppresser wasn't perfect. I took aim and squeezed the smooth Colt action. Fire and a deep *boom*! erupted at the end of my arm. Across the room somebody gasped and fell into something glass. Then he moaned and stopped making any noise.

I rolled to the left just in time before another gun fired in the direction of my muzzle flash. These boys were pros. Rolled and found the edge of the ladder. There was nothing to do but go down. I hit the bottom and frantically pulled out the metal hooks on the ladder. It crashed down into the shaft beside me. I retreated back into the tunnel, down the steps, into the next passage. Only the rough, century-old bricks of the wall guided me through the blackness.

I holstered the Python and fumbled in my pocket for the surveillance wire. Switched the battery on and whispered frantically into it.

"Mike, Mike! Officer needs assistance! Shots fired. At the Triple A Storage Warehouse. Yarnell's goons have me pinned down. I'm in the tunnels. They are heavily armed." I left the channel open and set it aside. I didn't really believe they were still monitoring me. I crouched down in the darkness and waited, the fear all over me. I felt the sweet ache in my abdominal muscles from Gretchen, and wondered why the hell I was doing any of this.

"There's no way out, Mapstone." It was James Yarnell. "You miscalculated your little blackmail scheme."

I pulled the Python out again and nestled it against my face, the coldness of the steel and the acrid smell of the four-and-a-half-inch barrel somehow helping keep down my fear.

"I went to see Max that night he was killed, but I didn't kill him," Yarnell said. "I told him he had to give up the Superior project. The banks were going to shut us down. We were leveraged to our eyeballs. We were going to lose everything. I was going to lose everything. Goddamned Hector. I hired his Mexican gang kids to make phone threats, set the fires, be my environmental terrorists—that way we could walk away from the project.

"But Max wouldn't play along!" he shouted from

the edge of the elevator shaft. "So I went out there that night, to try to reason with him. But he was already dead. I found him with that damned petrified wood driven into his heart. For all I know, somebody else was squeezing Max. Maybe you, Mapstone. Maybe you hired somebody to shoot me!"

He paused. "Any questions?"

I had a lot of questions, but I didn't say a word. I moved carefully back into the tunnels, navigating by memory, going in the opposite direction of the place where Andy and Woodrow had been entombed. I shuffled, trying not to kick anything and make a sound. The heavy mesh of a spider web caught on my arm and made me shudder.

Just then the lights came on and I was blinded just long enough. One of the goons dropped down into the shaft. He strafed the tunnel and something heavy tore into my left foot. My entire left leg was instantly consumed with a bone-deep, searing pain. I fell backward, firing in his direction. The heavy magnum rounds ricocheted viciously off the walls. The goon drew back, dropped to the floor. The Python clicked as it revolved around to a spent cartridge. In my panic, my fire discipline had turned to shit. Too many years away from the academy.

I had retreated to the big chamber, with its garbage and old citrus cases. I hobbled backward painfully, crashing into some wooden boxes, falling flat on my ass. There was no cover. No way out. I reached to my belt and brought out a Speedloader. Opened the cylinder. Steadied my shaking hand. Emptied the spent rounds. They fell like little bells onto the filthy floor. Steadied my hand. I dropped the Speedloader into the cylinder, turned the metal shaft and dropped six fresh rounds into the Colt. I swung the cylinder heavily into place just as the goon stormed into the room and leveled his machine gun at my head.

"Give me your fucking gun!" he huffed.

I was splayed out on the floor, surrounded by the debris of a half-century ago, a steady ooze of blood coming out of the top of my foot. I just stared at the Python and knew I was at the end. "You're not getting my gun," I forced out in a hoarse whisper.

James Yarnell stepped in behind him and shone a flashlight in my eyes. I could see a little chrome semi-automatic pistol in his other hand.

"The dentist's grandson." He shook his head, playing the light over my bloody left foot. "How much bad luck have you had this month, young man? You find things that were never intended to be found. And now you're dead." His expression was something between contempt and pity. "I never did like history classes. What's the point in looking back?"

I spoke to the barrel of the gun. "Sometimes you find unfinished business." They were lousy last words.

In the next ten seconds, the silence became just complete enough that we were all startled by a man clearing his throat.

Then the goon's right knee buckled in a way nature never intended. In the same instant, the room was overtaken by a huge explosion. The goon collapsed, screaming, holding a bloody mass where his knee used to be. James Yarnell retreated, weakly holding out his pistol. Out of the gunsmoke stepped Bobby Hamid.

He walked to the goon, kicked away his machine gun, and shot him again in the other knee.

"There, now you have a match," Bobby said hospitably.

"Bobby!" I winced.

"Dr. Mapstone, I am saving your life," he said evenly, then he faced James Yarnell, who by now was on the other side of the room, his back against the wall.

"This is fun," Bobby said, raising a gigantic, blue-steel automatic in Yarnell's direction.

"Don't kill me!" Yarnell pleaded.

"And why not?" Bobby asked, as if a party discussion had gotten heated and it was time for a new bottle of wine. "It sounds as if you have much to atone for, Mr. Yarnell."

"My family built this state!" he shouted.

Bobby shot him in the left foot, releasing a jet of bright red blood. The pistol and flashlight clattered off to the side, and we were in half-dark again.

"Don't speak, David," Bobby cut me off coldly. He walked over, retrieved the flashlight and set it on a carton overlooking Yarnell.

Bobby rubbed his fine chin and aimed at Yarnell's left knee.

"No!" Yarnell sobbed, clutching his mangled foot. "What do you want?"

Bobby chuckled. "You cannot possibly give me what I want. Dr. Mapstone, however, is more easily pleased. He would also tell you that you have the right to remain silent, that anything you say can be used against you." He focused his aim. "I suggest you start talking about this kidnapping. And please don't bore me, Mr. Yarnell."

Yarnell's eyes were wider than seemed possible for human eyes.

"It was Dad and Win together!" Yarnell blubbered. "They had to get Grandpa away from that little whore, Frances. She was pregnant again with his child. They were going to lose everything."

"Slow down," Bobby commanded.

"We brought the twins here. Then we went home. Talbott was told what to do, make the call demanding the ransom and pick up the money. After he gave the money to Uncle Win, he took Frances to the border."

I spoke through my pain. "Why would she go with him? He must have kidnapped her, too."

"No, no. She went willingly. She wasn't that bright. She didn't know anything about the kidnapping. Nobody did for days. Jack told her she would get to meet Grandpa in Nogales and they could be together. You've got to get me some help! I'm going to bleed to death."

Bobby raised an eyebrow. "So?"

Yarnell moaned.

I went on, "But the real plan was to have Jack Talbott kill her?"

"If it came to that," he said, his face contorted in pain. "Jack was supposed to drug her and get her an abortion. Then pay her to go away. He was given the money for that."

I asked, "So why was Jack Talbott executed and Frances Richie forced to spend her life in prison?"

"Jack tried to blackmail us," James said, forcing up some bravado. "The Yarnells don't blackmail."

Bobby stifled an exaggerated yawn.

"There was a time when we would have crushed you, towel head!" Yarnell yelled. Bobby mockingly put his hand over his mouth in shock, keeping the big automatic leveled. Yarnell said, "We couldn't have either one of them talking. Dad put the pajamas in a sack in the trunk of Talbott's car, just as a little insurance. Dad was smart that way. So if anything went wrong, and the cops searched Talbott, he'd look guilty and nobody would believe him if he blamed the family."

"And Frances?"

"Grandpa died thinking the little bitch had betrayed him. We made sure she kept her mouth shut once she was in prison."

"Really, how was that?"

"I'm dying here, Mapstone!"

"Put your hand over your wound. Apply direct pressure. I don't think you silenced Frances. I think she chose not to talk."

"You're full of shit, Mapstone. You're gonna tell me a broken heart over my grandfather shut her up? I'm finished talking. You're a deputy sheriff, even if you're a dirty one. So you have to arrest me, or arrest him!" He nodded toward Bobby without having the courage to look at him.

I said, "Frances didn't have the abortion."

"What are you talking about?" Yarnell started to gesture but stopped himself. Bobby kept the gun trained on him.

"She had the baby in jail," I said.

"That's...That's impossible. We paid..."

"Not enough, I guess. She had that baby and it was adopted," I said. "So the only thing this woman has left in the world is taken from her, but at least the baby has a chance to be safe and free. She knew if she said anything it might make the Yarnell family go after that baby. Mother love is powerful. Maybe it was the only thing left inside her after you and your family were through. Makes me wonder if there's another heir to Hayden Yarnell out there, maybe more than one."

"That's not..."

"They might have an interest in the Yarnell Trust after you lose every dime."

Yarnell stared past me and spoke in a monotone.

"When she was just his mistress, it was one thing. She got pregnant but Grandpa made Dad adopt the twin boys. Max was a little kid. He never knew. But Grandpa and that little bitch couldn't leave it at that. They loved each other." He made it sound like an unprecedented phenomenon. "After Grandma died, he was going to marry Frances…"

"When was this?" Bobby asked.

"Nineteen forty-one. My dad and Uncle Win couldn't talk Grandpa out of it. He was going to remarry and start a new family. He said he was sick of his sons and their gambling and failures."

"You were part of it," I said. "You also forgot to come back and get the two loose ends you left down here inside the wall. It must have been a hell of a way for little boys to die. Suffocating. In the dark."

Yarnell momentarily shook his head, and rubbed the bridge of his nose. "Dad had to do what he did. There was no other way. We were going to lose everything. Those boys weren't even his children."

Bobby glanced at me, something unreadable in his black eyes.

"Dad suffocated them in their sleep," Yarnell said. "That night. Then we carried them down here, to the tunnels under the hotel, and put them in the wall. The next day Dad ordered the tunnels sealed and closed the freight elevator. It would have worked if Dad and Win hadn't gotten at each other's throats about the gambling and the art collection. If he," Yarnell pointed at me, "hadn't found the tunnels."

He paused and swallowed hard enough that I could watch the saliva fall down his sweaty throat. "...If he hadn't found my goddamned pocket watch."

Yarnell looked around the bleak room, looked into the tunnel, as if for the first time. We all stopped and stared at him. The hard man brought low by unaccustomed pain and fear. Even the goon with both his knees gone stopped whimpering.

Yarnell added in a whisper, "They didn't suffer."

Chapter Forty-three

Christmas week. I stayed at Gretchen's apartment with my foot up, listening to Handel's *Messiah* on the CD player, foolishly mixing Macallan and painkillers, reading Burckhardt's classic *The Civilization of the Renaissance in Italy*. I had missed it in college. Now, it was pure enjoyment. It made me want to write and teach history again. I was glad to be alive.

Gretchen checked in on me from time to time, amazing me with what a man with only one good leg can accomplish. Peralta sorted out the Yarnell case, only making me write a few dozen pages of reports and statements. James Yarnell was under arrest for very current offenses: assault on a police officer, conspiracy to commit murder, giving a false report. Peralta's detectives were working on other charges. Peralta was outraged to be in Bobby Hamid's debt, and kept threatening to indict him for assault with a deadly weapon. Bobby would beat the charge, just like he had all the others. He could take care of himself, as I had chillingly learned. For a moment, the enemy of my enemy had been my savior. It made me feel strange.

The city settled into serious holiday business: the run-up to the Fiesta Bowl, high season at world-class resorts, packed five-star restaurants, a big golf tournament. The days were brightly sunny and the nights cold, magical. The smog wasn't too bad. The twentieth century ticked out its last days. In Willo, the winter lawns gleamed as if every blade of grass was lit up by electricity, and the neighborhood put out luminarias along all the sidewalks. Gretchen and I had our own celebration, two or three times a night.

◇◇◇

The bricks were set in place one at a time. It was done by a man's hand, a thick hand with copious hair on top, an ape's hand really. He ladled on the mortar and it ran off the sides like pancake batter. And I could only watch. It was dark and for a long time I watched with interest. So this was how bricks were laid. The hand moved very precisely. Every brick lined up perfectly. But I was inside, inside a tiny opening, so small I couldn't move. The wound on my foot seemed better, but my legs were inert. My hands were dead at my sides. And by the time I realized what was happening, every brick took away a little more air, and the hand kept laying them in place, and the mortar kept running like batter, and I couldn't breathe. I could only scream.

"David! Wake up, baby. Wake up. I've got you. You're safe."

Gretchen was next to me, stroking my face. "You were having a nightmare. It must have been awful."

I took big breaths and surveyed her large bedroom with relief. "I know, don't tell a dream or it might come true."

She held me close. "I have dreams about you and me, and I want those to come true, David. Oh, baby, you've been through so much. But you're safe with Gretchen. This awful thing is over. James is in jail. They killed that kid who stabbed Max with the petrified wood. It's over."

I let her rock me to sleep, my face nuzzling her russet-colored hair.

Then I came awake. I just stared into the dark for a long time.

◇◇◇

"David? Couldn't you go back to sleep? The holidays are so hard." She leaned over and kissed me, holding a hand against my forehead. "You feel clammy."

She got out of bed and brought me a glass of water. She looked more beautiful than ever: the ambient light playing off her hair; the shadows accenting the lovely planes and curves of her face, her robe open and revealing.

"What is it? You're upset."

I didn't want to speak, didn't want words or a voice to say them.

A wave of nausea just kept washing across me, again and again. But then I was letting her reach under the covers. It was a nice feeling.

"I know just what the patient needs," she said. I was hard as a twenty-five-year-old.

Grandfather used to say that corruption ultimately wasn't about payments under the table or anything so prosaic. It wasn't even about evil, at least at first. It was about what happened inside when a person got comfortable with what he knew was wrong.

"No," I said, pushing her away. She flashed those rich brown eyes and drew back.

I swallowed some acid saliva down my sandpaper throat and said, "How did you know Max had been killed with petrified wood?"

"David, what are you talking about?"

"We held back that information. Nobody knew how Max was murdered except the cops and the suspect."

"You told me, you goof!"

God, I wished it were true. "I didn't, Gretchen. I never told you that."

She didn't protest. She just watched me. We stared at each other a long time, until I looked away.

"If I call the city archaeologist's office, am I going to find out that there's no Gretchen Goodheart on the staff? That's what I will find, isn't it?" I swung out of bed and reached for my clothes.

"David, please! You're going to start the bleeding in your foot. What are you doing? It's the middle of the night."

"I'm going down to Phoenix PD and see if they have a city staff directory." In agony, I pulled my pants over my injured foot, then slipped on the sweatshirt.

"I don't work for the city." She sat back against the headboard and pulled her robe tightly around her. "I did help you, David. I helped you in ways you don't even know."

Why the hell was I starting to cry? I whispered, "You probably don't even wear a cowboy hat."

"I thought eccentricity would be disarming," she said.

"I was disarmed."

I waited for her to protest, to say she could explain, oh, God, how I waited. She just leaned forward, put her arms around her legs and rocked. With every throb of my foot the room and the world were collapsing around me.

"And the dolls. That was you."

Silence.

"So what organization, Gretchen? Who are you with?"

"What?"

"The FBI has been obsessed with eco-terrorism, and I thought they were overreacting. Apparently I was wrong. You used me to get close to Max." I was talking in short bursts. I couldn't do more. "That night, you probably used my name to get him to let you in. Tell me a former smoke jumper isn't strong enough to knock a man down with a kick or a punch, and then..." God, my foot was throbbing in pain. "...And then pick up an ornamental piece of petrified wood and plunge it into his breastbone."

"It's not like that." Tears were streaming down her cheeks. "I'm not with anybody but me!"

My clothes were on and I should have left. But I just sat on the other side of the bed, our body language nothing worse than a couple having a fight.

She said, "I never meant to hurt you."

The damned pulse against my eyes.

She came over, bent down and kissed me on the forehead, and then on the lips. I let her do it.

"I really love you," she said. "I thought you hungered for justice like I did."

"What are you talking about?"

"Do you know Max offered me money?" she said. "As if that could make up for anything."

All I could muster was a deep sigh. She took my hand and stroked it. I felt so tired.

"Three years ago, I learned that my dad had been adopted. He didn't know anything about the circumstances. It happened when he was a baby, so he has no memory of his real mother. A year ago, I learned I could never have children. It became really important to me to know where I came from. So it took some time. It took some money, and some other things. But I finally found Frances. She's my grandmother."

My foot was caught somewhere between the worst cramp you can imagine and the deep pain of a broken bone. I just let it throb.

"I said I was a law student looking into wrongful convictions, and they let me visit her. I knew she was my grandmother, my flesh and blood, immediately. But she was so far gone, she didn't even realize who I was. And then I learned the whole story. How the Yarnells had kept her in there for all those years. What they had done to her."

"So you murdered Max."

"Those are your words."

"God, Gretchen, stop lying to me. If you love me, give me the truth."

"I'm not sorry for what happened to Max, whoever did it. That's the truth."

"That's because you did," I said dully. "Then James Yarnell. I remember. You checked your watch that night, after we had dinner, and you suddenly left. You needed to be there when he was locking up the gallery and walking to his car. It didn't seem to matter to you, that night in Scottsdale, if you shot me along with him."

"If that had been me…if it had been, I'm a good shot."

"You have the perfect alibi for that night: dinner with your lover, the deputy." My mouth felt as if it were coated with acid.

Gretchen said softly, "Frances was a twenty-four-year-old girl who never did anyone harm. Her only fault was to fall for an old man who was betrayed by his sons! And then their sons carried it on. They could have stopped it any time. Just let her out and let her be. They had the money to let it go away."

"I guess they thought they were in too deep."

"They were evil," she said simply. "They had blood on their hands."

"That may be," I said. "But the punishment isn't up to us."

She faced me, her eyes fanatically bright. "How many more decades would we have to wait for your style of justice, David?"

"My style of justice?"

"How many?" she demanded. "You're the historian. The only thing necessary for the triumph of evil is for good men to do nothing."

"And there's no place for forgiveness?"

Her hands became fists and her voice rose an octave. "Tell my grandmother about forgiveness!"

"I can't imagine she wanted her granddaughter to live the same nightmare that she did. Don't you realize she stayed quiet all those years so your father would be safe, so the Yarnells would never even know about him?"

She sobbed softly. "Are you arresting me?"

I said nothing.

Then she kissed me, the most tender kiss of my life. It dawned on me that she could kill me, too, if she chose. Right that minute, I didn't care. I heard her whisper, "My God, we could have been good together."

I willed myself from her arms, willed myself out of the bed, willed myself out of the pain and desire to pass out. I grabbed the cane they had given me in the hospital and hobbled toward the door.

I stopped at the threshold of the bedroom. "How can you be sure you're right?"

"You know I'm right."

"I know I took an oath as a deputy sheriff. I know James Yarnell is under arrest, and we will prosecute him lawfully."

"Well," she said quietly. "You take your justice. I'll take mine."

Epilogue

Peralta didn't come home that night. The next morning, I found out why.

STRANGLER KILLED IN GUNFIGHT WITH DEPUTIES, the headline said. Photos showed Lindsey—it was a mug of her in uniform that was at least two years old—and Patrick Blair, looking gorgeous. And the strange, round-faced man who followed me that night in the Ford Econoline van. "Alleged serial killer," proclaimed type under his face. I looked at Lindsey's face and was suddenly afraid to read more. I felt a deep stab in my stomach.

I made myself read:

> *A 38-year-old Mesa man about to be arrested as the notorious Harquahala Strangler shot it out with sheriff's deputies Tuesday night. One deputy was wounded. The suspect, Mark Wayne Bennett, was fatally wounded.*

The firefight took place at the suspect's apartment on North Val Vista after sheriff's detectives attempted to serve an arrest warrant. After the suspect opened fire, Det. Patrick Blair was wounded. He was listed in guarded condition at Desert Samaritan Hospital.

Chief Deputy Mike Peralta praised Deputy Lindsey F. Adams, for saving Blair's life and preventing the suspect from escaping. Peralta said "substantial evidence" links Bennett to the slayings of 26 women in the Phoenix area. The alleged murderer had become known as the Harquahala Strangler because most of his victims were left in the Harquahala Desert west of the city.

On Christmas Eve, Peralta walked in the door just before six. I shook his hand and congratulated him on solving the case.

"From your new buddy."

He handed me a box with blue gift-wrapping. It was a bit smaller than the kind of hatboxes Grandmother once favored.

"Who?"

"Bobby Hamid," Peralta sneered. "You know, he closed the purchase on the Triple A Storage

Warehouse today. Says he wants to preserve the building. He's even going to excavate the tunnels." He eyed the package. "You going to open that or am I going to have to call the bomb squad?"

I slipped off the wrapping and opened a box filled with Styrofoam worms. I reached in my hand and caught the edge of something smooth.

"Good Lord, Mapstone," Peralta said.

It was a piece of Santa Clara pottery that glowed blackly in my hand. *He bought the building and he's going to excavate the tunnels, and take whatever might be hidden down there...*

"I'll be damned," I said.

Peralta looked at me a long time, then he just shook his head and walked into the living room.

"What I really want is a well-made Gibson," he said. So I hobbled to the kitchen and made drinks. When I came back out, the tree was lit and the picture window open to the street. Out on Cypress, the other Christmas lights glowed merrily back at us. I put on the *Messiah* again, the Boston Baroque recording. Peralta settled into the big leather chair, and I closed my eyes, reflecting on a year of so much change, so much loss, so many close calls and blessings.

Peralta wanted to read from the Bible, from

the Book of Luke, because that was the way his father did it on Christmas Eve. Peralta had his formal occasions, and deviation was unthinkable. It had been the same tradition with Grandmother and Grandfather. I retrieved the heavy King James Version from the bookshelves.

Peralta drew himself up in the chair and read, "And it came to pass in those days, that there went out a decree from Caesar Augustus…" He really had a beautiful voice, rich with intonations and possibilities.

Then he passed the book to me.

My voice was still raw from the talk with Gretchen, and all the wide-awake hours after that.

"And the angel said unto them, Fear not: for, behold, I bring you good tidings of great joy, which shall be to all people…"

Fear not. Be not afraid. When the *Pastoral Symphony* came around, I went to get Peralta's presents. Then I got him on his feet and took him by the shoulder. He glared at me uncomfortably.

"Merry Christmas, Chief," I said. "You need to be with Sharon, and she needs to be with you…"

He started to speak.

"No, that's the way it is on holidays," I said. "This is for Sharon." I put a package with avant-garde wrapping in his hands. "And this is for you."

A traditional wrapping, with the box of Anniversario Padrons I knew he would love.

"Call me tomorrow," I said.

He started to protest. He wasn't accustomed to being bossed around. But a small change softened his eyes.

"You'll be the next sheriff," I said. "I'm honored you're my friend."

"You're a good cop, Mapstone," he said. Then he gave me a rough *abrazo* and walked out to his truck. After he drove off, I stood for a long time on the quiet street. The sidewalks were marked with luminarias from Central to Seventh Avenue, gentle, warm footlights for the vault of metropolitan sky. They made me feel less alone.

◇◇◇

It was the way it should be. Holidays are for family. Mike should be with Sharon. Lorie Pope was back in New Jersey at her mother's. Kimbrough and his wife had a three-year-old at home this year. Carl the courthouse guard took the train to Los Angeles to be with his daughter. Hawkins was off in his soccer suburb, with his wife and his kids. Even Bobby Hamid had a wife and children and home.

And I was at home, in the house my grandparents had built, home to me and too many books, in my city, in the last week of the last year of the last decade of the last century of the millennium. I fixed a martini, limped back to the living room and willed myself not to cry alone. The arc of history is long but it bends toward justice. If that is so, then why did I feel such a hole inside me?

The doorbell rang.

I was ready to be angry at Peralta for chickening out. But when I swung open the heavy front door, Lindsey was standing on the step.

"History Shamus," she said. "You alone?"

I nodded.

"No snow and jingle bells?" she said.

"The first Christmas was in the desert," I said. "The desert never forgets that."

She took my hands. "You've been beaten up," she said.

"You've had some adventures, too. I read about you in the paper."

"You're right about one thing, Dave. Patrick Blair is a beautiful-looking man." She smiled. "A crappy shot, too. I found myself missing a man who would read me the classics in bed…teach me history and bring it alive…make me a martini…"

She started talking faster, trying to outrun the tears filling her eyes. "It's Christmas Eve. It's the time when we want to be home with our family, with the ones we love. The people who connect us to everything good we can be. And the one person in my life, the only person, who fits that description..." She almost didn't get it out. "...is you, Dave."

I was beyond words, so all I could do was take her in my arms and swear to God I'd never let her go. Take her in my house, in our house. Make peace with our individual histories and try to write a new one together. Hope for all the luck in the world. Let her into my cactus heart. It was cold in the desert that Christmas Eve, and it was enough that we could hold each other all night long.

To receive a free catalog of Poisoned Pen Press titles, please contact us in one of the following ways:

Phone: 1-800-421-3976
Facsimile: 1-480-949-1707
Email: info@poisonedpenpress.com
Website: www.poisonedpenpress.com

Poisoned Pen Press
6962 E. First Ave. Ste. 103
Scottsdale, AZ 85251

Printed in the United States
203138BV00003B/265-285/P